PRAISE FOR KENDRA ELLIOT

"Elliot's best work to date. The author's talent is evident in the character's wit and smart dialogue... One wouldn't necessarily think a psychological thriller and romance would mesh together well, but Elliot knows what she's doing when she turns readers' minds inside out and then softens the blow with an unforgettable love story."

—*Romantic Times Book Reviews* on *Vanished,* 4½ stars, Top Pick

"Kendra Elliot does it again! Filled with twists, turns, and spine-tingling details, *Alone* is an impressive addition to the Bone Secrets series."

—Laura Griffin, *New York Times* bestselling author, on *Alone*

"Elliot once again proves to be a genius in the genre with her third heart-pounding novel in the Bone Secrets collection. The author knows romance and suspense, reeling readers in instantaneously and wowing them with an extremely surprising finish . . . Elliot's best by a mile!"

—*Romantic Times Book Reviews* on *Buried,* 4½ stars, Top Pick (HOT)

"Make room on your keeper shelf! *Hidden* has it all: intricate plotting, engaging characters, a truly twisted villain. I can't wait to see what Kendra Elliot dishes up next!"

—Karen Rose, *New York Times* bestselling author

KNOWN

ALSO BY KENDRA ELLIOT

BONE SECRETS NOVELS

Hidden

Chilled

Buried

Alone

CALLAHAN & MCLANE
PART OF THE BONE SECRETS WORLD

Vanished

Bridged

Spiraled

KNOWN

A BONE SECRETS NOVEL

KENDRA ELLIOT

Text copyright © 2016 Kendra Elliot

Published by Montlake Romance, Seattle

www.apub.com

Amazon, the Amazon logo, and Montlake Romance are trademarks of Amazon.com, Inc., or its affiliates.

ISBN-13: 9781503949478
ISBN-10: 1503949478

Cover design by Jason Blackburn

Printed in the United States of America

For my girls.

CHAPTER ONE

The scent of smoke grew stronger.

Chris Jacobs strode through the woods, occasionally stopping to sniff the air and adjust his course. Ice cracked and crunched under his boots. Last night's storm had covered the previous day's foot of snowfall with a solid layer of ice. He stomped as he walked, breaking the thick crust, watching his boots sink deep into the snow, and wished his son, Brian, could experience the fun. He blew out a breath and the steam floated away. The air was still and silent. Dense gray clouds hovered at the peaks of the tall firs, blocking the treetops from his view.

More snow was expected at any minute.

He stopped and inhaled deeply through his nose. *The smoke is definitely getting thicker.* Beside him Oro paused and mimicked his master's scenting of the air. The skinny yellow dog didn't seem to mind the cold under his paws and walked lightly on top of the ice. He didn't leave Chris's side to investigate the brush or run ahead to check for squirrels as usual. He stuck close. Chris rubbed the dog's ears and wondered if he felt the tension in the woods. Chris had a sense of dread pressing against his forehead that made him want to go back to his isolated cabin, stoke the fire, and read a book. An intelligent brown gaze met his, and the dog whined in the back of his throat.

"Yeah. Me too, Oro."

The dog raised his nose and sniffed again.

"We'll find it."

Chris was accustomed to smelling smoke on his hikes through the foothills of the Cascade Range. Isolated cabins dotted the forest, and smoke from their wood stoves often crossed his path. This was different. The odor had invaded his cabin and awoken him this morning before dawn. He'd made himself wait until daylight and then headed out to find the source. Intermittent pleasant wood smoke was normal; this nonstop dirty-smelling smoke was not.

He'd bought the cabin eighteen months ago, looking for an occasional retreat from his home in the Portland suburbs. It'd been a calm spot in the constantly moving river that was now his life. During the summer it was a deliciously shady and quiet refuge; during the winter it was a secluded snowbound hideaway.

In other words, perfect year-round.

The cabin's heat came from wood and its water from a spring. Chris had spent the first month of ownership increasing the insulation and improving the pipes. No electrical wires

and no cell service. He'd viewed the absence of both as a benefit. Even though his financial means were dependent upon the
Internet, he loved to unplug from everything for long periods.
His closest neighbor was at least a mile away. Maybe more. It was
in that direction that he was currently hiking.

A half hour ago he'd eyed the thick blanket of ice and decided
to walk instead of possibly getting his truck stuck in the snow.
Depending on the weather, he usually hiked or ran several miles
each day, purposefully avoiding the other cabins. Today was a
hike. Each slow step required concentration and extra muscle.
He always wore orange, because some people didn't abide by the
hunting season's laws and dates.

He stepped out of the tall firs and into a small clearing. He
froze and then retreated backward into the dark of the woods, his
gaze rapidly processing the scene. In the open space the smoke
hung thick, trapped by low clouds that were heavy with snow.
At the center of the clearing was a burned-out shell of a cabin, its
walls smoking and steaming in the cold air. Black soot scorched
the walls above the windows where the heat had broken out the
glass. Several jagged holes had been torn in the shingled roof
where the fire had burst through but failed to take hold. At one
point the roof must have been covered in snow. Now frozen puddles circled the cabin, black icy cinders staining the white snow.

It was silent.

Chris moved cautiously into the clearing with Oro pressing
against his leg. The dog's ears lay back against his head; his tail
was tucked close. Chris understood. The black shell and burned
odors made the hair on the back of his neck stand up. The cabin
was similar to his own. One big rectangle that housed the living
space and kitchen, with a loft overhead for sleeping quarters.
The loft had sold him on his own cabin. One look at the glee on

Brian's face as he'd climbed the ladder and Chris had known the place belonged to the two of them.

Brian should have come with him to the mountains for the week. Instead he'd gone to Disneyland with his grandparents. Chris's mother had pleaded with Chris to accompany them, but the thought of dense crowds and noise eliminated that possibility. Brian had wavered, uncertain about leaving his father, but Chris had assured him he wouldn't be lonely. Most ten-year-old kids wouldn't have dreamed of skipping a Disneyland trip, but Brian was different. Up until two years ago, Chris had been his whole life. Now he had grandparents, an aunt, an uncle, and a school full of friends.

His son had bloomed under the attention, making Chris almost regret he'd hidden the boy from society for eight years.

Almost.

Please be empty.

Chances were good that this cabin was empty. The woods had been silent for three days while Chris had decompressed in his wilderness retreat. He'd caught a glimpse of the taillights of one vehicle during that time, but no people. Tourists flocked to the Oregon cabins during the summer; not so much during the winter. He started to circle around the smoking, steaming shell, thankful the trees stood back far enough that they hadn't been singed. The fire would have had a completely different result if it had happened during the summer.

He spotted an SUV with snow up to its bumpers about fifty feet away from the cabin as he came around to its front side. The windows were foggy and streaked with interior steam.

People.

The Suburban's blue paint was covered with a thick layer of ice. The snow below the driver's side doors was lumpy but also coated with unbroken ice, indicating it hadn't been disturbed since the ice storm.

Chris cupped his mouth and shouted, "Hello?"

Silence.

He slowly approached the SUV and yelled again, not wanting to sneak up on someone who was possibly armed. Inside the vehicle a gloved hand wiped the steam from a window, and he saw the blurry shape of a face behind the iced-over glass. He halted a good ten feet from the SUV, grabbed Oro's collar, and held his other hand up in a nonthreatening gesture. The door flung open and a woman hurled herself out of the vehicle. Under her pink knit cap, a tearstained face and red eyes were happy to see him.

"Please help us," she said in a raspy voice. "My mom's so sick and the truck won't start."

Not a woman. She was a teenager. Her youth apparent as she stumbled closer. He grabbed her hands as she started to fall when her booted foot hooked under a thick slab of ice.

"What happened?" he asked, looking over her shoulder at the silent SUV.

Her breath steamed in the air as she panted. "Do you have a car? Please get us out of here!"

"What happened?" he asked again, tightening his grip on her hands and meeting her gaze. The girl was terrified; her bloodshot eyes darted from him to Oro and to the burned-out husk of a building. She reeked of smoke. And worse. "How'd the fire start?"

"I don't know," she cried, her voice raw and choked. "Last night I woke up inside, and everything was in flames. I couldn't wake up my mom. I dragged her out." She burst into full tears, and he rapidly adjusted his grip to keep her from collapsing. She was dressed for cold. Boots, heavy coat, gloves, and hat.

Oro trotted to the vehicle door she'd left open. He stepped close, sniffed, and backed away, looking over to meet Chris's gaze.

What is inside?

Chris noticed the faint indentation of a trail from the cabin to the SUV. It wasn't individual tracks from boots; it was a wide, long groove as if something had been pulled across the yard before the ice formed. "Let's check on your mom."

The girl glanced around, wiping her nose with the back of her glove. "Where's your car?"

"I walked."

"What?" Fresh tears started. "How are we going to leave? *It's so cold.*"

He held on to her hand and stepped into the broken trail she'd created during her dash from the SUV. As he moved closer, the sour smell of vomit mixed with the odor of smoke. A figure was stretched out on the middle row of seats. Two amazingly thin but insulating emergency blankets covered the body. Stocking feet peeked out from under the shiny blankets.

No boots?

"What's your mom's name?"

"Gianna. Gianna Trask," she whispered.

He met the girl's dark gaze. "I'm Chris. You're both going to be okay."

The girl shuddered. "She kept throwing up. But she didn't stop breathing. My mom always says that's the most important thing," she babbled. "As long as someone keeps breathing and you do whatever it takes to keep their airway clear. I barely slept because I kept checking to make certain she could breathe."

He patted her shoulder. "You did good." He turned his attention to the still figure. "Gianna? You okay?" he asked loudly and shook a foot. He could feel the cold from her skin seep through the thick sock and dread swept through him.

Oh, no.

The foot moved.

Thank you, God.

He shook her foot again. "Gianna? Can you sit up?" He leaned into the vehicle and placed a knee on the seat. The woman stirred. The acrid vomit odor made him breathe through his mouth.

"Violet?" Gianna muttered. She shifted under the blankets.

"She's right here," Chris answered, assuming Violet was her daughter.

Gianna jerked, flung off the coverings, and thrashed, fighting to sit up. "Violet?" she croaked. Terrified brown eyes identical to her daughter's stared at Chris.

"Mom!" Violet leaned in next to Chris. "I'm here! He's okay. He's just trying to help." Her voice faltered, and Chris knew she'd abruptly realized she'd placed her trust in a complete stranger.

Chris backed up, relieved the woman was conscious, and Violet moved forward to kneel on the floor, taking her mother's hands. Gianna continued to stare at Chris. Her gaze alternated between terror and relief. A million questions flitted across her eyes. She looked past him at the steaming cabin and horror crossed her face.

"What happened?" she whispered.

CHAPTER TWO

Gianna couldn't catch her breath. Fuzzy images of fire, Violet's terrified face, and snow ricocheted through her brain, and she couldn't hang on to one thought long enough to feel grounded. She didn't remember Violet's getting her out of the cabin. Or the walk to the SUV. Or vomiting. Although all around her were the clear signs that someone had been sick. She perched on the edge of the backseat, her legs hanging out, as the stranger, Chris, rubbed her frozen feet. Her stomach twisted and churned, making her swallow hard.

Her head was killing her.

She pulled off her gloves and lightly touched her closed eyes with icy hands, breathing deep.

"Headache?" Chris asked.

Keeping her eyes closed, she nodded. "And I can't get warm." She wasn't used to feeling helpless and relying on someone else. The sensation was nearly as disconcerting as her nausea and loss of memory. Pain shot up her legs from his rough massage, and her eyes flew open as she flinched. He froze at her movement, his hand's heat seeping through her socks.

"That's a good sign," he stated.

She knew that but held her tongue. He was kind. She studied him as he ministered to her frozen feet, seeking a distraction from the pain in her head. Faded round scars dotted the left side of his neck and trailed up the side of his cheek to vanish under his black stocking hat. He hadn't shaved in a few days, which slightly hid the scars. A layperson might not notice them, but she was trained to notice all scars. To her professional eye, they were cigarette burns, and she wondered who'd tortured him. So far Chris was a man of few words, but he'd known the right ones to use. He'd calmed Violet and instructed her to get in the front seat with the dog and to hold the dog close under her jacket.

"Oro has body heat to spare," he'd told her. Now the dog and the girl watched closely as Chris rubbed feeling back into Gianna's feet. He'd tried unsuccessfully to start the SUV several times. He'd finally glanced under the hood and shook his head. "I'm no mechanic. I can't even begin to guess what's wrong."

"It was fine a few days ago," Gianna commented as feeling rushed back to her feet. "We drove up here from Portland and haven't driven it since then. Once it started to snow real hard, I decided to stay put."

"Understandable. We'll go back to my place. I know it's supposed to warm up tonight . . . hopefully enough to melt that layer of ice. I don't want to venture out to the highway. The roads are like skating rinks and I won't risk putting us in a ditch, but tomorrow the conditions should be better. We can head down to the ranger station and let them know what happened here." He glanced up at the low dark clouds. "Usually they'd spot the smoke and come investigate, but I suspect since the fire happened at night that they didn't see it and the clouds are blocking the residual smoke. We can leave a note on your dashboard with my name and address in case someone comes looking. Do you have boots in the cabin?" he asked.

"They should be just inside the door." She took in the blackened cabin structure, feeling shock roll through her system again.

How did we survive?

If Violet hadn't woken up . . .

Tears threatened and she swallowed hard as bile churned in her stomach.

"I don't think we should go in," she said. "It can't be safe. The roof looks ready to collapse."

"*We* shouldn't," Chris said. "I'll take a quick look."

"I'm sorry." Violet's voice cracked and her eyes filled. "I put on my own boots and coat, but I didn't grab yours last night. I couldn't think straight."

Gianna's heart hurt for her terrified daughter, and she reached out a hand to touch her cheek. "I'm just glad you're safe."

"I was so scared," Violet whispered. "You wouldn't wake up."

"How did it start?" asked Chris. He focused on her feet, but Gianna knew he was very interested in the response. She looked to Violet.

"I don't know." Violet sucked in a breath and tightened her hold on the dog. "The smoke in the loft woke me up. It was so thick, I could barely see. I called out for you and felt around, but you weren't in your bed."

Gianna nodded. The loft held two double beds. No privacy, but she'd welcomed the small space, hoping it would offer a chance to reconnect with her teen daughter, who'd been distant for the last six months. Violet had been horrified to learn she had to share a room with her mother.

"I crawled down the ladder and the kitchen area was in flames. You were crashed out on the couch and wouldn't wake up."

Gianna couldn't remember falling asleep on the couch. She thought hard, trying to recall what they'd done that evening, but even dinner was sketchy in her mind. "What'd we have for dinner?"

Violet's brows narrowed. "Meatloaf."

Gianna nodded, remembering she'd brought the homemade meatloaf with them, knowing it'd make an easy meal at the cabin. *Wine.* She'd had wine after the meatloaf. *How much did I drink?*

That could explain her headache. Shame and horror rattled her as she realized she might have drunk too much to respond in last night's emergency. One glass was sufficient to relax her; two made her extremely drowsy. *Did I drink more than that?*

She couldn't remember.

I could have killed us both.

This isn't right.

She looked away from Violet and met Chris's gaze. His calm hazel eyes didn't judge her, but she knew he had to be wondering if alcohol had been involved. She didn't need any extra judgment; she was piling on the guilt just fine.

"It's over. No one died," he said softly. He held her gaze another long second and then looked at Violet. "You were a real hero. It's amazing that you got your mom out of there."

"I was terrified," Violet muttered. She buried her nose in the furry top of the dog's head, and Gianna mentally thanked Chris for making her daughter sit with the dog. Pets healed. Had that been his intent?

He met her gaze again and gave a subtle shrug of one shoulder at her questioning stare.

"Do you have kids?" Gianna blurted.

Surprise and then pride lit his eyes. "My son, Brian, is ten. Oro is his dog."

Gianna noticed the lack of wedding ring. *Divorced.* "Is he at your cabin?"

"He's at Disneyland with his grandparents." Chris stood and brushed the snow off his shins. "I'm going to get your boots. We've got more than a mile to walk, and you're not going to make it unless we get your feet covered."

Gianna tentatively wiggled her toes, welcoming the lightning that flashed up her legs. "I can walk. Be careful in there." She wondered how stable the cabin was. All four walls were still standing, but the outside was well scorched and the roof looked like a cheese grater. A strong wind could knock it over. She couldn't see the far side, where according to Violet the kitchen had been in flames.

Did I start the fire with the propane oven?

Gianna shook her head and inhaled deeply to slow her heartbeat; she was never careless. Any fire had to have been a result of a malfunction of some sort. Chris plowed a path toward the cabin, stomping to break through the ice. Gianna glanced at Violet, who watched Chris with worried eyes, and a dark thought crossed her mind: she'd caught Violet with cigarettes twice in the past few months.

Had Violet been smoking?

Gianna hadn't found any recent evidence of cigarettes, and she had looked. Thoroughly. Snooping through her daughter's things and checking her cell phone had become necessary evils in her home.

Chris gave a hard shove on the handle of the front door. The door opened and he paused, studying the ceiling. He disappeared inside and Gianna held her breath. He reappeared seconds later with a pair of sooty boots, dusting them off with his gloved hand. A small shower of black dust floated to the white snow. He set them down and went back inside. He stepped out with her heavy ski jacket. He shook it and wiped it clean as he walked back to the women.

He handed the smoke-scented items to Gianna, and she thanked him profusely. He brushed aside her thanks, and she wondered if she'd embarrassed him. His face gave away nothing, and she recognized he was highly skilled at hiding his emotions. He'd briefly lit up while talking about his son, but that was the exception. He'd been calm and direct since she'd woken. Unlike his, her face revealed everything she thought, and Violet had inherited the trait. Or curse.

"I hope there's nothing else you can't live without for a few days," Chris said. "I'm not going back in there. The roof looks ready to fall in."

"My cell phone and purse are still in there, but I don't care," stated Gianna as she slipped her feet into her boots. "There's no cell service up here, and I'm not risking our lives for some possibly melted credit cards."

"I have my cell," said Violet. "It's been useless. I tried to call out all night."

"No one else was in the cabin, right? No pets left behind?" Chris asked, glancing at the cabin, his expression inscrutable.

"No," said Violet. "We don't have any pets."

Gianna laced up her boots and stood. A wave of nausea rolled through her as the clouds decided to release another round of snow. Not soft lovely flakes. These were tiny sharp flakes, almost more ice than snow. She pulled on her coat and winced at the overpowering stench of smoke. She turned and gathered up the thin silver blankets, hooking one around her neck. Gianna had always kept a small stash of emergency supplies in the vehicle and she wondered now if that forethought had saved their lives. "I'm glad you remembered the kit in the back," she said to Violet as the girl and dog trudged around to her side of the SUV.

"I forgot," Violet confessed. "I was desperate and digging through all the compartments, looking for a flashlight, and found them."

"Good girl." Gianna draped the other blanket over her daughter's shoulders. Violet's eyes filled. She flung her arms around her mother and hugged her tight.

"I was so scared," she choked out. "I'm so glad you're all right."

Gianna held her daughter, treasuring the heartfelt hug and the glimpse of the affectionate child that usually hid inside her maturing daughter. Hugs had been scarce for a long time, and her own eyes watered.

"Ready?" asked Chris. He'd written a note saying that everyone had survived the fire and giving his name and address, and set the piece of paper carefully on the dashboard. He'd stood back as she'd put on her boots, but she'd felt his careful gaze on her every move, weighing whether she was well enough to walk through the forest.

"Ready." She lifted her chin and met his gaze, ignoring the pain that pounded inside her forehead. She had a daughter to get to safety, and she needed to rely on this stranger. He turned and followed the broken trail she assumed he'd made when he arrived. She gestured for Violet to follow the man and she brought up the rear. Walking was slow. Their boots sank twelve inches into the soft snow under the ice. At first Gianna had to stretch her legs to follow his steps, but soon the holes grew closer together. She was touched that he'd noticed and shortened his stride.

Within sixty seconds she was exhausted and the sharp snow-flakes stung her face.

They'd nearly passed the burned cabin when Chris stopped, staring at tracks that led to his left. Gianna looked past him and noticed that the path they were on headed in a different direction. He glanced back at Violet.

"Did you make that path during the night?"

She shook her head.

Gianna stared at the broken ice and snow that led off to the east. *Chris didn't make the path?* Her gaze tracked the new path, which led straight to her cabin. She swallowed hard. "That's not the way you came from your place?"

"No." He pointed ahead to a break in the woods. "I came from this way. Have you seen anyone in the area? Who knows you're staying here?"

"No one knows except the rental agency," stated Gianna. "And we haven't seen a single person since we've been up here." The sight of another trail that led to where she'd slept with her daughter last night made her skin crawl. "Who could have made that? Violet, are you sure?"

"I didn't leave the cabin!"

Gianna wanted to run and put as much distance as possible between them and the trail. "It was formed after the ice storm. See? Someone had to break the ice when they walked. What time did that storm happen? Seven? Eight?"

"Let's get out of here," Violet begged. "I think someone looked in our windows and spied on us."

She was right. Gianna saw that the trail went to both of the lower-level windows and to the small porch.

"I didn't notice it when I first got here," said Chris. "I just looked at the damage."

Gianna's heart froze. "Did someone start the fire while we were sleeping?"

Chris met her gaze. "Very possible."

CHAPTER THREE

Chris wasn't surprised that it was after noon by the time they arrived at his cabin. Violet had kept up well, but Gianna had needed frequent stops and his arm to steady her steps. The mystery trail bothered him. Gianna hadn't mentioned it since they left, but he'd thought of nothing else. *Who spied on the women? Did that person start the fire?* He knew Gianna had to be wondering the same.

During the hike he'd nearly told her what he suspected had been left inside her cabin. He'd kept his mouth shut because of Violet.

Twice Violet had broken into tears on the trail, describing her terror and struggle to get her mother out of the cabin. Chris knew she'd be haunted for weeks, possibly years, by her trauma. From his own experience, talking it out was the best therapy. Her mother had comforted her and commiserated; Chris had stood back and stared at the trees, feeling like an intruder and trying to give them some privacy.

Memories flashed as he listened to Violet's fears pour out. Long ago he'd had a best friend for two years, someone to listen to all his terrors, someone who'd shared the same horrifying experience as he. That boy had died, and for over a decade Chris had had no one else. Then he'd met Elena. He could still feel her soft hands stroking his head on the dark nights when demons had sneaked up and destroyed his sleep. She'd never judged him. After Elena had died, he'd battled alone again until his sister and brother had dragged him and Brian into their daily lives and regular society.

Now Gianna and Violet huddled together under three blankets on his sofa while Oro pretended he was a lapdog. Gianna sipped coffee as Violet drank a cup of Brian's stash of hot chocolate. Both of them stared off into space, haunted looks on their faces. He'd lit every kerosene lamp, wanting to eliminate every shadow from the room.

Chris stoked up the fire in the wood stove, slightly uncomfortable with the silence. He didn't mind silence when he was alone; he treasured it. He avoided houseguests. The only people who'd been to his cabin were his sister, Jamie, and his brother, Michael. They understood he didn't make small talk. Thankfully, Gianna and Violet didn't seem to need a host; they simply needed to feel safe. He'd achieved that. He watched until the dry piece of wood he'd added caught fire, and then swung the iron door shut and twisted the handle to lock it. The wood stove gave off a pleasant smoky odor. Unlike what he'd smelled earlier.

As soon as he'd opened the door of Gianna's cabin, he'd known something was wrong. He hadn't simply smelled burned wood; he'd smelled burned flesh. He *knew* the odor of burning flesh; he'd smelled his own thirteen separate times. And he was haunted by the smell of other children's burning skin. It didn't matter who you were; when flesh burned, everyone smelled the same.

Someone or *something* had been severely burned in the cabin. In addition, there'd been an underlying odor of bowel. Like the smell of a burning latrine. He'd grabbed Gianna's boots and then her coat while scanning the inside, unwilling to move in any farther. Everything had been covered in ash. The upper walls were black and there was a dark path scorched up the wall from the kitchen stove. To his scant fire knowledge, that pattern indicated where the fire had started. From Chris's low point of view, everything in the loft was black and charred. No one would have survived up there. On the lower level of the cabin, the patterns and colors of the furniture were still discernible through the soot. His quick glance hadn't revealed the source of the foul smell.

How did he tell Gianna that he believed something in her cabin was dead?

He'd asked the women about other people and pets in the cabin, trying to make sense of what his nose had told him. Their answer hadn't satisfied him. He'd searched their gazes, looking for deception and awareness of the odor, or a fear that he'd seen something in the cabin that he shouldn't. Either they were gifted liars or they were unaware of what was in the cabin. He'd seen a traumatized teen with a need to be close to her mother after her harrowing escape. In Gianna he'd seen confusion, but it was directed inward, as her nausea and clumsiness perplexed her. During their hike he'd heard her quietly ask Violet if she'd placed the wine bottle in the recycling. Violet had given her an odd look, saying she hadn't touched it, no doubt wondering why her mother was concerned with a wine bottle when they'd nearly burned up in their sleep.

Chris had been just as puzzled by the question.

Now, in the warm cabin, Violet relaxed and her eyelids fell closed.

"Would you like to lay down on one of the beds upstairs?" Chris asked the teen.

Panic fluttered her eyelashes, and Chris felt a pang of guilt as he realized she'd remembered how she'd woken to find their cabin on fire. His cabin's layout was nearly identical to their cabin's.

"No, thank you. I'll just lie down over there. I didn't sleep much last night." The teen moved to the other couch, farther back in the big room. She stretched out under a blanket and closed her eyes, using a beat-up throw pillow to rest her head. Oro followed, spreading his body out next to hers. Violet scooted closer to the back of the couch to give him more room, wrapping one arm around the dog.

Within seconds her breathing slowed and deepened.

Gianna's gaze rested on her daughter, sad resignation in her face. She turned and caught Chris watching her.

"She'll be okay," he offered.

She took a deep breath and looked into her coffee mug. "It's possible she may have started the fire. Not intentionally, but I've caught her with cigarettes recently. Although I went through every bag she brought up here, I may have missed something," she said softly.

"But according to her, the fire started downstairs in the kitchen area. Not in the loft where she was sleeping."

"Maybe she threw a burning cigarette in the trash under the kitchen sink. I don't know."

"Did you ask her if she was smoking last night?" He knew Gianna hadn't; he'd been with them nonstop since Gianna had awakened.

"No. That trail in the snow shows that someone else could have started it." She glanced at her sleeping daughter. "I'm shaken at the thought that someone may have tried to murder us in our sleep."

Chris nodded. "I don't think your daughter started it. Someone else was clearly there." He paused. "When I went in to get your boots, it smelled like a body had burned inside," he said carefully.

Gianna stared at him. "What do you mean?"

"There's something inside. I could smell it. That's why I asked about pets or anyone else being with you. There's something dead in there and it burned in the fire."

"Are you sure?" Her eyes widened. "Why didn't you say anything?"

"I didn't want to in front of your daughter."

"We should have checked it out!" Gianna set her mug down on the coffee table, her back ramrod straight. "Someone may have needed help." She looked ready to hike back to her cabin.

"Whatever it was is dead."

"How do you know what a burned body smells like?"

"Trust me, I do."

Her gaze probed him. "I deal with death every day. Burned bodies, drowned, shot. You should have told me what you suspected."

He stared back, curiosity rolling through him. "What do you do?"

"I start with the Oregon medical examiner's office in a few weeks. I'm a forensic pathologist."

"You do autopsies," Chris said flatly. *I should have told her my suspicions.* "Christ. I had no idea. You didn't smell it?"

"I didn't smell a thing. Probably because too much was going on. But you're right . . . that smell is hard to mistake. We need to call the police."

Chris spread his arms. "We've got no cell service and we're stuck until better weather. I haven't heard the plows, and I won't risk the drive until then. We're on a low-priority road because there's only a few cabins up here. The last forecast I saw showed only a little snow coming after the ice storm rolled through, so I bet they'll plow it by tomorrow. We don't have many plows around here, and their priority is the highways."

"Do you have some sort of radio to call out with? I saw a ranger station out on the highway not too far from here. Can we reach them?"

He shook his head. "I don't have anything else. Someone from the ranger station might check on us, but we're used to waiting things out up here."

Her expression indicated she didn't like having her hands tied. She looked ready to drive through the snow and ice to the ranger station. He waited, watching her process every possibility. He knew she'd eventually arrive at the conclusion that they'd done all they could.

"There's really nothing else we can do about the fire right now, is there?" she asked.

"Trust me. I've been thinking about nothing else. There's something dead in that cabin, and it's possible the two of you were meant to die in there with it."

★ ★ ★

"We need to go back," Gianna stated, nervous that a death might have happened that close to her daughter. "If there's a body in there, we can't just leave it. We need to see if something can be done." She stood up and fought the wave of dizziness that swamped her.

Chris jumped up and held out a hand. Gianna didn't know if it was to stop her or give her something to grab to keep from falling. "You're not thinking straight. Remember that walk?"

She did.

She ignored his hand and sank back into the couch. "I'm not used to sitting around doing nothing. Especially when something horrible has happened."

Chris lowered himself back into his chair, his gaze penetrating. "You want to rush back to a scene where someone may have tried to kill you and Violet."

"Who would want to kill us? You're jumping to conclusions. We spent the rest of the night sleeping in my Suburban. Anyone who wanted us dead could have walked right up and taken care of it." She looked pointedly at him. "No one wants to kill us."

She wouldn't let him get in her head. She and Violet had survived a horrible night, but until she had proof that the fire had been deliberately set, she wouldn't panic.

"Why's there a dead body in that cabin?"

"You don't know that for certain," she argued. "You said you didn't actually see it."

"I *know* something was in there."

"Maybe an animal went in while Violet was getting me out. That could be what you smelled."

"I don't think animals rush toward fire and smoke."

Gianna threw up her hands. Clearly they were of two minds about what had happened. "I don't know what to tell you. Yes, there was a trail outside and I'm sure you smelled something that burned, but I'm not going to sit here and stress. Until we go back and look, we'll never know what happened. But you don't want to go back."

"You *can't.*"

Frustration raced through her. The stubborn man was absolutely right. She glanced at the wall clock. It was barely the middle of the afternoon. *He expects me to wait until tomorrow for answers?*

She picked up her coffee cup and leaned back into the couch cushions, faking an attitude of relaxation.

He exhaled. "I get your frustration. I feel it, too. But the smart thing to do is wait."

She nodded, tamping down her irritation at her situation. Waiting wasn't one of her strong points.

Chris got up. "I'll grill some sandwiches. Food always helps." He pulled a cast iron pan and a loaf of bread out of a cupboard. Oro lifted his head, his ears at full attention and his gaze on the food-maker.

"You'll be working with Seth Rutledge at the examiner's office?" Chris asked as he prepared the food on the small kitchen island. "And his anthropologist, Victoria Peres?"

Surprise washed over her. "You know them?"

"My brother knows them better. I've crossed paths with them a few times."

"Small world. I finished up a forensic pathology fellowship in New York City and saw Oregon was hiring an assistant ME. I did a visit and interview a few months ago and got the job." She paused, remembering her first stunning view of Mount Hood as her plane flew into Oregon. "I loved how clean the air smelled, and everything was green. I hoped Portland would be a good place for Violet and me to put down some new roots. Violet hasn't been herself. Her grandmother died six months ago, and she'd always been Violet's caretaker while I worked."

"A lot of people move here for a fresh start." He deftly cut thick slices of cheese and arranged them on the bread.

She watched, slightly surprised she'd told him about her mother-in-law's death. But they possibly had a long time to wait and nothing to do but talk. She was good at small talk, and he seemed like the type who didn't mind listening.

"Yes. And I wanted to get her away from where her grandmother died. I knew she wasn't going to cheer when I told her, but I didn't expect the outright anger."

"She left behind friends. Maybe she feels as if she left her grandmother behind even though her soul is long gone."

An air of sadness surrounded Chris, and she suspected he spoke from personal experience. It was on the tip of her tongue to ask who'd died, but she quelled her curiosity.

She didn't know this man. *Don't be so nosy.*

"Is there someone we need to notify that you're okay?" Chris asked. "If the roads are clear, we can call them tomorrow when we get out."

"I haven't been in town long enough to meet anyone other than a few people I'll be working with," said Gianna. "I didn't tell anyone we were coming up here."

He looked across the stove at her and raised a brow.

"I know," she confessed. "Not smart when you're heading out to the wilderness, but I didn't think my friends in New York would care that I was renting a cabin for a week."

"Violet's father?"

"Eddie. He's deceased."

"I'm sorry." Sympathy flashed in his eyes.

"It was a long time ago," she said softly. She knew the hole in her heart from Eddie's death had shrunk as small as it was going to get. She'd learned to live with the abrupt aches from the open wound. "This truly is a fresh start for us. It's just the two of us. My parents died a long time ago, and when Eddie's mother passed last spring, we felt very alone, but I saw it as a chance to do something new. Some people pack up their kids and move abroad. They go to Costa Rica and raise their kids while surfing. Others move to France and immerse themselves in a new culture and end up with bilingual kids. I'm too big of a chicken to do either one, but I thought I could handle a move to the opposite coast." She paused. "I don't think I made a mistake."

"Of course not. It's way too early to tell if it's a mistake."

His logical statement and serious face made her grin. Clearly Chris Jacobs didn't sugarcoat his words. She took a closer look at their rescuer. He'd removed his cap, exposing light-brown hair that needed a cut. She noticed it covered the scars on his neck and figured that was the reason he left it long. His eyes were a penetrating light hazel and studied her like a hawk's. They never gazed at anything for too long. Even when he sat perfectly still and his attention was on her, she knew he was aware of everything that moved in the room. She wondered if he ever loosened up or if he stayed in a perpetually alert state. She had a sense that one ear was constantly listening for noise outside. Twice he'd turned his head to the sound of ice breaking a branch a split second before the noise registered in her brain.

Does he ever relax?

"Maybe an animal made that other path outside my cabin," she stated.

He shook his head and placed the sandwiches in the pan. "Definitely human."

"We haven't seen anyone since we got here. I feel bad for the people who own that cabin. I can imagine there's fire danger during the summer, but I doubt they expected it in the middle of winter. Do you know the owners?"

"No."

"Do you live here?"

He gave a half grin and his face finally relaxed a bit. "Heck no. I like solitude but not every single day of my life. I have a place south of Portland. Brian needs the socialization he gets from school. I don't want him to be a hermit like me."

She studied him. "You're a hermit?"

He looked away. "No. I just like quiet. I homeschooled Brian for a long time and thought I was doing a good job until my sister Jamie set me straight. She's an elementary-school principal. Brian didn't have any friends his own age because we lived in a remote area."

"Violet occasionally begs to be homeschooled. Usually when she is having some sort of argument with a friend. Even if I had the time, I'm not the type of person who can do that and stay sane."

He gave a small smile. "It was good for us. But I did it only until he was eight."

"You haven't mentioned his mother."

His smile vanished. "She died a long time ago in a car accident. Brian doesn't remember her."

Gianna understood. Too well. "Violet doesn't remember her father either. Eddie's diagnosis and death happened within six months of her birth. She'd cry and cry about having no memories of her dad. That's when we'd take a few hours to go through every picture and video of him I have. It's never been enough, but it helps."

"I don't have any pictures."

She straightened. "None? How . . ." Seeing the closed look on his face, she let the question die. *It's none of my business.* "I'm very sorry," she said softly. She was truly sorry, and her heart hurt for the little boy who didn't have a single picture of his mother.

"I've drawn some. They're pretty accurate."

"That's lovely."

The conversation came to a sudden halt. Gianna didn't want to probe, and Chris clearly was done with the topic. Her brain raced for a safe subject. "Are you sure we can get out to the ranger station tomorrow?"

His shoulders straightened. "I think so. The plows should have been working out on the highways all day and hopefully they'll get to our road, but I imagine the ice has created some complications, so it might take longer. I'm just glad I wasn't back in the city. They were supposed to get hit with the ice storm, too. Nothing like a city full of hills and an unprepared population."

"Unprepared? They don't salt?" Gianna asked.

"Nope. And there are even fewer plows in the city than out here. Portland doesn't get enough snow to justify the purchase of a huge fleet. It's not like the East Coast. We just dig in and wait it out. You'll see."

"Dig in? For a tiny bit of ice?"

"Absolutely. Or for a half inch of snow. The kids love it. City schools cancel right and left." He abruptly stopped speaking and stiffened his shoulders.

The far-off crack and echo of a gunshot reached Gianna's ears.

And then another one.

Chris froze, listening as he held the metal spatula above the pan.

Gianna waited for a third shot that didn't come.

"Hunters?" she asked.

"Could be."

"Is it hunting season?"

"Doesn't really matter if it's not. People still shoot."

CHAPTER FOUR

Chris flipped the sandwich in the pan, barely registering that it wasn't golden enough. Every ounce of his attention was directed toward the outdoors, waiting for more shots. Closer shots.

None came.

He felt Gianna's gaze as she looked to him to determine whether she should be concerned.

He didn't know the answer.

He flipped the other not-ready sandwich and met her gaze, forcing a small smile. "Maybe someone's bored."

He ran through a mental checklist. There were four guns in his cabin. A pistol in the drawer to his right and three more weapons in the gun safe next to the couch where Violet slept.

Gianna didn't smile back. "Are we safe?"

"Yes."

"Are you armed?"

He pointed at the gun safe with his spatula. "Yes."

She stood and moved to a window, pushing aside the heavy curtain. Motionless, she stared out the window for a good thirty seconds. "It sounded pretty far off."

"I agree." Melted cheese oozed out of one sandwich and sizzled in the pan. "Hungry?"

"Starving." Gianna sat on a rickety stool at the kitchen island.

"You've been sick," he stated.

She frowned. "I wasn't sick until the fire. I seemed to have had a bad reaction to something I ate or drank, or perhaps to the smoke. My brain is seriously muddled and I honestly can't remember what happened last night."

Chris waited.

"I had only one glass of wine last night. I think . . . I really can't remember, but I feel like I've been drugged," she admitted.

He agreed. From his extensive surgeries, he'd had experience with every kind of prescription pain-killer and could recognize when someone was highly medicated. "You don't take anything?" he asked. He moved to her side of the tiny island, studying her eyes, trying to get a look at her pupils. Her irises were so dark that the pupils were hard to see. Violet had the same eyes. "Any sore spots on your skull?" He reached out and gently pressed in several areas. Gianna copied his movements, feeling her own skull.

"Nothing hurts. I wondered if I'd hit my head. That could cause the nausea and headache."

"So something was in your dinner. Or wine."

Silence dragged between them as they both glanced at the sleeping Violet.

"What kind of kids has she been hanging out with?"

"Not the kind who'd suggest she drug her mother," Gianna snapped. "Especially in the middle of nowhere. What good would that do her? She can't call anyone or text anyone."

Chris held up his hands. "Then what happened?"

"I don't know." Gianna leaned her head back. "I asked myself that during our walk. My arms and legs weren't behaving the way they should."

"I noticed."

"Maybe I inhaled something in the burning cabin that affected my motor skills and made me nauseated. But why didn't Violet experience it? I'm trying to rationalize *something* to account for it. There's got to be an explanation."

"Maybe," Chris echoed. Something had definitely affected Gianna. How it had gotten into her system was a mystery. Clearly she was the type of person who needed proof. He strongly suspected she'd been exposed to something that'd made her feel ill, but it appeared she'd need to see a blood test before she'd accept it as fact. He figured it was the scientist in her. She needed to weigh every possibility before drawing a conclusion.

It wasn't a bad trait, but he found it a bit frustrating.

"Back in New York, Violet had started hanging out with the wrong kids," Gianna said quietly. "I brought her up here so I could spend time with her without being interrupted every ten minutes by her instant messages or email. She's been very angry with me since we moved. Granted, it's been only a few months since we left New York, but I'd hoped she'd be over it by now."

Chris nodded. Teen angst and issues were foreign to him. He'd been a teen at one time, but his perspective had been severely skewed. Being held in an underground bunker for two years after being kidnapped by a child abuser had given him a history few people could understand. He kept it to himself.

"She looks just like you," he commented. The teen had Gianna's long sleek brown hair and dark eyes, but stood a good three inches taller than her petite mother.

Pride flashed in Gianna's eyes. "She does," she said simply.

Chris abruptly missed his son. Brian had the dark coloring of his deceased mother, Elena, but looked exactly like Chris as a child. "Violet was terrified when I first got there," he said. "She'd been awake most of the night, making certain you were still breathing, worried about keeping you from choking on your own vomit."

Gianna tilted her head to one side. "Poor thing. She's heard me tell too many stories."

"Stories?" Chris asked.

She gave a grim look. "Stories that naturally come from working with dead people every day."

"Ah," said Chris. "I bet you see some fascinating things."

"Most people say 'gross things.'"

"That, too." He deftly maneuvered a sandwich onto a plate and slid it in front of her.

"It looks incredible," Gianna stated. She took a look at her daughter. "I'm not waking her up. I suspect she needs sleep more than anything right now."

"She'll have plenty of time to eat. We're going to be stuck here for a while."

★ ★ ★

Gianna carefully inched down the ladder from the loft. Dim light filtered into the cabin from the moon outside. She'd slept, but had spent the last hour staring at the close ceiling with images of the destroyed roof of her cabin and the mystery path in the snow bouncing around her brain.

How did the fire start?

Is Chris right that it was arson?

She'd finally gotten up, hoping a glass of water would put her back to sleep. She stepped off the last rung, turned, and sucked in a breath.

Chris stood ten feet away.

"Jeez! You scared me to death." She tried to calm her racing heart. "Did I wake you?"

"No. I was up."

He didn't expand on his statement.

She silently stared back at him, caution creeping up her spine. She couldn't see his eyes in the faint light. "What's going on?" He was tense. Wide awake and standing where he could see out the front window and the side window at the same time. She knew the curtains had been drawn when she went to bed. Now they were completely open.

"Nothing. I don't sleep much. Sometimes I just like to listen so I'm aware of what's going on."

She listened and heard a whole lot of silence. "You're worried."

He looked away, and she realized he was still in the jeans and shirt he'd worn that day. Violet had napped for several hours and woken up starving around dinnertime. Chris had heated them a simple meal of leftover stew and steamed rice that both she and Violet swore was the best thing they'd tasted in months. Later Gianna had picked a mystery from his shelf of novels while

Violet entertained herself with games on her phone. Everyone had gone to bed early. Or so she'd thought.

"Did you hear someone outside?" *How long has he been standing like that? I've been awake for an hour and haven't heard a peep.*

"No. It's quiet."

She moved to look out the front window. Moonlight reflected off the snow, doubling its radiance. She scanned for fresh tracks and paths. The snow sparkled and the frozen branches of the trees glistened. It was beautiful, but marred by her knowledge of the burned husk of a cabin a mile away. And the odd mystery path. Turning around, she saw Chris still hadn't moved.

"You've been standing there all night, haven't you?"

"No."

Yeah, right.

"I slept on the couch for a while," he admitted. "I'm awake a lot during the nights out here. Actually back home, too."

"Why?"

He paused before answering. "I don't need much sleep. Never have."

His head moved slightly and the moonlight illuminated two of the scars on his neck. Gianna focused on the scars, wondering about his past, and decided not to ask more questions. If he wanted to play vampire, she wasn't going to stop him.

"Did you need something?" he asked.

"Just water. Unless you have something stronger."

A wisp of a smile crossed his face as he lit a lamp. "Sorry. Water it is." He drew the curtains.

The gas lamp would reveal us to anyone outside.

He poured some water from a refrigerated filtered pitcher, and she sat on the stool where she'd perched to eat her sandwich the previous day. *Is he always extra cautious or just tonight?*

"Sometimes I have a hard time falling asleep after a particularly rough day at work," she said to fill the silence. "I get images in my brain and can't let them go. I'm better about it now."

"Do you like your work?" Chris asked, pouring his own glass of water.

"I love it. I'm nosy and curious and it's fascinating to see how actions during our lives are reflected in the cells and tissues after death."

"What do you mean?"

"Well, a simple example is a chronic alcoholic. When I cut them open, I might find a liver that is almost crunchy, not spongy and flexible, and even after death their bodies still exude a sweetish alcohol smell. Or what about a smoker? Most people know smokers' lungs are hardened black lobes, right?"

He swallowed hard.

"What do you do?" She politely changed the subject.

"I write software and manage IT for a few small companies. I can do it from anywhere. I just need a computer and the Internet."

"Then you're obviously not working while you're up here."

"It's good for me to break away. Back home I'll automatically reach for my laptop even when I don't have work to do. Being disconnected forces my brain to do other things. Or simply be bored. We're raising a generation of kids that doesn't realize it's okay to be bored. They constantly crave stimulation. They're addicted."

Gianna agreed. Violet had been annoyingly vocal about the lack of Internet at the cabin and constantly played the games she'd downloaded to her phone.

"Sometimes it's good to simply listen to the silence," Chris added. He ducked his head a bit, and she wondered if he'd revealed more than he'd meant to about himself.

"How much school did you attend to become a forensic pathologist?" he asked. He sipped his water and leaned against the counter in the small kitchen area. His constant awareness had mellowed, and Gianna wondered if it was because she'd provided a distraction.

"Four years of college, four years of medical, four years of a pathology residency," she stated. "Then I spent two years training in New York in death investigation and autopsy pathology. During my residency I studied what every single cell and tissue in the body looks like. I also learned what they look like when things go wrong. I could have gone and worked in a nice quiet lab after that, staring in a microscope all day long, but that sounded a bit dull."

"You didn't want to be a regular doctor?"

Gianna grinned at the common question. *What is a regular doctor?* "I've found I prefer patients who can't complain, and I like knowing that I can't make them more sick by working on them."

It took a split second for her old joke to sink in, and then Chris gave the first full smile she'd seen from him. He wasn't a bad-looking guy, she abruptly realized. He simply had a way of not calling attention to any part of himself.

He wasn't shy; he was reserved, she'd learned. He had plenty of self-confidence but didn't flaunt it. He'd been comfortable with her daughter. Some people didn't know how to talk to teens, but Chris seemed a natural at it. He'd known exactly what to say to Violet to alleviate her fears.

Impressive for a man who claimed to avoid people.

"You studied computer programming?" she asked.

"No. I have a history degree, but I'm self-taught when it comes to computers. Everything I've learned came from books or online or from my own discovery when I'd stumbled into solutions while struggling with a coding problem."

"You like it?"

"Love it."

She nodded. She loved what she did, too. It was a hell of a path to travel to get to her position, and there'd been times when she'd nearly given up . . . usually when infant Violet had been up all night or Gianna realized she'd missed another school recital. She said a quick prayer for her passed mother-in-law. She never would have succeeded without her help with Violet. They'd been a household of three since Violet was one.

"Can you imagine doing anything else?" she asked.

"Never."

"I feel the same way. I swear I learn something new every day, and I get to solve problems. I find that very satisfying."

"I could say the same thing." He took a close look at her. "Are all your drugged-feeling symptoms gone?"

She took a quick inventory. "Yes, I feel nearly normal."

"We'll find out what happened," he promised. "To you and to that cabin. We'll get the police up here and check out the odor."

"Tomorrow."

"I can't promise tomorrow, but soon."

"Thank you for helping us." She hadn't questioned his intentions. At all. If he was a crazy recluse who'd convinced her and Violet that he was helping them when he was actually waiting to kill them in their sleep, she'd walked right into his trap. He didn't give off a crazy vibe. When she was with him she felt a quiet strength and determination. He didn't flaunt anything. It would be easy to let her gaze bounce over him in a crowd, but when he was alone in a room, a low hum of energy surrounded him.

He nodded. "Anyone would have done the same."

Images of victims on her table floated through her mind. "I'm not so sure of that. There're a lot of evil people in the world and others who simply don't care. Fate could have chosen someone else to live in this cabin."

"Do you believe in fate?" he abruptly asked.

She blushed, thankful the lighting in the room was poor. "Not specifically," she lied. She had a firm belief that everything happened for a reason, but didn't care to discuss it with other people. The belief belonged to her, one she held close to her heart. It wasn't a doctrine to share and debate with strangers. Or even her closest friends. To her, fate was made of iridescent colors and fresh air and warm breezes. It was something beautiful she clung to when life grew dark.

Fate had rescued her in the past.

"Things are placed in our paths for a reason," Chris said slowly. "I almost didn't come up here this week. I had some projects around the house I wanted to do while Brian was gone, but one morning I woke up and knew I should go to the cabin instead. I wasn't sure why. Nothing up here needed attention, but I didn't question my decision."

Fate rescued me again?

She forced a smile as a chill touched her skin. "You think you were meant to be here to get Violet and me out?"

"Yes."

She couldn't see his eyes, but knew he was looking directly at her. "I can believe that." She believed it 100 percent.

Someone looks out for me.

Flashbacks of another cold night, a long walk, and someone who'd helped her when she was ready to collapse sprung from a dark area of her mind.

You can make it.

Cold feet. Cold fingers. So tired.

Anxiety ripped through her, and she shut down the memories.

★ ★ ★

Chris had talked more in the last twenty-four hours than in the previous month.

At home Brian talked enough for the both of them. When Chris was a boy, he'd had the same habit.

Before.

Would he still be a talker if he hadn't spent two years with the Ghostman? Before he'd been kidnapped, he'd wanted to be a politician like his father, and boasted he'd be president one day. He'd been confident and self-assured, brimming with the brashness of youth.

Now the thought of being in the public's eye made him want to vomit. He'd learned to keep his thoughts to himself and silently observe. Don't rock the boat, but always be present. Be ready, flexible, and quietly alive. Stay in the background. Don't be prey. Retain the posture of the predator. Act when necessary.

Survival skills.

He rarely stepped outside his comfort zone. He did so only when the needs of his family dictated the action. He would kill to protect his family. Brian, Michael, and Jamie. He'd been forced to prove it.

Now he'd extended his circle of protection to Gianna and Violet.

Anyone would have done the same.

Gianna hadn't agreed that anyone else would have helped them, and he knew she was right. Chris didn't consider himself anything special, but only an asshole would have left the women behind. And one could have crossed their path. The world was a dangerous place. A person didn't need to travel to the Middle East to find danger. It was present in every American's backyard and looked perfectly normal at first glance. Even at second glance. The evil being who had stolen his life and murdered children had smoothly interacted with society for years.

During that time Chris had hidden, terrified the Ghostman would find him again. He'd moved on in his life, keeping a low profile and constantly looking over his shoulder. When Brian came, Chris kept him in seclusion to protect him from all predators.

His greatest fear was that he'd learn he'd placed his son in danger's path by letting him move about in public. He had frequent nightmares about Brian's being in the hands of a killer or snatched off a public street.

He shuddered.

Gianna finished her water. "I'm going back to bed." She paused. "You should get some sleep."

"I will."

She didn't move, and he felt her disbelief. She opened her mouth and closed it, changing her mind about speaking. Knowing what his sister would have said, Chris guessed she was about to argue with him. Instead she looked toward the drawn curtains. "It's very dark outside. And too quiet. I struggled to sleep in the cabin because of the silence. I'm used to some sort of noise."

He understood.

She continued, "When it's this still, I find myself listening hard for a sound. Any sound. I think it makes my brain work harder and keeps me awake. Then my mind is off and running through a million different things."

Even in the poor lighting, he saw the stress around her eyes. She turned away and headed toward the ladder back to the loft.

"Good night, Chris."

She disappeared and he heard her murmur a few words to Violet, and then the cabin was still.

He stood in the silence and listened.

CHAPTER FIVE

The next morning Gianna poured coffee as she watched Chris scramble eggs.

Somewhere there's a woman missing out on this guy who likes to cook.

Gianna had been up for five minutes. Long enough to wash her face, pull her hair into a ponytail, and rouse Violet. The odor of coffee had filled the cabin. Violet had refused to open her eyes when Gianna woke her until her brain registered the smell and sound of frying bacon.

"Good morning," Chris said.

"Good morning," Gianna echoed. "What's the weather doing?"

He lifted a brow as he stirred the eggs. "It's definitely warmer. Doesn't look like we'll be getting more snow. The snowplows haven't come down our road yet, but maybe they will later."

"Good!"

Chris stiffened and then abruptly turned to look out the window.

It took Gianna a few additional seconds, but she heard the faint roar of an engine. "That sounds like a snowmobile."

Chris nodded. "A few people have them up here. I've been thinking about getting one. It would have been handy yesterday." He set down his whisk, turned off the stove, and walked over to the window near the front door.

Gianna noticed he stood to the side of the window, out of sight of anyone who might be approaching. Tension had filled the room, confusing her. *Shouldn't we be relieved someone is out and about?* The engine noise grew louder and Chris stood immobile, his gaze focused out the window. His right hand twitched at his side as if he wished to grab something.

His shoulders relaxed. "It's one of the rangers. He may have found the note I left in your vehicle. Or he's just checking on everyone in the area."

Gianna wrapped a throw around her upper arms and moved to look out the window. A man in a heavy coat removed his goggles as he strode toward the door of the cabin. His coat had patches showing the insignia that identified him as an employee of the US Forest Service. Chris opened the door as the ranger stepped onto the small covered porch.

"Good morning," Chris said as the ranger stomped the snow off his boots.

"You Chris Jacobs?" The ranger was rather short, with a narrow face and a thick beard. He touched the brim of his hat at

Gianna as she peered around Chris, who'd blocked most of the doorway with his body. Chris nodded at the ranger.

"I'm Francisco Green with the forest service." He paused, looking back and forth between Gianna and Chris. "I found your note in the Suburban at the Abell cabin. What the hell happened over there?"

★ ★ ★

Chris watched the forest ranger politely accept the coffee Gianna handed him and wrap chilled fingers around the mug with a sigh. He'd asked them to call him Frisco.

The three of them had taken a seat at the small table after Chris invited Frisco inside. The ranger had serious eyes and Chris had yet to see him smile, but he'd shown concern over Gianna and Violet's escape from the cabin.

Frisco hadn't mentioned the burning flesh odor, and Chris wondered if he'd looked inside the damaged cabin. Probably not. The cabin shell was an accident waiting to happen.

Violet emerged from the tiny bathroom, her face damp from a wash, and joined them at the table after grabbing a slice of bacon. She wrinkled her nose and shook her head when Chris asked if she wanted coffee.

"We're not sure what happened," Gianna said. "My daughter and I were both asleep when the fire started. She woke first and managed to get me out."

"Get you out?" Frisco repeated. He scowled and scratched at his beard.

Chris ran a hand over his own three days' worth of light stubble and briefly pictured himself with a full beard.

Nope.

Gianna looked down as she traced a gouge in the table with her finger. "I couldn't wake up. I honestly don't even remember her getting me out of the cabin, and then I vomited several times during the night as we waited in the car. There's a possibility I was drugged."

"What?" asked Violet, her eyes opening wide as she stared at her mother. "What are you talking about? How were you drugged?"

Chris studied her for any signs of guile; he saw none. The girl seemed sincerely stunned by her mother's comment.

Frisco's dark eyes silently scrutinized Gianna, and she squirmed. His stare was intimidating, and Chris figured the ranger didn't get much back talk while handing out tickets to overzealous fishermen and hunters.

"I know it sounds ridiculous," she said. "But I didn't take any medication, and I'm nearly positive I had one glass of wine last night. I didn't do anything that should have rendered me nearly useless. The only conclusion I can come up with is that I was somehow drugged."

"Nearly positive?" asked Frisco.

Annoyance flashed across Gianna's features. Twice the ranger had simply repeated what she'd told him. Chris understood. The man didn't want to put words in Gianna's mouth, but he wanted more answers.

"I can't remember. I know better to drink more than one glass. I'm tiny; alcohol can knock me on my ass with two glasses. It's ingrained in me to never have more than one drink."

"It sounds like you were knocked on your ass last night," Frisco stated. He took a long look at Violet, who stared right back at the ranger. "You see your mom drink?"

"I saw her with a glass of wine. That's normal."

Gianna coughed.

"I mean, it's not odd for her to have a glass of wine in the evening, but I've never seen her drunk," Violet amended.

"How do you think the fire started?" Frisco asked.

Violet raised a shoulder. "When I saw it, most of the flames were in the kitchen area. Something went wrong there. Maybe some bad electrical?"

Chris held Gianna's gaze and tipped his head in Violet's direction, hoping Gianna understood he wanted to bring up the odor in the cabin but wasn't sure about doing it in front of her daughter. She glanced at her daughter and shrugged.

"Did you look inside the cabin?" Gianna asked Frisco before Chris could speak.

Frisco shook his head. "I read the note that everyone got out and headed right over here. I wasn't about to go near it. It looks ready to cave in."

"Chris thinks there's a dead body inside. He stepped inside and could smell it."

"What?" Violet reeled back in her chair. "What are you talking about?"

Frisco's gaze shifted to Chris.

"Something with burned flesh is in there. I could smell it. They didn't have any pets, and I can't imagine that a wild animal headed in after the fire was already started. That tells me something human has to be in there."

"That can't be right," said Violet. "How could someone have died in there? It was just the two of us . . ." Her voice trailed off and she met Chris's gaze. "That's why you were looking at that other path. You think someone was there."

"What other path?" asked Frisco.

Chris told him what they'd seen outside the cabin.

"I think I need to go take a look and see for myself," said the ranger.

"Can we get out to the ranger station to make some calls?" asked Gianna. "The fire department should also be notified if there is a body in there. They have the professionals to investigate how it started."

"Nothing's been plowed but the main highway. And they did part of it only because of the accident. I'm doing all our patrols by snowmobile today."

"What accident?" asked Chris.

Frisco lifted his brows. "Big pileup about ten miles west of here. About twenty big rigs and a dozen cars. No traffic has gotten through since last night. What a fucking mess. It was all that damned ice." He looked to Violet and Gianna. "Pardon my language."

"The highway's only two lanes wide out there," Chris commented.

"Yep. Didn't take much to block it and create the biggest snarl I've ever seen. You can't even head east and cut to the north, because they've closed the highway along the gorge due to ice. South is the only option, but that'll take you four hours out of your way—if you make it. My understanding is that the ice is even worse down there." He glanced around the cabin. "How are you set for food and heat?"

Violet paled. "We're stuck here? For how long?"

"It's supposed to warm up. Not too much longer."

"We've got plenty of food, wood, and propane," Chris said, mentally taking inventory. "But that also means we can't get the police out here."

"I want to look inside that cabin before I call the sheriff's department. Who knows what could have made that smell," said

Frisco. "The county has a big enough mess with that wreck. And things are a general mess back in Portland, too. According to the news, the city has a lot of power outages and several of the streets are impassible from the ice."

"Can you get another person on that snowmobile?" asked Chris. "I'd like to go with you."

"No, I should go," asserted Gianna. "I'm the best person to take a look if there's a body."

Surprise crossed Frisco's face. "And why is that, ma'am?"

"I'm a medical examiner. Dead people are my business."

He stared at her for two seconds before shrugging. "No arguing with that."

★ ★ ★

Frisco was a daredevil on a snowmobile. Full speed ahead with no concern about anyone coming around a turn. Gianna hadn't ridden one in years and clamped her arms around his waist in a death grip. Memories of a wild high-school boyfriend with a motorcycle popped into her head. The same boy had taken her snowmobiling countless times. Looking back, she wondered how they'd both survived.

She'd never autopsied anyone who'd died in a snowmobile accident, but that was because she'd worked in Manhattan. No doubt an examiner from Montana or Idaho would have interesting snowmobile accident stories to tell.

They made it to the cabin within a few minutes; the winding curved driveway to her rented place stirred up her nausea as Frisco cut the hairpin turns as tightly as possible. Her heart stopped as they came within sight of her vehicle. Someone had smashed the driver's window.

All of Chris's concerns from the previous day shot through her brain.

Someone else has been here.

"Holy shit!" said Frisco, spotting the mess. "I was just here an hour ago and it didn't look like that." He slowed the snowmobile next to her Suburban and pulled a turn to reverse direction before they stopped and dismounted. They both slowly scanned the woods, Frisco resting his hand on the butt of the weapon at his waist. With the snowmobile abruptly silenced, the woods seemed eerily quiet.

Gianna's gaze halted on the burned cabin. *Would someone hide in there?*

Are we being watched?

The broken vehicle window simply made her sigh. There had been nothing to steal out of her old Suburban and there was nothing she could do about the damage right now.

"Maybe they were desperate. Perhaps their vehicle's snowed in and they needed to get to town." She scrambled to find a possible explanation for the broken window. One that didn't alarm her. "I don't know why the Suburban won't start."

"No one's driving this out of here even if it would start. You wouldn't get past the first turn in the road. The snow's too deep. This was done by a jerk who was looking for something to steal."

"Well, all they found was an owner's manual. And my grocery bags."

"I wonder what direction they came from." Frisco gestured at the tracks Chris, Violet, and Gianna had made the previous morning. "I saw that path when I was here earlier." Then he pointed at the far-off path that led east. "Is that the track you guys spotted when you left?"

"Yes, we made the ones that head west," Gianna said. "But there're definitely more prints now than when we left. Think he . . . or they . . . could be in the cabin?" she asked in a low voice.

Frisco looked in the cabin's direction. "Hello!" he shouted, making Gianna jump. "I'm with the forest service! Does anyone need help?"

They waited. His shouted words were swallowed up by the woods and snow. They didn't echo. They simply vanished.

"Anyone here?" he shouted.

Silence.

Frisco shrugged. "Either they don't want to be found or they took off after breaking your window."

Gianna felt as if a dozen eyes watched her from the woods, but she turned her attention back to her sad vehicle.

"Let me look in the truck first." Frisco peeked through the windows, checking the back row of seats and the cargo area. "All clear."

The vehicle was nearly ten years old but ran like new. It'd acquired a few extra squeaks and rattles since she'd first bought it, but it'd had no real problems until it had refused to start for Violet last night. "Are those marks from your snowmobile?" Gianna pointed at distinctive grooves in the snow and stepped carefully over to her vehicle.

"Yep. That's where I turned when I came by earlier. And those are my tracks where I walked over to your vehicle. You were smart to leave it unlocked for me to find the note." He winced and gave her an apologetic look. "I locked the doors after I found it. Maybe they wouldn't have broken the window if I'd left it unlocked."

"You did the right thing." She sighed. "Wish I had some duct tape and plastic, but it's not a priority right now." She eyed the cabin again, curious about what might be inside.

Frisco slipped a small camera out of his pocket. "I'll take some pictures before we make any new paths."

"Good idea." Gianna was a fan of as many pictures as possible when it came to collecting evidence. She'd testified in court several times and had found photographic evidence could be the determining factor when life insurance companies fought against claims. She'd seen a routinely snapped autopsy photo win a case for a mother with four young children after the death of her husband. Frisco took pictures of her truck's window and the jumbled mess of deep footprints in the snow. He slowly expanded his range of shots, taking some far images of the cabin and then focusing on the path that'd been forged between the vehicle and cabin. Gianna followed as he moved closer to the cabin. She inhaled through her nose, searching for the odor that had convinced Chris someone had burned inside. She smelled only burned wood.

The mystery path traveled east from the cabin and away into the woods. Frisco took some close-up images of the prints in the snow, and from the cabin's small porch he took a few of the path. He yelled again, asking if anyone needed help. Silence. "Let's see if it looks safe to step inside for a few minutes."

Gianna was ready. She hadn't worked in a few weeks and the familiar excitement climbed up her spine, as it did when she received her daily assignments in the morgue. She'd been unable to get the possibility of a death in the cabin out of her mind ever since Chris had mentioned the smell. *A puzzle to solve.* She put her hand on the door handle and turned it, giving the door a push. It stuck.

"Let me try." Frisco stepped forward as she moved back out of his way.

He turned the handle and pushed against the door with his shoulder. It flew open and ash billowed up from the floor.

Gianna's heart dropped as she took in the blackened interior. "Ohhhh."

We're lucky to be alive.

The odor of death slapped her in the face. Burned death. It was unmistakable. A combination of barbecue and sewer. Chris hadn't been wrong.

"Dear Lord," muttered Frisco. "He wasn't kidding." He blocked Gianna as she tried to move past him. "Hang on a second."

She stopped and took another look at the ceiling. Large pieces of roof hung from the burned holes.

"Someone's walked in here since the fire." Frisco pointed. "Look at the footprints. Is that from you guys?"

Gianna studied the large prints that led toward the back of the room. "Chris went back in to grab my boots. I don't think he walked that far. My boots were right by the door and he didn't want to be inside any longer than necessary." Dread crept up her spine.

Who was here?

Did they set the fire?

"I want to take some pictures before we tramp through here," Frisco stated. "I don't want our prints mixed up with those."

She nodded.

Frisco took wide angles of the entire room and then closer focused shots. Gianna spotted her cell phone and purse near the far couch. Both were barely recognizable. All color was gone, and they were partially melted and buried under ash. There was nothing she wanted from either object. She didn't get attached to physical things; in her mind everything was replaceable. "Do you think it's safe to go in?" she asked.

"I think it's okay. It doesn't look like any parts of the ceiling have fallen since the fire went out. Let's take a look and see if we can find what's causing that smell and then get out."

"It's coming from the back of the room," she stated. *Where the footprints lead.* The first floor of the cabin was a deep rectangle with the bathroom at the rear and the kitchen to her left. The main room had a fireplace and two comfy couches. From their viewpoint they could see everything except the interior of the bathroom, the loft, and the area behind the farthest couch.

Frisco took measured steps across the great room, carefully photographing his way in. Gianna glanced behind them, seeing their footprints added to the existing path in the ash. The ranger's shoulders tensed as he stepped past the second ash-covered couch.

He looked down and crossed himself.

Gianna held her breath and stopped beside him. The figure on the floor behind the couch was in the traditional pugilist's pose of a burn victim: arms and legs drawn close to the body from the heat contracting the muscles. Some of his clothing had melted; some had burned. It was clearly a male body—his frame, boots, and masculine skull stating his sex. His head was charred, his hair mostly gone, and the bone of his skull exposed.

"Know him?" Frisco asked.

"No . . . I don't think so." He was burned beyond recognition. *How did the man sneak into our cabin?* "I don't understand . . ." Gianna couldn't speak. Had the man been in the cabin as she lay passed out on the other couch? Or had he entered after Violet had dragged her out? She crouched to get a closer look, part of her itching to get him cleaned up and on a table. "Look there." She pointed at the base of his skull. Mixed in with the burned hair, roasted flesh, and ashy bone, she could see two holes in his skull. Frisco took another step and bent down beside her.

"Well, hello there," he said softly. He pointed his camera at the head and took several angles. "It looks like our boy had a confrontation with a couple of bullets."

"A confrontation implies he saw it coming," said Gianna. "I don't think he saw it headed toward the back of his skull." Her mind spun with more questions. *Who shot him? When was he shot? Why is he in* my *rented cabin?*

"I don't think there's much more we can do here," Frisco stated as he stood. "Let's get you back to the other cabin, and I'll call the state police. This is above and beyond my job description."

Gianna reluctantly straightened, unable to pull her gaze from the murdered man. Shock slowly built in her lungs. She'd seen a lot of violence in her career, but none that'd occurred this close to her and Violet. She veered away from her pathologist mind-set and let her mothering side take over. "Oh, my God. What if Violet had gotten hurt?" Her knees shook at the images that raced through her brain. "Why is he in here?"

Frisco shook his head. "You'd be the first person I'd ask."

She whipped her face toward him. "I don't know anything about this."

"I know that," he said, pointedly holding her gaze. "But if I was an investigator who'd just been handed this case, you'd be the first person I would question. You *and* your daughter. Are you ready for that?"

Dread touched her spine, but she kept her face neutral and remembered how she'd dealt with officers back in New York. "Of course. We don't have any idea how this happened. It will be frustrating for the investigators, but we aren't going to be much help."

"It could be that your daughter saw something."

"She didn't see anything. She was totally surprised when Chris brought it up."

"Maybe she doesn't realize she saw or heard something important. She was clearly rattled by the whole experience. Once she's calmer and can think back on what happened, she might recall something."

Gianna nodded but inside she tried to calm down about how close the assault had been to her daughter. As traumatizing as that night had been, Gianna believed Violet would have noticed a man in the cabin.

"Let's head back. I was about to ask if you wanted to grab anything, but it's probably best not to touch anything. The investigators aren't going to like that we entered."

"Tough," muttered Gianna. "I'll tell them we did them a favor by making sure it was human and not calling them out to discover Smokey the Bear had died in here. I don't need anything from inside." She felt a bit naked without her driver's license and credit cards, but she was due to get an Oregon license, and new cards could be ordered. She moved to the front door and stared at her Suburban as Frisco took photos of the footprints they'd left across the floor of the cabin. A clear record of where they'd been.

Frisco stepped beside her and took a few more pictures of the snowy paths. "I love the quiet cold days like this," he said. "Everything is silent and sleeping. You have to cherish that feeling to live up here. This isn't a life for people who need constant action. Our year-round residents know how to change with the seasons. Winter means settling in and being prepared to wait things out."

"I don't mind it for a few days," answered Gianna.

Frisco nodded. "That's why we get a few tourists during the winter. They crave the adventure of being snowed in, but once it's continued for more than a few days they start climbing the walls."

Gianna thought about Chris Jacobs. He seemed the sort who could last for weeks in the solitude.

"We were lucky Chris came along," Gianna said. "We would still have been sitting in my Suburban when you arrived this morning."

Dread shot through her at the thought of having spent that much more time without heat. *Would we have survived?* A dizziness rocked her as she imagined hour after hour of dropping temperatures. She bent over and rested her hands on her thighs, putting the image of Violet slowly freezing to death out of her head.

A spray of warm moisture and small fragments covered her face and shoulder. She twisted away reflexively as the sound of a gunshot filled the silent forest. A hole punched through the cabin siding beside her, and she lunged to the side after she heard the second shot, leaping off the low porch and landing on her belly in the snow, knocking the air out of her lungs.

She looked over her shoulder. Half of Frisco's head was gone.

Brain matter and blood.

That's what sprayed me.

His body slumped in a heap on the porch. Horror paralyzed her, and she fought to find a breath.

He's dead.

I can't help him.

I'm next.

Get away.

Her brain shifted into flight mode as she looked forward at the forest.

The shots came from the woods.

Did he shoot the man inside?

Run. Snowmobile. Now. For a brief second she considered dashing back inside the cabin. *That will protect me for ten seconds. Leave now.*

Gun. Keys.

Voices screamed in her head as she forced herself to scramble to her hands and knees and crawl back up on the porch, keeping her head low. Her hands shook as she flipped the snaps on the holster that held Frisco's gun, and she yanked on the handle. It didn't move. *Push first.* She pushed down on the butt of the gun and felt the holster's safety release. She slid the weapon out of the holster and shoved it in the deep pocket of her coat. She mentally thanked the cop who'd shown her how the release worked when she'd teased him in the morgue, saying that she could snag his gun. Frisco's tiny camera lay beside him. She grabbed it.

Keys. Still in the ignition.

Go. Now. She took a deep breath and sprinted to the snowmobile, dashing awkwardly in the snow, thrusting her boots into old footprints and nearly falling several times as her boot tip caught on the lip of the ice. Every second she anticipated a death-blow in the center of her spine, and her ears strained to hear the next shot over her gasping breaths.

She flung herself on the snowmobile, fumbled with the engine switch and choke, and turned the ignition. It purred.

★ ★ ★

He ran.

He hadn't expected it to go down that way.

She was supposed to be dead. Instead she'd survived the fire and someone else had just died. He'd been unable to fire again as he realized the man who'd collapsed from his bullet wore a uniform.

Did I just shoot a cop?

More sweat ran down his sides under his coat as he pushed through the branches and deep snow. Pain shot through his lungs as they begged for oxygen. He wanted to throw the rifle aside, let it be buried in the falling snow, but he knew it could be traced to him. Instead he cursed it, blaming the gun for the man's death and now his aching lungs.

I fucked up.

It was supposed to be over. All of it. But he'd made a mistake. He'd planned to tell his father that he'd found the cabin burned to the ground and the woman dead, and that he'd put the old man out of his misery with a gunshot to the head. But she was *alive*.

And it was his fault.

How am I going to fix this?

His father wasn't going to be happy.

He'd keep his mouth shut about what'd just happened until he'd found a solution. Luckily he had a handy scapegoat.

And he'd follow Gianna Trask and finish the job.

CHAPTER SIX

"Do you mind if I make some more eggs?" Violet asked.

Her mom had taken off a few minutes ago with the ranger, and Violet was painfully aware that she'd been left in the confines of a remote cabin with a man she knew nothing about. Her hands were restless and she needed something to take her mind off her mother's safety. Yes, she'd left with a forest ranger, but she was going back to *that* place. The place of flames, smoke, fear, and cold. Violet had woken up twice last night, terrified that Chris's cabin was on fire, but everything had been silent. Now she couldn't get the idea of a burned person out of her head, and she needed something to do to fill the awkward silence.

"Go ahead. I had to toss the ones I made earlier. I forgot about them once the ranger showed up." Chris stood near the front window, watching the direction in which the two had vanished on the snowmobile.

"I can make a big batch of scrambled for both of us."

Chris turned to look at her. "That'd be great." He smiled, but it was one of those adult smiles intended to make kids and teens feel like everything is okay. Violet had known how to recognize them since she was four.

Everything is not okay.

There might be a body in our cabin?

She put the thought out of her brain. Surely her mom would be safe with the ranger. Oro jumped off the couch and planted himself just outside the kitchen area, watching Violet as if she'd offered him eggs, too.

"Is he hungry?" she asked. She took the egg carton out of the skinny refrigerator and snooped through the cupboards until she found a medium-size bowl and whisk.

"I'll feed him." Chris poured some kibble in a bowl on a mat near the door. Oro watched his movements and then turned his dark eyes back to Violet.

I'd prefer eggs to dog food, too.

She studied Chris out of the corner of her eye as she broke the eggs and whisked them together. He stayed a solid ten feet away from her at all times. Part of her appreciated his efforts to make her not feel threatened, but another part of her wanted to roll her eyes. The man was clearly a gentleman. He might look rough around the edges with his scars and faded jeans, but his manners were impeccable. She didn't feel unsafe around him, just curious and awkward.

"How long do you think they'll be?" she asked.

"Can't say. If there's a body in there, I imagine your mom will want a long look."

"Absolutely." Violet wrinkled her nose. "She's obsessed with death." She knew he was right. Her mom had a tendency to lose track of time in her work.

"Obsessed with death or the human body?"

Violet thought about it. "You're right. She can talk non-stop about what bodies do when they're in certain situations. Sometimes I have to tell her to stop. I'm used to it, but it's embarrassing if I have friends over or we're out in public. Sometimes she forgets that not everyone is used to seeing gunshot wounds or rotting flesh."

"There's no way you're used to hearing her talk about it," Chris stated. He took a stool at the far end of the island as Violet poured the eggs in a pan.

"I know how to tune things out. Most of the time, she doesn't bring up her work, but sometimes I think she gets distracted by the science of it all and can't keep it to herself." Violet met his calm gaze. "She really likes her job."

"You don't?"

"Sometimes I wish she worked in a bank."

He grinned. "My dad worked in a bank. I can't think of anything more boring. One of my dads," he corrected.

A small spike of pain hit Violet's heart and rapidly faded. She looked down at her eggs and kept the whisk moving through the yellow slimy mass over the low heat. "Is that your son?" She tilted her head at an enlarged photograph on the wall. It showed a dark-haired boy wrestling in the snow with another man. The colors were vivid against the white snow, and she could almost hear them shouting in laughter. Happiness radiated from the picture.

Chris looked at the photo and smiled fondly. "Yes, that's Brian and my brother, Michael."

Violet studied the details. "They both look like you. You all have different coloring, but I can see the resemblance in the eyes and the faces.'"

He looked away under her scrutiny, but she saw he was pleased by her observation. She felt the same way when people said she looked like her mom. Her mom was gorgeous, and Violet had always loved that she referred to Violet as her mini-me—even after Violet grew taller than she. It was something no one could ever take away from them.

She saw nothing of her father in her face, and her mom agreed. It often felt as if she'd been created solely from her mother's genetics. It hurt. She swallowed hard and stared at the eggs.

Please stay safe. She didn't need to lose another parent.

"He's an only child?" she asked.

"Yes."

"I've always liked being an only child," Violet stated. "I have friends who hate it and say they wanted someone to play with when they were younger, but I've always been able to entertain myself. I didn't feel a need for siblings."

Chris nodded, but she suspected he wondered at the truth of her statement. When she'd needed one, her grandmother had been a wonderful playmate, and when her mother was home, Violet had always wanted to spend time with her.

"It must have been hard to leave your friends behind in New York."

Her head jerked up. *Did my mom already tell him?* "Yes. I've lived there all my life, and my mom decided to uproot me during my junior year. I think anyone can agree that's not cool." She stirred her thickening eggs. "I miss my friends. Texting and

Skype help but I've lost that since we came up here. Do you think we'll be able to go back to the city today?"

He took a piece of cold bacon, bit into it, and chewed, looking out at the light snow. Violet couldn't read his expression.

"I doubt it. The warming trend they forecasted hasn't appeared yet. If they don't get the roads plowed, I'm not sure how my truck will be in the deep snow, and I hate to risk it until we have to. And with that big accident Frisco told us about, there's no point in even trying. If we get out to the main highway, we'd have to turn around."

Her eggs looked perfect. She scooped a big serving onto a plate and handed it to him, nodding at his sincere thanks.

She dished up her own plate and they ate in silence for a few minutes. Oro scooted closer, moving his focus to Chris and his plate. Violet had always wanted a dog. Her best friend's dogs were big, goofy, joyful animals who celebrated whenever Violet visited. She'd always thought it'd be cool to have someone over-the-moon excited to greet you every time you came home. Oro wasn't goofy; he was calm. But she noticed he was aware of every movement made in the cabin. Just like his owner.

She watched Chris eat and realized the awkwardness she'd felt earlier was gone. She still had a bit of anxiety over her mom, but she'd absorbed some of Chris's calm. He finished nearly all his eggs and scraped the remainder into Oro's bowl on top of his dog food. The dog finished the eggs in a split second and left the kibble. Oro picked a new spot to sit and fastened his stare on Violet.

"Did you even taste the eggs?" Chris asked the dog. Oro didn't look away from Violet.

A far-off gunshot sounded from outside. Chris turned to look out the window and the tension in the cabin abruptly returned. Another shot sounded.

"That sounds pretty far away," Violet said. *Mom?*

The sudden stiffness in Chris's back alarmed her. *Is he worried?* "I imagine you hear gunfire up here pretty often?" she asked hopefully, wanting him to alleviate her fears. They were in the middle of the forest; shouldn't gunfire be normal?

"Sometimes," he said. "Not as much this time of year. We heard two shots last night, too." He gave her that small don't-worry smile again. "Someone's probably bored."

"Are we safe here?" Violet blurted. "Is my mom safe? Do you think that was the ranger's gun? What if something's happened to them?" She turned and rinsed her plate in the tiny sink as a small blanket of fear covered her shoulders. She wanted to run out the front door and go search for her mom.

We're in the fucking middle of nowhere.

"Hey, we're okay—" Chris started.

"I know *we're okay*, but what about my mom? They might be hurt," Violet snapped at him as she turned around. Guilt flooded her. "I'm sorry." She wiped the island with a damp cloth, unable to keep her hands still. "I have a tendency to say whatever is going through my head."

"That's not a bad thing," Chris said. "Gunshots will make anyone concerned."

"Mom says I need to use the filter between my brain and mouth more often."

"I've never had that problem." He raised a brow at her. "Most people complain that I don't tell them what I'm thinking."

Violet believed it. The whole time she'd been around him, she'd had no clue what was going on in his head. She had been able to tell he was happy when he looked at the picture of his son and brother, but she didn't know what he thought about their current situation. He was almost annoyingly calm.

"What about the gunshots?" she pressed. "Shouldn't we do something?"

"Do what? Run out and try to find someone with a gun in the middle of the woods? We're safest right here. Frisco probably knows every inch of this forest, and I noticed he handled that snowmobile like he'd been born on it. I felt confident about letting your mom leave with him."

"Do you have a gun?" Violet held her breath.

He gazed at her for a few seconds. "Yes."

She exhaled. "That's good." She felt a tiny bit better and focused on cleaning up the egg pan. She and Chris and Oro had finished every bite, she noticed as she remembered her mom hadn't eaten before she left. *I'll make more when she gets back.*

"I won't let anything happen to you," Chris said solemnly. "Your mom trusted me with your safety."

She glanced over her shoulder at him. His face was deadly serious. Clearly he was taking his role as protector to heart. Violet had already mentally moved on to plans for filling her time with some baking. When she was bored or nervous, she baked. "I know," she said. "It's okay. I'm not nervous anymore," she lied. "Do you have baker's chocolate?"

"I don't think so. Could you substitute hot chocolate mix?"

Violet bit the inside of her cheek, holding back a laugh. "I'm afraid not."

She heard the far-off hum of the snowmobile a split second after Chris turned his head toward the front door. *Thank goodness. They're coming back.* She rushed to the window and looked down the long drive, willing her mother and Frisco to appear. A tiny figure on a snowmobile came around a curve and Violet squinted. *Is Mom driving?*

"Where's the ranger guy?" she asked out loud. Chris silently watched over her shoulder as the snowmobile came closer to the cabin.

Violet stared. Her mother's pale-green coat had stuff on it. Red stuff.

"What the *fuck*?" Chris muttered under his breath.

He strode to the door and yanked it open.

★ ★ ★

Chris leaped over the porch steps, his vision locked on Gianna.

She stopped the snowmobile and jumped off, nearly tripping as her boots sank into the snow.

"What happened?"

"Frisco's dead." Gianna gasped between pants as she stumbled toward him. "Someone shot him. At the cabin."

He grabbed her forearms. Her eyes were wide, half her face covered in a light spray of red. A heavier spray covered the shoulder and front of her coat. She followed his gaze. *"Oh, my God."* She yanked one arm away and smeared the mess more with her glove. He pulled her hand away from the blood.

"Mom!"

Gianna looked past him. "I'm okay. I'm not hurt." Chris thought her voice was extremely calm for that of someone who'd just witnessed a violent death.

"Whose blood is that?" Violet squeaked.

Gianna swallowed. "It's Frisco's. He's been shot."

"What? Is he okay?"

She blinked at her daughter, her mouth moving but no words forming. She shook her head at Violet.

Chris tightened his grip, pulling her attention back to him. "What happened?" he repeated. He led her up the porch steps, wanting to get out of the exposed yard. She pulled away from him and yanked off her jacket, holding it out from her as if it were poison.

"I don't know. We had just stepped out of the cabin when someone shot at us. Twice. I managed to get out of the way, but Frisco . . . and they broke a window of my Suburban. *Someone is over there. We need to go to the police,*" she pleaded with Chris. "And there was a dead man in the cabin—he'd been shot and burned. That's what you smelled."

Violet clamped a hand over her mouth and stared at her mother in shock.

Chris's brain shifted into analysis-and-survival mode. "Did you see the shooter? Did they have a vehicle? Was there just one person?"

"I didn't see anyone. Or a car," Gianna forced out. Her pupils were dilated and Chris saw a vein pound at the side of her neck.

If they come by foot, it could take half an hour to get here. We left a clear trail to my cabin yesterday.

By vehicle, they could be here any minute.

"Let's get inside," he ordered. He gave Violet a small push on her shoulder. Her wide-eyed gaze was still locked on her mother's bloody face.

"No! We need to go to the police!" Gianna argued, planting her feet.

Chris pointed at the snowmobile. "That won't hold three of us." He thought about his vehicle in the shed and for the hundredth time analyzed the depth of the snow and ice. *It might handle these conditions. Or would I be risking our lives even more?* Basic survival rules indicated that they stay with the shelter, but the murder had changed the rules. "Who do you pick to stay here alone?"

Gianna looked from him to Violet, who'd stepped just inside the door and into some semblance of cover. She stared back at her mother.

Indecision fluttered across Gianna's face.

Chris had already done the analysis. He wouldn't let the two women leave on their own, and he wouldn't leave anyone behind in the cabin. That left the three of them hunkering down. *Unless we risk traveling through the snow in my vehicle.*

At least he was well armed.

"Can you shoot?" he asked Gianna in a low voice.

She pulled a gun out of the pocket of the bloody coat. "I took this off Frisco after he went down. I wanted something to protect myself with. But no, I've never shot one."

Crap.

"Inside." He took the weapon and coat from Gianna. They entered the house and he locked the door. "Violet, would you check all the locks on the windows? And close all the shades." They should already be locked, but he needed to cross the verification off his mental list.

He spread out the coat on his kitchen island, keeping the human-tissue spatter from touching the surface. He grabbed a roll of paper towels to tackle the worst of the goop.

"You can't do that! That's evidence!"

He met Gianna's gaze. "If we have to leave the house, this coat is all that stands between you and freezing to death. Do you want some of this cleaned off so you can use it or do you want to save the coat for a crime scene technician?"

She didn't answer.

He handed her the roll of paper towels, and strode across the room to his gun safe and spun the dial. After a moment of silence, he heard the tearing of a paper towel and the soft sounds of her jacket being wiped. He felt like an ass, but someone had needed to get her brain thinking in the right direction. *Survival mode.*

He'd spent years in survival mode, always looking over his shoulder and lying awake at night waiting for sounds that indicated he and Brian had been hunted down. When the assassin finally arrived, his preparation had paid off, and he and Brian survived.

When the assassin had Brian in his grip, Chris had learned he was capable of taking human life.

He pushed away the memory, but the adrenaline raced through his veins again and he welcomed the reminder to keep his guard up—even when his ghost had been eliminated. Frisco's murder proved that evil still moved in the world. Avoiding society as much as possible didn't prevent horrors from touching Chris's life.

The buzz in his veins was familiar. Like a song he hadn't heard in a long time. His skin tingled with an awareness that he'd nearly forgotten, and he wondered if his reflexes had grown rusty. He pulled a rifle, a double-barreled shotgun, and another pistol out of the locker. His primary weapon lay in a drawer in the kitchen island where Gianna silently worked on her coat.

Why didn't I grab that first?

Rusty.

He lay the three weapons on the counter next to Frisco's weapon and reached around Gianna to push in on a nearly invisible drawer. It popped open, and she gaped at the gun inside. He hadn't worried about either of the women finding it. It was on an end away from the other drawers and required a special release. Brian knew how to open the drawer. Chris had schooled him early in gun safety and use. His son had a healthy appreciation for the power of guns and treated them with respect.

"What the hell is going on?" Gianna said under her breath. She tossed a bloody paper towel in the garbage and ripped off another. She dampened it and attacked the smears on her coat. She'd removed 90 percent of the matter and it looked good enough in Chris's opinion, but she scrubbed at the brownish discolorations with fervor. He watched her hands and saw them tremble.

"Who knows you're up here?" he asked quietly. He'd asked her the same question yesterday, but he wondered if she'd have a different answer now.

Her hands stopped midscrub and wide brown eyes met his. "What are you asking?"

"I'm asking if there is someone who'd like to hurt you or Violet," he whispered.

Her horrified gaze flew to her daughter, who sat on the couch with her knees up under her chin and Oro pulled tightly to her side.

"No one wants to hurt us," she hissed at him.

"Think hard. You've been possibly drugged, nearly burned, and now shot at. *Think!*"

"We just happened to be in the path of some crazy people in the woods! I'm not a target for anyone!" She kept her voice to a harsh whisper, glancing nervously at Violet to make certain she hadn't heard.

She could whisper all she wanted. Chris suspected Violet knew and heard a lot her mother didn't want her to. He studied Gianna's expression, searching for deceit, and didn't see it. But he did see doubt; his questions had rattled her, and he wondered if she was playing down his concerns in an attempt not to alarm Violet.

It's time for both of them to be alarmed.

"I think someone is focused on you or Violet," he stated slowly. "And I'm going to operate as if they're coming here next."

"Operate? What the hell are you?"

"Someone who knows how to stay under the radar and protect myself."

Silent eyes searched his. "What happened to you?" she whispered.

He shook his head. "No time for that now."

CHAPTER SEVEN

The flash of pain in Chris's eyes vanished immediately. He might have scars on his neck and face, but he had even bigger ones on the inside. Scars that'd toughened him into some sort of robotic human. He'd barely shown any emotion since she'd returned. He'd acted and spoken as if people were shot every day and they just needed to follow a checklist to handle the situation.

Gianna didn't know whether to pity him or be thankful.

A little of both.

She blew out a breath and looked down at her coat. It was ruined. Her scrubbing had pushed the blood deep into the fibers and she knew it'd never come out. She didn't care; she had no desire to wear the coat again. Frisco's open skull flashed through her mind. She'd seen a lot of head injuries come across her table, and she'd neatly opened plenty of skulls. But she'd never been present when lives had been obliterated.

Oh, Lord.

Her vision tunneled, and she leaned forward on her hands as her knees suddenly felt liquid. Chris grabbed her shoulder and shoved a stool against the backs of her thighs. She sat and rested her forehead on the countertop, waiting for her blood pressure to normalize.

What if the shot hit me instead? What would have happened to Violet?

"Mom?"

"I'm fine. Just a bit dizzy all of a sudden." To her ears, her voice sounded too high.

Chris rubbed at her shoulder. "Take your time," he said softly. "It'll pass. It's just everything catching up with her," he said to Violet, who'd moved off the couch.

She thought back to Chris's question. "The agent who rented me the cabin is the only person who knows we're here," she said quietly. "I may have mentioned to some friends back home in New York that we were taking off for a few days, but I never said where we were going. I mainly said something to let them know why I wouldn't be answering any calls or emails. Same with the new office in Portland. I only said I was going to be unreachable for a while." Her vision started to clear, and she sat up to meet his serious gaze. "That's the truth."

He nodded. "Can you think of anyone who'd be angry or upset enough to want to harm you? Did you piss anyone off because you didn't report the autopsy results they wanted to hear?"

She understood his question. Relatives didn't want to hear that their loved ones had committed suicide or indulged in dangerous behavior that'd taken their lives. Sometimes a relative would swear their loved one had never, in their entire life, touched the drug that had shown up in the tox report. Or Gianna wouldn't be able to pinpoint a cause of death—it happened. Concrete evidence was always needed. She couldn't assign a cause of death based on her suspicions. She'd been questioned on her results several times; it came with the job. Yes, there had been people who had disliked her results, but not enough to want to harm her.

I don't think they would.

"What? You've thought of something."

"I'm sure it's nothing," she said hesitantly. She'd firmly put the Sullivan case out of her mind, but Chris's prodding had brought it to the forefront. It was the only one—that she was aware of—that would fit his description. The Sullivan family had a few nuts in its tree. "I don't think this is the time to sit down and analyze my past, right? I don't want to make guesses about the past, and we need to worry about the *right now.*"

"True." His gaze prodded her.

"Trust me. I haven't thought of anyone who'd come three thousand miles to burn down a cabin in the woods." *Truth.* "Frisco said that the county sheriff's department had their hands full with that big pileup on the highway. Maybe that's where we should go, to be near some police. We need to let them know what's happened, and we can't just leave Frisco out there."

Indecision briefly flashed in his eyes.

He stepped over to a window and pushed the curtain to the side with one finger to see out. Gianna held her breath, trying to be as silent as possible as he listened. "We'll be leaving a glowing trail of where we went. Anyone will be able to see our tracks."

"They can already see our tracks. If they're on foot, they can follow the path the three of us made yesterday. If they drive, the snowmobile tracks are pretty clear."

"You said you didn't see a vehicle, right? Did you see any other tracks in the road when you rode over with Frisco?"

She shook her head. "Some snowmobile tracks, but I assumed they were the ones Frisco made while coming here. No vehicles."

"How bad were the roads?"

"Bad. If not for those extra-tall markers, I wouldn't have known where the sides of the road were." It was the last thing she wanted to tell him, but he needed the truth. Only he knew the area well enough to decide if leaving the cabin was worth the risk. She had only a hazy idea of where they were located. "How far to that big wreck?"

"Frisco said ten miles to the west. But first it's a good eight miles out to the main highway, where he said the plows had done some clearing."

What if we try to drive out and get stuck?

"That many miles isn't horrible if we get stuck," Gianna said slowly. "We walked a mile yesterday. We could manage if we had to come back to the cabin on foot."

"I don't want to get stuck and have the wrong type of help show up either. Or have a new storm suddenly dump another foot of snow. The forecast we heard is days old. It could have been updated and completely changed."

Gianna's head was about to explode. *"What are we supposed to do?"*

"I think we need to wait, Mom," Violet said quietly. "I know you feel you need to take action—you're always like that—but Chris is right. We need to sit tight. I know he can face anything that comes."

A surprised and thankful expression lit Chris's face as he looked at her daughter. Violet was right. Gianna was an action person. She always thought things through first, but she usually leaned in the direction of taking quick action. "Damn it." She gave Chris a side-eye. "We'll hole up for now."

He nodded. "I think it's the right thing to do. We can always leave later if we have to."

If we're able to.

"Do you think someone will come?" she asked softly, not clarifying that she meant someone who meant to do them harm.

He nodded again, his eyes stating he knew what she meant. "I do."

Her stomach churned.

"But we're ready. No one's getting past me."

"Do you think those shots we heard yesterday are related?"

"I have no idea. Could have been someone fooling around."

"Oh!" Her hand slipped into the back pocket of her ski pants. "I grabbed Frisco's camera. He took some shots of my Suburban and the cabin. Do you want to take a look?"

Chris took the camera and popped out the memory card. He moved to the rear of the cabin and grabbed a laptop off a small desk against the wall. He set it up on the island and placed the card into a port. They waited.

"You had the presence of mind to grab his camera *and* his gun?"

"Taking his gun was my first thought, since someone was firing at me. The camera was right next to him on the porch."

The pictures opened and Chris rapidly scrolled through them. He sped past images of a fender bender, a dead buck, and a garbage-strewn campsite. Sunny weather was present in the first pictures on the card, and then clouds and rain took over. When snow started to show up, Chris scrolled more slowly. He stopped on a number of pictures of a birthday party. Frisco was front and center, a yellow-and-red party hat on his head and other rangers in uniform making goofy faces beside him. A photo of a cake with his name.

"Shit," muttered Chris. He continued scrolling.

He paused at more snowy background pictures. Another dead deer, its red blood splattered on the snow. A shot of Gianna's Suburban from the rear, her New York State license plate easy to read. Gianna leaned closer to the screen.

"He took that picture before he drove over here. Look . . . you can see the glass of the driver's window. It's solid."

Chris nodded. The next image was the note he'd written with his name and address. *Where did Frisco put the note?* A chill shot through him; the note with his personal information was probably in Frisco's pocket—available to anyone who examined the body. *Fuck.*

Then there were two images of the burned cabin and an image of the Suburban's broken window. "Did he shoot those cabin pictures when you went back or did he take them before he came here?"

Gianna thought hard. "I can't remember. I was focused on the broken window."

More shots showed the broken trails and boot prints from the Suburban to the cabin. The pictures abruptly changed to the darker interior of the burned cabin.

"Violet, don't look at these." Gianna looked over her shoulder at her daughter's wide eyes. "Just for a minute."

Violet nodded and turned away, crouching down to pet the dog.

Frisco had taken three shots of the dead man. The last one was a clear shot of the holes in his skull. Chris pressed his lips together in a tight line but said nothing. Gianna studied the body with a professional eye.

"Did you recognize him?" Chris asked almost soundlessly.

Gianna shook her head, but her mind raced. *Do I know him? But can't tell?* She reached out and scrolled back to the first picture of the body, seeking something familiar. "I don't think I know him," she whispered back. She didn't explain that his face was unrecognizable—Chris would know she was going by his clothing, his build, and what was left of his hair.

Again she searched the body for something to trigger a memory.

"We need to get to the police," she said again.

Chris didn't answer. He scrolled through more pictures of footprints in the ash on the cabin floor and then stopped at wintry photos that'd been clearly taken from the porch. A few shots focused on the mystery path Chris had spotted.

They were the final photos on the memory card.

He died seconds after taking those pictures.

Chris was still silent.

Violet asked, "How long were you there?"

"Not long," admitted Gianna. "I wonder if we scared someone away from the cabin when we arrived."

"And they shot at you to get you to leave? Maybe there's something else in there they didn't want you to see? So they won't come here," Violet stated firmly. "They just wanted you to go away."

"I can't put any weight in that theory, Violet. They murdered a ranger, there's a dead body in the cabin, and they shot at your mother," said Chris. "They have to assume we'll tell someone about that."

"Maybe the fire was also started to get us to leave," added Violet. "I'm sure they know someone will come to investigate, but perhaps they just needed us gone for a little while . . . I don't know why . . . but maybe they needed a window of time to do something over there without us present. You know . . . dig up the buried treasure under the floorboards. Or to get the body out of the cabin before anyone got a good look at him."

Violet's theory spun in Gianna's brain as she picked it apart and studied it from every angle. She didn't see a reason it couldn't be true. A small sense of hope went through her. *Maybe no one will follow us here.*

A glance at Chris's determined face told her he disagreed with what Violet had said.

And no way in hell would he let down his guard.

★ ★ ★

Gianna silently watched as Chris paced the cabin a few times and then turned to face her and Violet, a decision clear on his face. "We need to be prepared to leave at a moment's notice. I want to get the truck ready and packed. If it looks feasible, we'll go."

She and Violet glanced at each other and then nodded at him.

Gianna followed Chris across the deep snow to the detached garage, struggling to balance the two snow shovels on her shoulders and stay upright as she stepped in his tracks. To call the building a garage was probably a compliment. It appeared to be a large, long shed on the verge of tipping over. As they drew closer, she saw that parts of the roof had been replaced and a series of solid locks placed on the vehicle-size door. The paint job looked like it'd been finished in 1970.

Chris constantly scanned their surroundings, the rifle in his hands. Gianna tried not to breathe too hard, worried he couldn't hear the sounds of the forest over her pants as she followed him through the deep snow. Nonstop flurries had fallen for hours and now there was nearly another foot of powder on top of the ice crust. So much for their predicted weather warm-up.

Packing the food had been assigned to Violet. While listening to Chris's directions to her daughter, Gianna had had the impression he was preparing for four nights in the woods instead of a simple drive out to the highway.

Nothing wrong with being overprepared.

Or else he believes we're going to get stuck.

Chris worked on the series of locks, and Gianna dug into the snowdrifts that were deep against the door. He finished the locks and plunged his shovel into the snow after carefully studying the woods. He heaved aside a giant scoop of powder. "We just need to move enough snow to slide up the door," he grunted.

"Are you sure we can drive your truck in this?" she asked.

"No."

Shit. "We need to rethink taking the snowmobile."

"It's too tiny. There's no room for three of us and there's Oro to think of. I was surprised Frisco got the two of you on it."

"Could the snowmobile pull something? Would it have enough power if we rig something behind it?"

Chris stopped shoveling and stared at her. "You're brilliant. Why the hell didn't I think of that?" He tackled the snow with a renewed vigor. "I have two plastic sleds we could pull behind the snowmobile. Brian and I use them all the time."

"If we get out to the highway on just a snowmobile and sleds, we might not be able to go much farther," Gianna pointed out.

"That's why I want to try the truck first. If we can make it out to a plowed road in the truck, we should be able to get to town on our own. You can drive the snowmobile, and I'll drive the truck with Violet and Oro. That way we'll all stay together. We'll pack a bunch of rope and put the sleds in the bed of the truck, and we'll use them if we need to." He grinned as he tossed aside a shovelful of snow. "Now we've got two options to get us out of here. Nice thinking, Gianna. Eight miles. All we have to cover is eight miles to get to the main highway."

"Towing us on sleds could be a strain on the snowmobile engine," Gianna said.

"I don't think it will be too bad. Think of how easily things glide on top of the snow. Once we get moving, it shouldn't take too much. There're a few uphill sections of road going out to the highway . . . that might be a different story, and we might have to do some walking, but most of it is downhill or flat. My fingers are still crossed we can get pretty far with the truck." He hurled another load of snow. "But pulling something behind the snowmobile is the best idea I've heard all day."

They worked silently for a few moments. "One of my cases made me think of it," Gianna said quietly. She hadn't been able to get the old images out of her mind for the last two minutes. "A ten-year-old girl. A snow day off from school. Her dad was towing her and her brothers behind his quad on sleds in the snow, but he was going too fast and took his corners too sharp. The centrifugal force during a sharp turn slammed her and her sled against a small stone wall."

Chris had stopped shoveling and was watching her intently. "She didn't survive?"

"None of my cases survive."

"How do you work on kids?" His gaze bored into her. She had a well-rehearsed answer for his common question.

"I care about them. I know that when they're on my table, they'll get the tenderness and compassion a child deserves. I want their parents to know that their children are handled with sensitivity. Just as I'd want Violet handled, so I give my best."

He held her gaze for a few seconds. "You do, don't you?"

"Every time. I'm human and I'm a mom. The tragedy of some of the cases kills something inside of me, but I counteract it by giving back to the child and family with my actions. Not all of us can do it. Usually within an office you know which cases are not good for certain people to work on. I have a type of case I don't care to work on and they keep them away from me. It's not uncommon for examiners to struggle with child autopsies, but I take pride in doing them. An abused child needs someone to speak for him."

He turned back to the snow and dug. The set of his jaw told her she'd struck a nerve.

"I think this is good enough." Chris set his shovel aside. He'd leaned the rifle against the door of the garage while he worked, but Gianna had noticed that he never took his gaze from the woods for more than a few seconds. If someone wanted to shoot at them, the two of them would be easy targets, but they'd agreed to take the chance. He handed her the rifle and bent down to pull up on the giant door handle. The door stuck. He grabbed the handle with both hands, planted his feet, and yanked. It slid upward, its horizontal panels neatly arcing up and into the garage in its tracks.

A set of rectangular headlights stared back at her. The old Ford truck was tall; its giant black tires had huge teeth designed for getting traction in deep snow. She didn't know the technical term, but she recognized what her friends would call a "redneck truck." If any truck could handle the snow, this was it. But she understood his doubts; the snow was deep. If those big tires got stuck, they could be stranded.

She crossed her fingers.

His garage was as immaculate as she'd expected. Everything in its place. "Help me with these," he said as he started to load a few small concrete blocks into the back of what seemed to be the longest truck bed Gianna had ever seen. "It needs some weight over the back wheels." Together they added a dozen blocks. Chris grabbed a few pieces of wood, two sleds that were hanging on one wall, and several lengths of rope, and stowed them in the bed near the cab. Sliding open a garage cabinet door, he pulled out two heavy-duty canvas duffel bags and added them to the truck's bed. He saw her watching and said, "Emergency supplies."

She wasn't surprised. The man had *always prepared* tattooed on his forehead.

He also pulled out a helmet and a few pairs of ski goggles. "For the snowmobile." Gianna nodded. The falling snow had bitten into her eyes and skin on her trip back without Frisco. She hadn't cared much at the time.

Together they shoveled the drifts into a semblance of a ramp leading out of the garage. Once they'd eliminated the drifts, Gianna estimated the snow's depth to be about two feet. How deep would the truck sink? Was it even possible to drive in snow that deep?

He added their two snow shovels to the bed. "Let's see how she does."

★ ★ ★

It'd been a hard decision, but Chris finally felt it was worth the chance. He'd kept picturing his old Ford stranding them in deep snow, but with Gianna's suggestion about Frisco's snowmobile, they now had a solid backup plan. He never liked to make a risky decision without a secondary option. Walking ten miles wasn't a practical secondary option.

Gianna's gaze had rested on his duffel bags, but she hadn't asked questions. He had a second set he kept at his home in Portland and a smaller version in every vehicle. Foodstuffs, flashlight, batteries, Leatherman tools, tarps, blankets, fire starters, to list a few. In other words, peace of mind.

They both held their breath as he started the engine and drove out of the garage. The big tires bit into the snow and the truck groaned as it sank and pushed through the deep white fluff. Chris clenched his teeth. He'd never driven in this depth, but the truck managed. He drove carefully from the garage and parked as close to the cabin porch as possible. His brain filled in the details of the landscape that were buried under the snow, and he steered to avoid the border of small boulders he knew lined the driveway. He loved the old truck. It'd been through hard times and had the scrapes and dents to prove it, but it kept going. Sorta like him.

They stomped the snow off their boots on the front porch and went in to check on Violet. The cardboard boxes he'd set on the kitchen island and asked her to load with food were full. He'd shown her how to use the shotgun before they'd left for the garage, believing it was the best option for her even if the kickback was strong. She didn't need to aim that much if she was threatened; she just needed the guts to pull the trigger. Her face had paled as he explained how it worked, but she'd paid attention, listening closely and nodding at the right moments. The shotgun was still by the door where he'd placed it when he and Gianna had left.

Violet was nowhere in sight.

"Violet?" Gianna called, looking up at the loft.

Silence.

Chris's heart rate increased.

The teen stepped out of the tiny bathroom at the back of the cabin, wiping her eyes, and he took a deep breath.

Gianna hurried over to her daughter and took her hand. "What's wrong?"

Violet slowly shook her head, staring at the floor. "I don't feel good. I thought I was going to throw up."

Gianna slipped her arm around the girl's shoulders and hugged. "It's anxiety. You know it gets to you. This has been stressful and now we're about to make it worse."

Violet brushed her eyes and took a quick glance at Chris, lowering her voice. "This feels different. I think I ate something. Maybe the bacon . . ." Chris heard her and did a mental check of his stomach. He'd eaten nearly half the bacon and felt fine.

"I really think it's your nerves," said Gianna with sympathy. "There's been a lot to take in this morning."

"My legs are shaky."

Gianna guided her to the couch and the two women sat. Chris grabbed the garbage can and set it next to the teen. She gave him an embarrassed look.

Should we be leaving if she's sick? Is Gianna right and it's just nerves?

He glanced back at the shotgun and wondered if his little lesson had been more than she was ready for.

We need to leave.

The thought hung above his head. He'd been arguing to stay at the cabin for twenty-four hours, feeling it was their best decision, but now he felt the opposite. And the feeling was growing stronger with every passing moment. It'd felt wrong outside; he didn't know how to describe it, but there was a tension in the woods similar to what he'd felt when he first saw the burned cabin.

Everything is wrong.

He wasn't a slave to his instincts, but he listened to them very closely. "Is she going to be okay?"

"Yes," said Gianna simply, keeping her gaze on her daughter. Her expression ordering her daughter to agree with her.

"I don't know if I can walk . . . if we have to walk," Violet said slowly.

"We shouldn't have to do much walking," Chris said. He told her of her mother's idea about the sleds and relief flowed through the teen's eyes. "Let's finish packing."

He directed them to carry the food and the heavy coats he kept at the cabin. He fought the urge to pack every blanket and all his firewood into the truck. *Eight miles. Nothing could happen where we'd need all that within eight miles. I know where we are and where we're going.*

He had accurate maps of the terrain in his truck, and he knew that once they made it close to the highway, they'd have cell phone reception.

I can do this.

After a careful scan of the area, he followed them out of the cabin and locked the door behind him. It felt like a useless gesture. If anyone wanted to break into the cabin, they could.

They threw their supplies into the back. He snapped his fingers at Oro and pointed at the open door of the cab. The dog leaped in and sat in his usual place on the passenger side. "In the back." The dog followed his gesture and scrambled over the center console to the rear bench seat of the extended cab. Chris brushed the snow off the passenger seat. Gianna gave her daughter a hug, and Violet got into the vacated seat.

Gianna had goggles around her neck and the helmet in her hand. Her brown eyes were confident and he wished he felt the same. "I'll follow you," she stated. "Good luck." She stepped through the snow to Frisco's snowmobile.

Chris watched her go. She looked like a child wearing an adult's helmet as she climbed on the machine. He settled into the driver's seat of the truck and started the engine.

Violet stared at the two long stick shifts on the floor of the cab and struggled to buckle the limp seat belt. "How old is this truck?"

"Old," stated Chris. "Close to twenty-five years. They don't build them like this anymore."

The look on Violet's face said she didn't find his words reassuring.

We have to get out of here.

He looked out across the faded red hood, hearing an echo of words in his mind, spoken by a young boy decades ago. Determination flowed through him.

This time they'd *all* survive.

CHAPTER EIGHT

Violet wanted to cry.

Her stomach wouldn't calm down and twice she'd nearly lost the eggs she'd eaten for breakfast. Each time she thought about food, it made her stomach worse, and now the stress level in the cab of the truck was more intense than it'd been in the house. She held her breath and clutched the handle on the cab's door. Chris's jaw was clamped shut and his arms jerked with each turn of the wheel as the truck bounced and heaved its way through the drifts. The trip was slow. Twice Violet had looked back, surprised to see how short a distance they'd moved. At least they were still going forward and the heater in the truck blasted hot air in her face.

She wished her mother were with her. Gianna was following on the snowmobile with no apparent problems. Violet wished she'd asked to ride behind her mother. Riding on the snowmobile might be colder, but no doubt it was smoother.

A deep lurch in the snow flung Violet against the door.

"Geez," she muttered. Chris hadn't flinched, his concentration on the road . . . actually the lack of road.

Chris wasn't nervous; he was focused with a laser-beam intensity that Violet found both reassuring and slightly terrifying. Their journey rested on his skills. There was nothing Violet could do to help their situation.

No wonder my stomach's in knots.

She'd spent too much time feeling out of control over the last few months. First her grandmother's death and then her mother's announcement that they were moving. All the way across the United States to some city that didn't even have a subway system. She'd never been to Portland before, and she'd never seen so many beards in her life. And the beards were on guys barely older than herself. They weren't old men; these were guys who discussed the IBUs of their beer and spent hours wandering through a used bookstore that occupied a full city block. And bikes—the nonmotorized kind—were everywhere on the roads. Several times her mother had nearly hit one, before she learned to check her right mirror before making a right turn.

Violet missed her friends, her school, and their skinny, tall house with the kind neighbors. But most of all she missed her grandmother. It was a soul-deep lonely ache. For the last six months, each time Violet had walked by Nana's bedroom it'd felt startlingly empty. She'd begun avoiding that part of the house.

Nana had died in her sleep. A heart attack, her mother said. One day she'd been fine and the next she'd been gone. Each day after school last spring, Violet had stepped into their home and opened her mouth to greet Nana, only to realize the house was empty. Her mother was at work most days, but she had cut back her work schedule after Nana's death.

She missed Nana with every ounce of her being. No more scents of dinner cooking or the welcome sight of her kind smile after a boring school day. She'd always wanted the gossip about Violet's girlfriends and asked what boy she was interested in. Her mother never mentioned those things. Her mother asked about grades and homework. It wasn't until Violet had missed a curfew last summer that her mother took an interest in her friends. Too close an interest. She'd discovered Sean had been arrested for possession and cracked down on Violet's time with him.

Violet had already figured out Sean was a loser, but when Gianna had ordered her not to see him anymore, it'd made her bitter. Nana would have asked her what Sean did to make her life better and how he made her feel. Gianna saw a one-time drug arrest and put her foot down, claiming that she knew where drug users ended up: her table.

Violet's eye-roll during that conversation had gotten her phone confiscated for two days.

I didn't deserve that.

She was honor roll. She didn't do drugs. Sure, she'd tried cigarettes; hadn't everyone?

I'm a good kid. Why does she treat me like the losers at school?

Now she sat in the cab of a truck with a stranger, worrying that someone had tried to hurt them. *Why us?* She'd listened while Chris questioned her mother about people who might be angry with her. She'd waited for Gianna to mention her ex, Owen, but it'd never happened. Even Violet knew that relationship hadn't ended well. Her mother kept her dating life extremely private. She wouldn't introduce Violet to a man unless they'd been dating for a few months. Over the past ten years, Violet had met two men. There'd been more, but Gianna hadn't brought them home. Owen had been the second man, and Violet had met him in the days after her grandmother's death.

He'd introduced himself at Nana's funeral. Violet had stared at him, trying to place the familiar name, but her mind hadn't been functioning right. Her grief over Nana and being exposed to her first funeral had created dark curtains that concealed many corners of her memory.

"I'm a friend of your mother's. I never knew your grandmother, but I know how important she was to you." Owen had held his hand out and Violet automatically shook it. She'd never shaken so many hands or been hugged by so many people she didn't know. She looked up into Owen's face, but he was staring across the room at her mother, admiration in his eyes as her mother consoled a white-haired woman.

It clicked.

This is Mom's current guy.

"Pleased to meet you," she recited. "Thank you for coming." She'd heard her mom repeat the line a dozen times and had adopted it as her own. She didn't have the energy to personalize each interaction. The constant pity in everyone's eyes had worn her down. Their well-meaning but grating comments made her want to scream.

"You must miss her so much."

"She's in a much better place."

Fuck you! she wanted to scream. *Yes, I miss her! I don't care that she's in a better place; I need her here! My heart is breaking and I have to stand here and smile at all of you!*

"Your mother said you were very close to your grandmother. That she'd practically raised you while your mother went to school and work," said Owen, still watching her mother.

"Yes." Behind one of the hazy curtains in her brain, the curious daughter in her emerged to size up Owen Thomas. *Tall. Not too bad looking for an older guy.* The hand holding a cup of coffee had dirt under two of the fingernails, and he'd missed a spot on the side of his neck while shaving.

He still hadn't looked her in the eye.

Eye contact, my Violet. She heard Nana's voice. *Always look directly in the eyes of the person you're talking to. It shows respect. It doesn't matter if they're an adult or a child.*

She waited for him to look at her, recalling the facts her mother had mentioned about this man. *Owns a consulting business. Never married. No kids.*

After a moment of silence, Owen jerked his gaze away from her mother and met Violet's patient stare, his eyes widening the smallest bit. Did he realize she'd caught him being rude? He shook her hand again. "I'm very sorry for your loss," he said rapidly. "Maybe we'll meet again." He nodded at her and left.

A small chill vibrated through her chest as her gaze followed his dark suit as he walked across the room to her mother.

I don't like him. Nana wouldn't have liked him either.

He stopped beside her mother and possessively placed a hand on the back of her arm, just above her elbow. Gianna gave him a grateful smile and introduced him to the woman she'd been speaking with.

Owen immediately made eye contact with the woman.

Violet grew light-headed, as if the room had lost its oxygen, and she no longer heard the low murmurs of the mourners. She was alone. Standing in a room full of strangers and her mother's friends, she was invisible, yet everyone's gazes rested on her as one. She wanted to retreat behind thick doors and rip off the smile that'd frozen in place. Then she wanted to cry—and have Nana stroke her hair like she'd done when the boy she liked had asked her best friend to the holiday dance.

Her recollection vanished as the truck's right front wheel abruptly dipped downward and Violet pitched forward, the seat belt digging into her chest. Oro's bulk slammed into the back of Violet's seat and he yelped.

"Fuck," Chris muttered under his breath.

The truck stopped. Chris threw it into reverse. The truck vibrated and groaned. He twisted the steering wheel and tried again.

It didn't budge. Oro softly whined.

Violet watched the snowflakes gently land on the windshield as Chris wrestled with the truck's gears. A few moments later he paused.

"We can try to dig out, but I suspect it's snowmobile time for all of us."

★ ★ ★

Chris yanked on the ropes, confident they'd hold.

He glanced over at Gianna, who was having a quiet conversation with Violet. The teen was pale and holding her hands on her stomach. Her seat belt had wrenched her in the gut when the truck stopped. He'd felt both front wheels catch and rise within a split second of each other. Then the right front wheel had suddenly plunged down and brought the truck to a crooked halt.

The culprit was a downed tree across the road. It'd been completely hidden by the depth of the snow, but the snow on the far side of the tree hid an air pocket. His right front wheel had sunk through the false peak, bottoming out the truck and effectively trapping it. He'd need a tow truck to get it out. And probably a chain saw.

The wind blew small flakes down his neck, sneaking them past his high collar as he surveyed their backup plan. The snow had been steady, but it was the wind that was the worst. It'd grown stronger over the last hour, turning the flakes into flesh-biting ice, and the constant sway of the fir trees gave him the impression that the forest was moving. Gianna's snowmobile tracks had already been obliterated. The road before them was a smooth white swath weaving between the tall firs. With the light snowmobile, it shouldn't be too hard to get to the highway.

He'd tied the two plastic toboggans together. They were cheap toys he'd picked up somewhere, but one of the best purchases he'd ever made. He, Brian, and Oro had spent joy-filled hours sledding with them near the cabin. Now they would possibly save their lives. He set a duffel on each one and figured Gianna and Violet could hold them. He wasn't going anywhere without the supplies. He packed as much of the food as possible onto the toboggans and the back of the snowmobile. With the bitter wind, it would be a freezing ride without the protection of the truck's cab. The snowmobile's gas tank was a quarter full. He had no idea how much the tank held, but by simply eyeing the machine he estimated it couldn't be more than ten or twelve gallons.

What kind of gas mileage does a snowmobile get? While hauling two full sleds?

More than enough to get them to the highway. How far they'd need to go on the highway was another question. At least there should be some traffic out there.

Unless they cleaned up the accident and closed the highway until the storm passes.

It'd happened before.

He checked his cell phone. Still no service. As soon as a bar appeared on his screen, he would call Michael. His brother was the best means of getting them off the mountain. There was no way they were driving a snowmobile sixty miles into the city, and because of the storm and accident, it was possible that the forest rangers and Clackamas County Sheriff's Office wouldn't have the resources to give them a ride to town.

The wet sound of retching filled the quiet forest. He spun around to see Violet bent over and Gianna supporting her forehead with one hand while resting another on her back. Gianna's brown gaze met his and she shook her head the tiniest bit. She didn't look too concerned.

Sick? Food poisoning? Nerves? The seat belt?

Oro headed toward the women to investigate. *"Oro!"* Chris called the dog back, fully aware of what dogs were willing to eat. Oro spun toward him and perked his ears. "C'mere, boy." The golden dog rocked through the deep drifts, purposefully tossing snow in the air with his nose.

At least one of us isn't worried.

"Ready?" he asked Gianna. She nodded at him and held up one gloved finger, asking for a moment. Chris studied their backup plan, pleased with the results. The rope towline should pull the sleds with no issues. He simply needed to be careful when stopping and cornering. It would get them where they need to go. Gianna directed Violet to one of the toboggans.

They'd agreed the teen should wear the helmet. The girl sat down, put on her goggles, and gripped a duffel. Oro promptly sat in the front of her sled, his eyes and ears stating he was ready for fun. Violet patted the dog and gave a weak smile. The first Chris had seen all morning.

"That's his usual seat," Chris explained. "He loves sledding."

Gianna took a seat on the other sled. "Let's go." She pulled her hat down and her scarf up over her nose and mouth to her goggles. Through the clear plastic, her gaze said she had complete faith in their success.

Chris took a deep breath and started the engine.

★ ★ ★

A windshield would have been nice.

Gianna kept her head down, thankful for the goggles. The wind was nearly unbearable. It blasted right through her scarf and gloves. She'd tried facing backward during part of her ride, but it'd nauseated her. Violet rested her helmeted head against Oro's back, using the dog to block the gentle snowflakes that turned into stinging pieces of ice upon impact with skin. Oro didn't mind the cold.

Twice they'd dismounted and walked up hills when the engine groaned with its load. Chris would drive the snowmobile to the top of the hill, then walk back down, breaking a path for them. For the first five steps she'd welcomed the change and relief from the cold wind. Then she'd simply been miserable.

Violet was quiet. Gianna was 90 percent certain that nerves had upset her stomach back at the truck. The teen hadn't complained about the cold or the hikes up the hills, making Gianna simultaneously proud and worried. Her pace was a bit slow, but she didn't ask for a break. When they got back on their sleds after the second hill, Violet had promptly closed her eyes and leaned forward against the dog. Gianna noticed that Chris kept an eye on her daughter but didn't ask questions.

Their progress was slow. She and Violet had learned to use their heels to help slow the sleds when Chris needed to stop or take a sharp turn. Frankly, the sleds worked so well, she wished they hadn't wasted energy on the truck. But once they got out to the highway, she knew they'd wish they had the Ford. After what felt like hours, the tall firs lining the narrow road opened up to a wider highway.

Chris raised one arm in exultation and Gianna cheered. Violet's smile was wan, but Gianna could feel her relief. Along the edge of the highway, a tall berm of plowed snow made for some tricky maneuvering to get to the road. Clearly the snowplows hadn't even attempted to plow the road to their cabins, and had simply passed it by. *Frisco.* The forest ranger's face filled her mind, and she said a silent prayer for the kind man who'd clearly gone out of his way to check on them. Without his snowmobile they'd still be stuck in the cabin or in Chris's truck. With a murderer running around.

With a burst of teen energy, Violet ran out into the center of the road and spun on one foot, her arms in the air. A mother's instinct urged Gianna to tell her to get out of the road, but it wasn't necessary. No cars. No sounds of traffic. The highway was typically two lanes wide but was currently plowed to a width of one and a half. It hadn't been disturbed in hours; a couple of inches of powder rested on top of the packed snow. No tire marks.

"They must have closed the highway," stated Chris. "The accident must have been worse than Frisco realized." He pulled out his phone. "Yes! I've got coverage." He immediately dialed and held the phone to his ear.

Violet checked hers. "I've got coverage, too." She looked at her mom. "Who should I call?"

Gianna considered calling her uncle but then rejected the idea. They'd argued the last time they spoke. He'd wanted her to move to California instead of to Oregon, claiming she needed to be near family. She didn't want to admit that she'd stranded herself and Violet during their first month in their new state. No matter how much she loved the man who'd raised her after her parents' deaths, it would trigger a million questions she didn't have the energy to answer. "We'll let Chris make the calls." Violet gave her an odd look but slid the phone back in her pocket.

No one knows we're here.

If she and Violet had died in that fire, how long would it have taken before someone missed them? A week? She had a scheduled phone call with her uncle on the first of the month, no matter the day. So he wouldn't have noticed until she missed their call. She had close friends back in New York, but they knew she was slow to answer emails and texts. She wasn't the type to call and chat for hours with friends on the phone.

Her empty life spread out in front of her.

Would her new employer have been the first person to notice they were gone?

She'd moved to the West Coast with the intent to make a fresh start, and that fresh start had nearly killed her and her daughter.

I'm not reckless.

Not like them.

For years she'd heard the stories about her parents. The adventurers. The beautiful people. So many friends. So little time.

Gianna had been their trophy child. Photos showed a serious girl who always had a bow in her hair and was dressed to match her mother. Having a daughter hadn't slowed down her parents. They simply took her with them. Before she was six, she'd been to Australia, Italy, Russia, and Japan. She didn't attend kindergarten; her parents had felt it was a waste of time. Instead they filled her world with books and travel. When it was time for first grade, the carefree travel stopped, and they stuck to winter and summer vacations for trips. Gianna remembered her introduction to the monotony of school. Suddenly she'd been forced into a structured schedule and immersed with children her own age. Before, it'd been the three of them and her parents' adult friends.

She'd thought everyone lived as she did.

She met children who'd never been in an airplane and never swum with dolphins. At first she'd talked about her experiences, until her teacher had pulled her aside and asked her not to brag, because not everyone had the money that her family did and she was hurting other children's feelings.

Gianna hadn't realized her family was rich. Nor had she realized she was bragging. Humiliated, she'd kept her mouth closed.

Soon it'd no longer mattered.

Overcome with a soul-deep need to connect to her daughter, she reached out for Violet, pulled her close, and touched her forehead to Violet's. The teen held the familiar pose for a long second. "We're gonna be okay now, right, Mom?"

"Yes."

★ ★ ★

Chris told the 911 operator about the deaths. She'd wanted him to stay on the line longer, but he'd told her they needed to get to shelter and would be at the closest ranger station. Next he called his brother, and the sound of Michael's voice was as heartening as making it to the highway.

He relayed a condensed version of their situation.

"I can be there in less than a half hour. I'm on the far east side of the metro area looking into a story," said Michael.

"What if the highway is closed?" Chris asked.

"It is closed," answered Michael. "All the mountain passes are closed. They've been closed since last night, because there were wrecks all over the place."

Chris knew that wouldn't stop his brother. The investigative reporter had a way of getting whatever he wanted.

"What about in the city?"

"Portland is fine. We warmed up and now there's just nasty slush everywhere. It's the Cascades that are still trapped in low temperatures and snowfall. You say these women don't know how the fire started?"

He heard the interest in his brother's voice. There was nothing Michael liked better than nosing into odd situations. He pushed and prodded until he found answers that satisfied him.

"And she didn't see who shot the ranger?" Michael asked. "Did they keep shooting at her?"

"She took off."

"They didn't follow her?"

"We didn't wait around to find out. Once we figured out how to get out of there, we left. But they could have been as trapped by the snow as we were. If they were on foot, and if they knew where they were going, they could have made it to my place before we left. I didn't want to wait any longer to find out."

"Are you armed?"

"What do you think?"

Chris imagined the gears turning in Michael's head.

"I'll reach out to the state police, but I know they're stretched thin right now."

"Somebody needs to get to those bodies," Chris muttered.

"They're not going anywhere," Michael stated.

"I can't stand the thought of them left behind." Despite the cold, sweat formed on his forehead.

"It's all right," Michael said quietly. "You're not leaving anyone behind. It was totally out of your control."

Chris's vision started to tunnel slightly. "It's not right. Somewhere someone is wondering about them."

"They'll be taken care of. We know exactly where they're at and in this weather, nothing is going to disturb them. You did everything you could."

"Maybe we shouldn't—"

"*Chris.* Listen to me. Sit tight. The police will investigate. You did the right thing getting out of the forest. Remember that someone shot at her—what's her name?"

"Gianna. Gianna Trask, and her daughter is Violet." He turned to see Gianna watching him from several yards away. Her arms were wrapped around her daughter, but her focus was on Chris's phone call. His vision cleared and he recognized the familiar drain he'd started to circle.

Violet turned her head to look at him.

These two are safe.

"Thirty minutes," said Michael. "Start driving down to the ranger station. You'll probably get there before me. Keep an eye out for my vehicle."

Chris looked up and down the deserted white highway. "Not a problem."

CHAPTER NINE

He needed to clean up the loose ends.

He hadn't found the device his father wanted. His father had been convinced the subject would make contact with the woman, but it'd never happened. He'd kept his distance and simply watched, monitoring all electronics, wondering if the subject was communicating with the woman in a way they hadn't foreseen, but everyone involved had believed the subject would talk to her in person.

How could he not?

It'd come down to time. And the cold. It'd been fucking cold and miserable and the subject still hadn't approached the woman. He'd grown tired of waiting and launched an interrogation.

He'd been ordered to keep his distance, but who would have expected several feet of snow and then a damned ice storm? The interrogation was the right move.

And his father was far, far away.

Right now he was running rogue, changing the plan, and the freedom was exhilarating. He needed to feed his own fascination first and then he'd implement his father's plan and make everything right. He could make both happen.

Gianna had been a welcome surprise in this assignment. Surveillance was typically tedious, but from the first moment he'd spotted her, he'd wanted her. She'd become an object, one he wanted to own. Usually his wealth could buy him anything, but she hovered out of his reach. Flashing his cash wouldn't turn her eye. Plus his father had ordered her death.

Accepting his father's orders, he'd tried to kill her. But he'd failed twice.

Was fate speaking to him?

Maybe he was meant to have her first . . .

Lust shot through him. He needed to put his hands on Gianna. He needed to explore and feel the energy that radiated out of her.

He'd make it happen.

His past had taught him to follow his instincts.

He'd spent most of his life wandering aimlessly in one small part of the world, searching for his place and his purpose. He hadn't found it. Instead he'd found trouble. He'd been attracted to the wrong people, wanting to experience the danger and energy that oozed from their pores. He'd wanted people to look at him with fear and worship. Instead he'd been set up to take the fall.

I was used.

The knowledge still heated his brain and sent waves of anger to his extremities. His father had had to step in and hustle him out of the country before he ended up in prison for the rest of his life. Part of him had hated his father, who had made success and power look effortless. He'd spent most of his youth believing that he could achieve the same. Every sports car and privilege their wealth had provided, he'd taken for granted, and then his poor decisions had nearly destroyed every advantage he'd received.

Once his feet had touched American soil, he'd known deep in his heart that here he could recreate his father's success. His father still financed his life. His family's fortune paid for his glitzy apartment and shiny car. But it wouldn't be long before he could provide for himself.

He had the brawn, the brains, and the looks to make it happen. He dressed the right way, and Americans loved his accent. That plus credit cards and the right car made American women practically jump in his bed. At first he'd believed he'd conquered the American dream. Then he realized the women simply wanted to spend his money. They were sneaky bitches. Praising him to his face and then laughing about him to their friends. Fakes. Every last one of them. He learned to be more selective in his companions. He didn't want a stable of easy lays who pretended to enjoy themselves in exchange for a shopping spree; he wanted respect . . . fear . . . and admiration.

The real stuff.

He'd abandoned the cheap whores and nonstop partying crowd, searching for quality. Gianna Trask was quality. People respected her. She was smart and cautious and had stood in the limelight and then chosen to reject it. He'd never had a woman like that in his bed before.

What kind of person rejects fame?

His lust and curiosity were both engaged. His obsession growing beyond that with any other woman he'd pursued. He needed to have her to get her out of his mind and system. Then he could fulfill his father's orders.

He'd been following her for weeks. His orders were to watch for the subject who'd double-crossed them. The subject had been seen traveling to Oregon, but they'd lost his trail, and their intelligence indicated that he would meet with Gianna. She'd been easy to watch. She hadn't started her new job yet, and had spent most of her spare time unpacking her moving boxes and sightseeing with her daughter. He'd set up shop in an empty rental house directly behind her new home. Watching from the windows that allowed him a direct line of sight into her bedroom and family room.

No one came to visit.

He'd followed her to Starbucks and the grocery store. Carefully keeping his face from her sight. But the more he'd watched, the more he'd needed her to know he existed. He could feel the pressure still building inside him.

His father still needed the device. Had the man passed it to Gianna? When? He'd searched the old man's clothing and found nothing.

One of the Trask women should know where it was.

He couldn't fail his father again.

★ ★ ★

Before Michael Brody arrived at the ranger station, he suspected he knew more about Dr. Gianna Trask than his quiet brother, who'd been with her for the last twenty-four hours. A couple of quick phone calls at the start of his journey had yielded fascinating fruit by the time he'd come upon the massive wreck that'd closed the highway.

Gianna Trask had a unique legacy. At one point when she was very young, she'd been in every gossip magazine and on every national news show. But her fifteen minutes had been brief. She'd been a child when her parents had died in a manner that'd caught the nation's attention. According to the old articles his assistant had dug up, Gianna Trask had no recollection of the car accident.

Every molecule in his body ached to interview her.

She had to remember *something*.

She'd done well for herself, considering her tragic past. A respected forensic pathologist. A daughter who did well in school. Michael's sources had rapidly dug under a lot of rocks.

Why did she choose Oregon? She's barely settled in and ends up adjacent to two murders?

His thoughts had raced as his Land Rover handled the snowy roads with ease, churning past dozens of abandoned cars. Drivers had patiently waited on the sides of the road for the highway to reopen, but when the word had gone out that it would be closed down for at least twenty-four hours, they'd discovered their vehicles couldn't manage the drive back to town. There was a dystopian feel to the highway. Lonely and deserted. Police had long since cleared out the people, and for many miles Michael felt like the only human alive.

A single well-placed call had cleared him to pass the accident. The primary wreck was a sight. Semis, cars, trucks. Some of their makes and colors unrecognizable. Even with the state troopers' orders to let him through, the one he talked to still gave him crap. "Don't make more work for us. If you get stuck, we don't have the time to come find you. We just got the last body out an hour ago. This investigation is going to take days."

"I'm going only a few miles and then turning around. Think of it like I'm doing you a favor to get out this stranded group."

The trooper wasn't amused. "Make it fast." He directed Michael to a narrow path through the disaster that'd been cleared to get the ambulances in and out of the snowy scene.

Michael drove slowly, fighting his desire to stop and take photos of the burned-out husks and crumpled vehicles. He transferred his reporter's instincts back to the topic of Gianna Trask. There was a story there; he knew it. Even if the shooter in the forest turned out to simply be a local nut with a gun, no one had publicly interviewed Gianna in decades.

She was a survivor.

Just like Chris. Michael shook his head. Knowing his introverted brother's silent ways, he suspected Chris and Gianna had no idea how much they had in common. A lot had changed in the years since Chris had come back into Michael's life.

Two decades ago Michael's brother Daniel had vanished along with several other children and their school bus driver. Chris Jacobs had lived. Nearly dead, he'd stumbled out of the forest two years later with no memory of what had happened. Michael had hated the boy for surviving while his brother was still missing.

But the survivor had a secret. He was Daniel Brody and had assumed Chris Jacobs's identity to protect the very public and political Brody family from a killer. The real Chris had died while escaping with Daniel from their captor. Chris had kept his mouth shut, protecting his secret for years, interacting as little as possible with society as he tried to heal and live as his deceased friend.

While looking for Chris two years ago, Michael had fallen for the real Chris's sister, Jamie, and then discovered his secret.

Because he'd lived longer as Chris than as Daniel Brody, Chris had kept the stolen name. Now the three of them were a tight-knit but incestuous-sounding family.

Michael wouldn't have had it any other way. He'd gained his brother, a nephew, and the love of his life during that hot summer.

Michael understood the stress that had been in Chris's voice when he talked about leaving the ranger and the other shooting victim behind in the forest. As a teen Chris had had his heart ripped to shreds when he'd been forced to leave his dead friend behind in the woods to escape their kidnapper.

Even after Chris had accepted that he no longer had to hide, he'd refused help coping with his guilt. He'd tried a few therapists at Jamie's urging, but it never lasted. Talking wasn't Chris's strong point.

Good thing Michael could tell what his brother was thinking with a single glance. Jamie could, too.

A squat building appeared on the side of the road, a sign marking it as the ranger station. It'd taken him nearly an hour to reach the location. A figure moved to the center of the snow-covered highway and waved his arms. *Chris.* Michael smiled, relief flowing through him. A golden dog danced into the road, jumping in circles around the black figure. Two other figures stood outside the building, one in a pink coat and another in pale green. It appeared they'd just made it to the ranger station.

Michael slowed to a stop and stepped out of the SUV. A rare grin beamed on Chris's face. Michael pulled him into a bear hug and pounded on his back. "Here I am, saving your ass again." He turned to greet the two women.

Gianna Trask was tiny. Her direct brown gaze studied him as Chris made introductions. Violet was her mirror image, only slightly taller and with that youthful freshness of a teenager. Oro planted his front paws on Michael's chest, a final set of dark eyes that were grateful to see him. "Hey, boy." He rubbed the happy dog's head.

"Thank you so much for coming to get us," Gianna said. Michael sized her up. "Confident" and "competent" were his first impressions. A large brown smear covered part of her coat. His gaze locked on it and her gloved hand brushed it self-consciously, but she said nothing.

How close was she when the ranger was shot?

"We were just about to go inside," Chris said. "But let's put our stuff in the back of your truck."

He was already grabbing two large duffel bags from a pair of sleds. He lifted the back window to Michael's SUV and loaded them in. Violet scrambled to grab a few boxes of food and supplies. "How much did you pack?" Michael asked.

"I didn't know if our trip would take three hours or three days," said Chris. "I was prepared for both. I'll feel more secure once I see pavement, but for now I'll settle for some heat inside the station."

Gianna and Violet chimed in their agreement.

Two pale-green forest service trucks were parked in front of the building, their tracks hidden in the new snow. Chris grabbed Gianna's arm as she nearly lost her footing in an icy spot.

Michael blinked.

Nah. He's just being polite.

But the length of time that Chris had looked at Gianna after she'd slipped had been more than polite.

Michael glanced at Violet, who'd hung back to hook a leash onto Oro's collar. The teen hadn't seemed to notice anything. He waved them all ahead and brought up the rear as they tramped up the snowy path to the door and walked right in.

It was as if they'd stepped back into the 1970s. The ceilings in the waiting room were uncomfortably low and the fake wood paneling had discolored from years of sun. The tile floor reminded Michael of an old grocery store, and the seats of the folding chairs had lost their padding. Down the narrow hall to the right, a man stepped out of an office and headed their way. "Can I help you?" The heavyset man wore the tan-and-green uniform that Michael associated with the forest service.

Chris stepped forward, holding out a hand. "Phil, right?"

The ranger shook his hand and squinted at Chris. "Yeah, you own the place up on Road 359, right?"

His brother nodded. "Right. You helped me out with some permits."

"Glad to see you're not snowed in," Phil said. "Frisco is out making rounds to check on people in the area."

Chris and Gianna exchanged a look.

Phil picked up on the tension. "What happened?"

"Frisco came out to my place this morning," said Chris. "He'd already been to the Abell cabin where Gianna and Violet were renting." He gestured at the two women. "The Abell cabin burned down the night before last. These two were lucky to get out. I smelled the smoke and went over there and brought them back to my place. When Frisco and Gianna went back to the Abell place this morning, someone shot at them."

"What?" Phil's thick brows shot halfway up his forehead.

"Frisco was killed."

Phil stared for a long moment at Chris, and then looked to Michael, who nodded. "You're saying Frisco Green was murdered this morning," he said slowly. "Are you fucking kidding me?"

"No," said Gianna. "I was on the porch with him when he was shot. I managed to get out of there with his snowmobile."

Phil tilted his head to one side, considering her. "Maybe he wasn't dead. Did you check? Maybe—"

"I'm a medical examiner," Gianna cut in, her voice cracking. "His head injury was lethal. He died instantly." She sniffed and wiped her nose with her glove. Violet stepped closer to her mom, their shoulders touching.

"I need to make a call," Phil said slowly, his gaze moving between the adults as if hoping one of them would say they were kidding. He started to take a step back to the hallway.

"That's not all," said Chris. "Someone was murdered inside the Abell cabin. Or murdered and his body left in the cabin."

Phil froze, his wide eyes blinking slowly, reminding Michael of an owl. With a small turn of his head, he yelled down the hall. "Jason?" His gaze stayed on the group. "You're telling me you're reporting two murders. Frisco and who's the other one?"

"We don't know," stated Chris.

The group went silent. Michael heard a chair with squeaky wheels down the hall. A second man appeared and headed their way. Jason was young, his skin red with acne, and Michael wondered if he was old enough to drink. The young man's eyes lit up when he spotted Oro, and his gaze lingered on Violet as he joined the group. Chris frowned.

"Have you heard from Frisco today?" Phil asked, still looking at the adults.

"Not since he left this morning."

"I need you to take a statement from these folks while I try to reach someone at OSP."

"I'll grab a notepad." Jason left.

"I know you guys are swamped with the wreck toward town," Michael said. "I passed it coming up here. OSP is helping out with it, too."

One eyebrow rose this time. "How'd you get past the road-block? They're not supposed to let anyone through."

"I know the right people to ask, and I wanted to get these guys out and back to town. But you'll need to have someone go back to the cabins and figure out what happened."

"With an active shooter possibly hanging around?" Phil shook his head. "I'll contact OSP to handle it."

Jason reappeared, a yellow legal pad in his hand. "Why don't you head back this way and we can use the conference room. I started a fresh pot of coffee."

They started to follow the young ranger.

"Jason," Phil said. The ranger stopped and looked back. "It appears that Frisco was murdered this morning and that these folks witnessed it. There was a shooting at the Abell cabin."

Jason didn't move as his face whitened. "Is that true?" Jason whispered, looking at Chris and then Violet. The young man seemed to shrink inside his uniform.

Violet nodded, her eyes wet.

He looked at all their faces a minute longer, seeing the con-firmation, and his expression grew numb. Jason gestured for them to follow as he turned down the hallway. Phil stepped into an office and closed the door.

Chris waved the women in front of him and followed. Michael had already reported the deaths to his contact at the Oregon State Police. Hopefully Phil's call would speed up the response and they'd get some investigators on the scene.

★ ★ ★

Three hours and several pots of coffee later, they were still wait-ing for the OSP detectives to show up.

During the long wait, Chris felt sorry for Violet, who'd stretched out on the ragged couch in the forest service break room. She'd fallen asleep in minutes. Gianna cast longing looks at her sleeping daughter, and Chris knew why she wasn't sleeping. Too many questions buzzing around her brain; he had the same problem.

Who shot Frisco?

Whose body is in the cabin?

He and Gianna had been watching old DVDs of the TV show *Friends*, because there wasn't cable or dish service in the remote station. "I could never decide if I wanted to be Monica or Rachel," mumbled Gianna, during an episode with Tom Selleck. "Neither one was quite right."

"I never wanted to be any of the guys," answered Chris. "They weren't exactly role models."

"Who did you idolize growing up?" Gianna asked.

Chris glanced through the window at Michael, who was pacing outdoors and gesturing as he spoke on his cell phone. "Hard to say."

"Try."

She rested her chin on one hand, a small smile on her face as she waited for his answer.

"Well, Schwarzenegger was always the hard-ass."

"But presented unattainable standards."

"True. I liked Nicolas Cage. He was a geek but always won."

"The nineties were great for Cage. I can watch *The Rock* over and over."

He smiled. "One of my favorites. Sean Connery. Ed Harris. Good stuff." Movies had been an escape for him after the two years he'd spent underground in the hands of a kidnapper. In the movies the bad guy always got his due. And the heroes weren't always tough guys like Stallone and Schwarzenegger. Chris's favorites were the heroes who had everything going against them and defeated the bad guys with their brains.

"I always like the females who were nerdy scientists," said Gianna. "I have a weak spot in movies for the underdog and for women who were discounted because of their looks. They would rise up and kick butt every time."

"Is that why you went the science route?" asked Chris. He didn't think so, but he wanted her to keep talking. Their forced time together had fostered an easy intimacy that he hadn't experienced with a woman in years.

Someone simply to talk to.

"Hell no. I continued with science because I couldn't get enough of anatomy and physiology in high school. Other students thought dissecting cats was disgusting, but it was my favorite class. Getting to see how the muscles and tendons work beneath the skin? Fascinating."

His high school had offered the same class. Chris hadn't taken it, but he clearly recalled the smell from when he'd passed by the classroom on dissection days. He'd stuck to computer classes. Computers didn't smell.

The OSP detectives and Michael chose that time to step into the room, and Chris immediately missed the aura of companionship that had developed. The end of his time with Gianna was in sight. He wasn't ready to part ways.

Michael made introductions. "Major Crimes Detectives Henry Becker and Nora Hawes. Hawes and I met during a murder case a year ago," he said, indicating the tall woman. Nora Hawes appeared to be in her forties and looked like a young Helen Mirren. She shook their hands, said pleasantries, and handed them a business card as Chris tried not to show surprise at her lack of an accent.

Henry Becker was younger and looked more like a ski instructor than a detective. He let Hawes do most of the talking, but Chris noticed he didn't miss a word.

Gianna woke Violet and the three of them told their story for the umpteeth time.

"Can we see the pictures?" Becker asked. He had the smallest hint of an accent that made Chris think of Canada. Or somewhere near the Dakotas.

Phil brought out a battered laptop, and Chris popped the memory card into the port. He sat back as the detectives studied the photos, occasionally asking a question. When they got to the images of the body, Gianna leaned closer to the screen and increased the size of the photos. Phil and Jason looked away. "His burns are fourth degree," Gianna stated calmly. "Black and white and charred to the bone."

"I didn't know there was anything beyond third degree," muttered Becker.

"I'd call some of them third degree, too." She pointed at the picture, her voice in lecture mode. "See where this yellow layer is exposed? That's subcutaneous fat and—"

"Mom, please." Violet tilted her head at Jason, who was striding out of the room.

Gianna glanced at the other listeners. Hawes shrugged. "Doesn't bother me. Go on."

The next image popped up. "I don't think you need my professional opinion on this one," said Gianna.

"We've seen a few," agreed Hawes as she leaned closer to study the bullet holes in the skull. "What's this?" She touched a perfectly round ash-covered spot near the victim's neck. Gianna shrank the image slightly, trying to bring the edges of the spot into focus.

"Looks like some sort of medallion on a chain. Does it show in the other shots?" She automatically moved to the next pictures and stopped on one. "I didn't even notice it. I was looking at the entry holes."

"How do you know they're not exit holes?" Chris asked.

"The angle of the bevel. It gets smaller as it goes through the bone. Only on this photo can you see it clearly. I noticed immediately when we were in there." She increased and decreased the size of the photo, trying to get a good look at the medallion. Chris estimated it to be a good two inches in diameter.

"That's rapper-size jewelry," stated Becker. "Unless it's one of those medical alert things."

"Not like any medical alert I've seen before," stated Gianna. She frowned at the screen and continued to adjust the image.

"It has some sort of swirly design on it. Can anyone make it out?" asked Hawes.

Gianna was silent, staring at the medallion.

Becker touched the screen. "This part of the design looks like the tip of a bird's wing. Could it be military?"

"We'll figure it out later," said Hawes. "It's nearly dark. It's going to have to wait until tomorrow, when I can get a team in there to clear the area. We aren't going to investigate until I'm certain no one will shoot at us, and I can't assign anyone to keep people out of the area in this cold weather overnight. I hate to leave the scene exposed, but there're too many factors working against us right now. So I've given strict orders for no one to be let through on the highway." She raised a brow at Michael. "No one."

He gave her a grin.

CHAPTER TEN

"Gianna?"

She forced her eyes open in the vehicle, abruptly aware of a heavy warmth across her lap, and her hand automatically stroked the dog's fur. Chris had turned around in the front passenger seat and was looking in her direction. She couldn't make out his eyes in the dark.

"We're almost to your house."

Looking out the window, she recognized the street adjacent to her own. Some minor slush had accumulated along the roadsides, but the streets and yards were clear. It'd been dark when they left the ranger station. Michael had slowly followed the Oregon State Police detectives past the scene of the pileup.

They'd all gaped at the burned and smashed vehicles. The emergency vehicles were gone and two county patrol cars had stayed to turn around any drivers who tried to continue along the highway. A lone tow truck had been pulling a crumpled car up onto its truck bed with a winch.

Once they'd passed the accident, the roads had improved. Gianna remembered how heavy her eyelids had felt and how she'd closed them just for a minute.

Or so she'd thought.

She awakened Violet.

"Can you get in without your things?" Michael asked.

Gianna finally felt the loss of her purse. Up in the forest, it hadn't seemed important, but now she was back in the real world. "There's a keypad to open the garage."

He stopped at the curb and relief flowed over Gianna at the sight of her home. She'd owned it for only a few months, but she adored the house and the new beginning it symbolized for her and Violet. The outside lights were on and transmitted a sense of peace. Violet opened her door and started to slide out, no doubt thinking of her bed and good Wi-Fi.

"Wait," stated Chris.

Gianna stopped, her hand on her door handle.

"Does the window next to the front entrance always look like that?" he asked. Michael bent over slightly to look past Chris at her home.

"Violet, get back in the truck," Michael ordered.

The girl silently obeyed.

Gianna slid across the seats, pressing up against Violet, trying to see out her side of the vehicle to the window in question.

A spiderweb of cracks glistened in the glass, catching the light from her outdoor lamps and highlighting a large jagged hole.

"Oh, shit." Gianna's brain wouldn't accept it.

"Someone broke the window," said Violet. "Mom, why would they do that?" She started to softly cry.

Gianna pulled the girl close, her heart breaking for her daughter, who'd had one shock after another in the last two days. She squinted at the hole in the window; it was right at the height of the front door handle and lock. Clearly they hadn't simply broken a window. Someone had gotten into her home.

Chris called the police.

Why is this happening to us?

"Can anything else go wrong?" Gianna muttered.

"Is this normal for you?" asked Michael quietly. Because of the streetlights and the dark in the vehicle, he was simply a silhouette in the front seat.

"What's that supposed to mean?" snapped Gianna.

"Some people attract drama." He shrugged. "It's like they have a magnetic force that constantly brings bad luck into their lives." He turned toward her, and she could faintly make out his eyes.

He knows.

"The last two days have been horrible," Gianna stated. She closed her mouth. Chris had told her his brother was an investigative reporter, and she knew how to deal with reporters. Rule number one was to not speak to them. Every few years one would call her out of the blue, wanting to update the story of her life. She always refused and threatened to call her lawyer if they pestered her again. She'd had more phone numbers in her life than a call center. Once she received one of those nosy calls, she got a new number.

Violet opened her mouth to speak, and Gianna squeezed her arm.

Quiet.

She closed it.

"These have been bad days for you," said Michael. "Someone tried to burn down a cabin with you two in it. Someone left a dead body in your place—almost as if they were trying to pin his death on you. Someone took a shot at you. Now it looks like someone broke into your place. I'd be very concerned."

"I'm sick over what's happened. This is the last thing I need. And no, this isn't normal in our lives." She tightened her grip on Violet's shoulders, her anger growing at the man who was simply stating the obvious.

"Someone will be here in a few minutes," said Chris. He turned to look at Gianna. "Don't take Michael's questions personally, but he does have a point and it's related to the same one I've asked a few times. Why would someone target you?" He pointed at her home. "This isn't a damned coincidence. They knew you were up on that mountain and they knew where you live. What's going on?"

She stared back at him, the truth of his words slamming into her brain. Violet shuddered under her arm.

"Mom?" she asked softly.

"I don't know what's happening," she whispered.

★ ★ ★

After a thorough search, the two Portland police officers declared no one was in her home. Gianna knew most break-ins didn't warrant more than the filing of a report. Crime scene investigators didn't rush over to take fingerprints and trace evidence. But once the officers realized the break-in could be tied to two murders, they agreed to call an investigator and refused Gianna entrance to the home.

"I won't touch anything," she argued. "Let me at least look to see if anything is missing."

The officers exchanged a look. "You'll have to wait until the detective says it's all right. I don't want any evidence disturbed before the detective takes a look. He should be here within an hour." The older one grinned. "They hate getting called out at this time of night. But from what you've said, we need to take precautions."

Gianna wanted to cry. Pressing for an investigation had promptly gotten her locked out of her own home. She'd been aching for the safe haven. Her home symbolized comfort. The place where she and Violet could catch their breath and let down their guard.

The haven had been ripped away and she felt adrift.

The chaos in the forest might have followed them home.

Where can I keep Violet safe?

"What's it look like inside?" she asked. "Is stuff broken? Is it trashed?" She held her breath, hoping they'd tell her that it appeared some kids had broken in to drink and break things.

Please tell me it doesn't look targeted.

"I noticed there's a computer monitor in an office, but the tower is missing," stated the younger officer.

Violet moaned. "That has my school stuff on it."

"And there're a lot of files piled on the floor near a filing cabinet in the same room. Did you leave it like that?"

Gianna shook her head, unable to speak. The intruders had left the extremely expensive computer monitor but stolen the hard drive containing her personal information. *Not random.* She mentally reviewed what parts of her life had been neatly filed in the cabinet and now had been examined by a stranger.

Tax forms. Mortgage information. Health insurance.

"Outside of that room I thought everything looked very neat," said the other officer. "For a break-in, it's one of the cleanest I've seen."

Not teenagers. Who's doing this to us?

"Kitchen was neat, the bedrooms didn't look disturbed," he continued. "The closet in the master bedroom was open, but it's a walk-in."

Her heart stopped. She always kept that door closed.

"You're gonna want to protect against identity theft. That's the big thing these days," said the younger one earnestly.

She nodded numbly, feeling that this was larger than simple identity theft.

"I can't get any clothes?" Violet asked.

"Not tonight. Are you going to hang around and wait? I hate to say it, but sometimes the investigators can take forever to get here. You don't have to stay. Can you two go to a hotel or a friend's for the night?" he asked kindly.

Not without my credit cards.

"They can stay at my place tonight," said Michael. "I'll call Jamie. We have more than enough room."

"I don't want—" Gianna started.

"You're not imposing. End of discussion."

She met Chris's gaze, and he nodded at her.

It's just for one night. And I'll feel calmer with more people around Violet.

★ ★ ★

Once he saw Michael and Jamie's home, Chris finally relaxed. He'd been on high alert for too long and he could feel it in every cell of his body.

"I'll run you home once she's settled," Michael said quietly to Chris as he pulled the SUV into the driveway of the little house. Michael had moved into Jamie's place soon after they'd become a couple. Chris and Brian had lived with them for several weeks before finding a house close by, and they had dinner with them at least twice a week. Essentially it was Chris's second home.

Jamie stepped out of the front door as they came up the front walkway. She kissed Michael and moved to hug Chris.

"I'm glad you're safe," she whispered in his ear.

"Hey, little sis," said Chris.

"What?" Violet's voice sounded right behind him. "I thought Michael—wait a minute. Who are the siblings here?"

Chris turned and saw the confusion on Violet's face as she studied the three of them. "Biologically, Jamie is not my sister," he explained. "I'll let Jamie tell you the whole story later. She does it best."

Michael gave a small smile as he addressed Gianna. "Chris doesn't like to talk about himself."

"I figured that out."

Jamie hustled the women into the house and down a long hallway to her guest room. Chris heard her launch into the abbreviated version of their past. He knew Jamie would skim over the darker aspects of his story, but anyone who spent a little time on the Internet would easily discover the horrors he and the other children had suffered at the hands of the Ghostman. Suddenly he wanted to be the one to explain his past to Gianna. He wanted to sanitize the information, assure her that he was still a normal, functioning human being.

Normal? Him?

Would she see him differently if she heard the truth?

"Hey."

Chris turned at Michael's voice, realizing he'd been staring down the hall long after the women had vanished, regrets and fears overtaking his thoughts.

"How much do you know about her?" his brother asked.

Chris recognized Michael's full-on investigator voice. "She's going to start at the medical examiner's office soon. They haven't lived here long."

"That's it? You spent all that time with her and that's what you know?" Michael narrowed his brows.

"She likes her coffee black. And Violet was hanging with a bad crowd at her old school."

"And here I thought you'd be a good addition to the private investigation practice I want to open."

"You said I'd be in charge of the computer side."

"But you need some basic curiosity about people. Where are your instincts for asking questions?"

"I'm not nosy." Annoyance shot up his spine. "You don't know what it was like up there, she and her daughter were in a crisis. I wasn't about to ask their life history."

"Well, I did. As soon as you gave me her name, I had people digging."

"What? Why?"

"Because two people are dead and you're involved."

"I'm not—"

"Not directly involved, but I wanted to know who'd thrust themselves upon your mercy."

Curiosity swirled in his brain. "You found out something," he stated.

"When Gianna was eight, her parents were killed in a car wreck. Gianna was with them when their car went off a cliff and down a hundred-foot drop. That little girl crawled out of the wreck and all the way back up to the road. Then she walked over two miles in the pitch dark in the middle of the night until she found a house."

Chris couldn't speak.

Michael nodded. "Yeah, that's how I felt. I remembered the story once I was reminded of it this morning. Her story was all over the national news. She survived when everyone else died."

Like me.

"Hard to miss some of the parallels to your past. A lot of the same elements."

Memories poked at his brain and he fought them back. Day after day of imprisonment in that bunker below the dirt. The faces of the other children he'd believed had been set free but who had been murdered instead. Pushing through the dark forest, half dragging the real Chris Jacobs, terrified neither of them would survive. The sight of the farmhouse where he'd finally found safety.

"Chris!"

"What?"

"Jesus Christ. You look like you're about to faint."

He turned away from his brother as his vision started to narrow. He braced his hands on the hall table and breathed deep.

Michael's hand gripped his shoulder.

He flinched but didn't pull away. *It's Michael.*

"I'm sorry, Chris. I didn't realized it'd hit you like that. I'd hoped it'd be better by now."

"This is better." He forced a laugh. "A few years ago you'd be stepping over my pool of vomit and have a black eye for touching me."

Michael let go.

"No. Don't."

Michael put his hand back and gripped harder. "You've come a long way. I can see it. Jamie does, too. And you're raising Brian to be an amazing kid."

The mention of his son's name nearly made his knees buckle in longing and sheer terror because the boy was out of his sight. Panic shot through him. *Is Brian okay?* Sweat started under his arms and the air in the house suddenly grew thin. He met Michael's gaze.

"Have you heard from Cecelia today?" Chris asked.

Understanding crossed Michael's face and he pulled out his phone. "No. Need to talk to Brian?"

"Yes."

Chris counted the seconds between his breaths, trying to calm his heart, while Michael called their mother, his phone at his ear. The moment went on too long, and he felt sweat run down his side.

"Mom? No, everything's okay. Chris needs to talk to Brian."

Michael handed the phone to Chris. He held his breath until he heard the sleepy voice of his son.

Chris moved to the family room and sat heavily on the couch. The abrupt absence of stress left a stabbing pain in his left temple as he listened to his son talk about the Tower of Terror ride. He made encouraging comments, not fully listening to the excited chatter.

Brian's fine.

He listened for a few more minutes, ended the call, and noticed Michael was staring at him with hawklike intensity. Chris closed his eyes and sank back in the cushions.

He didn't have the energy to tell his brother to knock it off.

★ ★ ★

"So Chris's name is actually Daniel Brody. And Michael Brody is his real brother," Violet said slowly, trying to make sense of the confusing story Jamie had just shared. "And your brother—the real Chris Jacobs—died when he was a young teen."

Jamie nodded.

"But back then you hadn't seen your brother for two years and Chris—our Chris—assumed your brother's identity after he escaped from their kidnapper."

"I know. It's hard to believe," said Jamie. "I look back now and I'm still stunned."

"How long was he in the hospital after he was found?" her mom asked.

"Months. He looked like a walking skeleton when he returned. For a while the doctors weren't sure he'd survive."

"He was held and tortured for two years?" Violet whispered, remembering the scars on the side of his neck.

"It's amazing that he had the presence of mind to keep up the charade after he escaped," Gianna said. "He must have been terrified the kidnapper would come after him and the Brody family."

Violet thought about the quiet man she'd spent the last days with. *What is it like to have someone want you dead?* "No one figured it out for all that time?"

"Not until someone discovered the remains of the other missing children from the kidnapping. All the children were accounted for except for Daniel. Everything started to crumble at that point. Michael wanted to know why his brother's remains weren't found with the other children's."

Violet liked the way Jamie smiled when she said Michael's name. Even though the story was horrible, just saying his name clearly made her happy.

"So Michael did what he does best," said Jamie. "He snooped and poked and prodded until he got answers."

"That's how you met?" Violet asked.

"Yes."

"And Chris is like your brother now."

"I was only ten when he escaped from his kidnapper and came to live with us. He's the only brother I've known since then. I understand my real-life brother died . . . and I feel his loss. But Chris has filled that hole for decades."

It made sense to Violet. It was hard to miss what you didn't remember. Sometimes she wondered if she should feel more loss over her maternal grandparents' deaths, but they'd died when her mother was eight. She carried a tiny bit of guilt for not missing some people she'd never known.

But she missed Nana every day.

Gianna sat on the guest bed beside her and hugged her. Violet sniffled and realized she had tears on her face. "I'm really tired," she mumbled.

"And I've been talking your ear off for ten minutes," said Jamie. "I brought the two of you some pajamas." The tall woman smiled at Gianna. "Clearly you'll have to roll up the legs."

"I'll be asleep. It won't matter. Thank you so much." Her mom yawned. "Tomorrow we'll figure out what is going on."

An image of the blood on her mother's coat popped into Violet's head. She'd nearly forgotten that they'd left two dead people up in the forest.

CHAPTER ELEVEN

He'd gone against his father's directive.

No one told him what to do.

Even his father. He would get the job done, and it was time he followed his own initiative. The end result would be the same: he'd recover the device. But now he was doing it his way.

Gianna Trask would be taken care of. He was pleased she hadn't died in the fire. Yes, she would still have to die at some point, but until then he would enjoy every minute.

Breaking the front window at her home had been a risk. But he'd been watching for so long that he'd ached to set foot where she walked every day. He'd seen her and Violet load their vehicle, clearly leaving for a few days, and had decided to take a chance. He had a tracker on her vehicle; he could catch up. That night in the dark, he'd broken in. It had almost been too easy; the home had no defenses. Something he'd checked thoroughly before risking an alarm.

The home had a faint cinnamon scent. He'd gone immediately to the kitchen and looked for evidence of previous baking. If she'd made cinnamon rolls, she'd taken them on her trip. He didn't use his flashlight, finding his night vision sufficient in the dim home. He'd poked through her kitchen drawers and cupboards. There was an absence of the junk that he'd noticed in most people's homes, the little things that accumulated over time that people hated to throw away. It made sense. She'd been in the house for only a short while.

He wandered to the upper level of the house, stopping first in Violet's room. Black walls greeted him. Noticing that her blinds were closed tight, he turned on his flashlight to a dim level, and realized the walls were actually dark purple and covered in posters of young men. Movie stars, bands. He recognized a few. A strong perfume filled the room. The type he associated with certain clothing stores at the mall that catered to teens who lived in hoodies and lace and shorts. He turned off his light and backed out of the room. The teenager held no interest for him; she was a child.

His interest lay in the bedroom at the back of the house. The room he'd watched every day for three weeks. He kept his flashlight off and moved to the center of her master bedroom, inhaling deeply. No overpowering scents. Large windows filled the back wall of the room, with her bed positioned at the bottom of one. On sunny days she'd wake to the sun on her face.

He knew she kept her blinds lowered from the top, keeping the bottom halves of the windows covered and blocking curious gazes from ground level. But from his second-floor spy nest, he could see her if she walked about the room, constantly moving in and out of his view. It simply tantalized him, making him want to see more.

He moved to the window and spotted his favorite spying position in the empty home behind hers. *Does she ever wonder who lives in that house? Wonder if they watch her?* He picked up a pillow and pressed it against his face.

He caught the faintest odor of shampoo or face cream. A store-bought scent. Annoyance rolled through him. He'd wanted to know what her skin smelled like, what her favorite shirt would smell like after she slept in it. He stepped into the master closet, pulled the door closed, and turned on the light. The odor of leather was the primary smell. Shoes, jackets, and purses were lined up on her shelves. He peeked in a bag on the floor, his mind spinning as he spotted lingerie with the tags still attached.

She's never worn these for anyone.

He shoved the bras and panties into his coat pockets.

He rifled through her filing cabinet, grabbed her computer and a few other knickknacks, and then vanished silently out the door. He hadn't found the item he was looking for, but he had a few mementoes that'd made it worth his while.

★ ★ ★

To Gianna's surprise, the next morning Chris strode into the home during breakfast and took a seat at the table with her,

Michael, and Jamie, helping himself to the stack of waffles like he did it every day.

Maybe he did.

"Have you heard from the Portland police detective?" he asked her.

"Michael reached out to him first thing this morning," Gianna said. Chris looked better than he had yesterday. Like he'd actually had a good night's sleep. He probably thought the same thing about her.

"What'd he say?" Chris's hazel eyes studied her over the rim of his coffee cup, and she thought about Jamie's story from last night. After Violet had gone to sleep, Gianna had asked Jamie a few deeper questions. Jamie had been frank. And the story of Chris's two years of torture was disturbing. *Soul-deep damage* was one of the phrases Jamie had used. *Still recovering.*

Gianna had lain awake for a long time, reviewing the events of the last forty-eight hours. Jamie's story had filled in some holes and explained some of Chris's behaviors.

No wonder he was constantly aware of his surroundings; he'd been on guard since he was a child. Her heart had ached as she thought about the young teen who'd lost his innocence too early. He'd become a strong man. One who was sensitive and caring. If the damage had been too deep, she didn't think he'd be the dependable person she'd seen.

Clearly he'd healed. But how much?

Sunshine streamed into the cheery kitchen nook where they ate, and Gianna noticed he'd shaved. Chris Jacobs cleaned up nicely. "He's getting in touch with Hawes and Becker. He wants their opinion and to compare notes," she said.

"Have you heard from the two state detectives?"

"Yes. I talked with Hawes. She said they were just getting ready to enter the cabin. They had a team clear the surrounding area first, determining the shooter was gone so they could start their investigation."

"What about tracks? Spent casings from the shooting? Did they figure out where the shots came from?" Chris asked.

"Slow down," Gianna ordered, waving her fork at him. "Hawes didn't tell me anything except that they felt it was safe to begin. We'll hear what they found."

Chris looked antsy. Like he wanted to drive back up into the Cascades and look over the detectives' shoulders.

"She said they'll try to get the bodies to the medical examiner's office by this afternoon."

"You'll be there for the autopsies, right?" asked Michael.

Gianna blinked. "I don't think that would be right."

"Did you ask Dr. Rutledge? I doubt he'd have a problem with you observing. And I assume either Hawes or Becker will be there, too. It'd be a good time to hear what they found."

Clearly Michael likes to push boundaries.

"I'll think about it." The more she thought about it, the more she wanted to attend. She'd been unable to get the murdered burn victim out of her head. She'd wanted to spend more time studying the photos and discussing them with the detectives or the brothers, but Violet had always been around, so she'd bitten her tongue, not wanting to upset her daughter more. The fact that Gianna hadn't noticed the medallion when they'd first found the body bothered her. She was a trained observer; she was supposed to notice the details that other people missed. She didn't believe in making excuses for herself, but she'd been through hell before finding the body. And she hadn't been on the job at that moment.

She was deeply curious to find out the identity of the dead man in her cabin. Maybe another set of eyes at the autopsy would be a good idea. Once they identified him, hopefully that would lead to who had put her and Violet in danger. If they'd been targeted, she wanted to know *why*.

"Mom? Grandpa wants to talk to you." Violet stood in the doorway to the kitchen, holding out her cell phone.

Gianna rose out of her chair. "Did you call him?"

"I texted him when we got here last night. He must have just seen my message."

"What does he know?" she asked softly.

Violet shrugged. "Everything."

Gianna silently moaned. She'd hoped to control the elements her uncle heard of the story. She wasn't in the mood for a lecture about moving. She loved her uncle, but he tried her patience. Saul Messina was a good man. He'd taken her in after the death of her parents and raised her as his own. He'd never married, but had dated a wealth of kind women who were always eager to mother the orphan. Some of them had been genuine; some not so much. Gianna had learned early how to tell the fakes from the sincere ones. And she had learned to not get attached.

She reluctantly accepted the phone and stepped into the hallway, seeking privacy. "Saul?"

"Gianna? Are you all right?" Her uncle still had a hint of Brooklyn in his voice, even though he'd lived in Southern California for thirty years. Homesickness hit her in the gut and she wiped her eyes. She'd lived in New York for only a few years, but the combination of his familiar voice and the realization that she'd truly left behind everything she'd known overwhelmed her.

"We're fine, Saul. We were very lucky. I owe my life to Violet."

"What's this about you being shot at? And possibly drugged? I'm telling you, Gianna, that state has some residents who are a bit feral. Are you sure the two of you are okay?"

"We're fine, Saul. The police are going to handle everything. We were just in the wrong place at the wrong time and neither of us got hurt." She hoped Violet hadn't told him about the personal items missing from her house. She didn't need Saul worrying any more than he already was.

"You know how I felt about the two of you moving there. This doesn't put my mind at ease at all."

He'd been very vocal with his disappointment when she'd accepted the job in Portland, even though it'd placed her on the same coast as him. She suspected the only city he wouldn't complain about her moving to was Los Angeles. "It's a good place to live. I won't judge it by what happened."

"Do you need to come home for a while?"

She sighed. Saul's house hadn't been her home for almost two decades, but he still referred to it as if she'd just left yesterday. "I don't think so. Violet has school and I start my new job soon."

"Don't know what you see in that wet state. You should have picked somewhere with sun."

"I made my choice. We like it here."

"Violet doesn't sound too happy."

Irritation brought up her chin. "Any new school is hard. It doesn't matter what state it's in."

She refused to argue with him. They'd already beaten the subject to death.

"I'm coming up there. You need some family around. Violet says you're staying at some stranger's house because your home was broken into. I've already called the Benson Hotel and arranged for you to have the presidential suite for a few days. If you're not going to come visit, I'll come there."

"Saul, that's not—"

"Don't argue with me. Someone needs to make certain the police are doing their job, and you're too nice about it. I can get results."

Anger burned in her chest. Saul always threw his weight and money around to get what he wanted. He'd made a fortune in the temporary worker industry and was known for burying the competition when there was something he wanted. Now he wanted to handle Gianna's life. They'd butted heads for decades over his pushy behavior.

Gianna had learned to pick her battles with her uncle, and decided to stand down on this one. She had a feeling Detective Hawes could handle Saul just fine. "You take the suite, Saul. There's nothing wrong with my home. The police should be done with it today." She crossed her fingers.

"Well, I've hired a security company to take a look at it today. If you insist on staying there alone, I want to know you have the best defense."

Gianna closed her eyes, fighting the need to bang her forehead against the wall. "Thank you, Saul."

She ended the call after getting his travel information. Saul would be taking over Portland by six this evening.

Hopefully, Portland was ready.

"You okay?" Chris asked, moving into the hallway. Gianna wondered how much he'd heard.

"You look like you need to hit something," he said.

"My uncle can be a bit infuriating," Gianna replied.

"I take it 'infuriating' is a polite term?"

"Absolutely. He's a freight train, barreling full speed wherever he pleases. Right now he feels the need to come supervise my life and stir every pot I own."

"Sounds like he cares about you."

"That's not what I need to hear right now."

"Okay . . . sounds like he's a pushy son of a bitch."

"That's better."

"This is the guy who took you in after your parents died?"

Gianna swallowed. Someone had done some research. "Yes. He's my father's brother."

"But he's not related to Violet's grandmother who died."

"No. That was her father's mother."

Chris was silent, and Gianna took a close look at him. Even though he'd lived through hell, he hadn't lost his humanity. He cared. He was probably selective about whom he cared for, but she knew Violet and she were now included.

Other people could have come out of his experience and been bitter the rest of their lives, turning their backs on everyone. Chris looked forward. There was an optimism about him that she suspected had everything to do with his son.

His heart was good.

"The Portland police detective called back while you were talking with your uncle."

"Damn it." Her to-do list was getting longer and longer. "I need to get a new cell phone. Today."

"He wants to meet at your place in an hour."

Gianna nodded, "I can do that." That'd give her time to replace her cell phone. "Crap. I need—"

"I'll drive you." His eyes were kind.

"Surely you have things you need to do today."

"I'm my own boss. I gave myself the day off."

Gianna exhaled, grateful for his generosity. "After this meeting, I need to rent a car."

"Jamie asked Violet if she'd like to stay here for the morning, and Violet said she would. She seems a bit fascinated with my sister."

"Violet's interested in teaching elementary school. I suspect your sister will be bombarded with questions about her job as a principal."

"Jamie will love that."

"Can we leave in five minutes?"

"I'm ready when you are."

CHAPTER TWELVE

Chris thought Portland police detective Drew Sanchez didn't look old enough to buy cigarettes. He'd greeted Chris and Gianna and invited them into Gianna's home like he was the owner. Chris saw the amusement in Gianna's expression, but she didn't say anything. Not that she could get a word in edgewise. The detective talked like he'd drunk a triple espresso on an empty stomach.

The three of them stood in Gianna's home office. It was a pale room with white crown molding, white wainscoting, and a huge white desk. The walls were a faint blue, and he wondered if she'd simply kept the decor from the previous owner.

In Chris's opinion it didn't fit Gianna's personality at all. To him she was about color. He'd envisioned a home full of deep reds and yellows and purples. He'd always associated people with colors. Jamie was the cool, calm green of her eyes. Michael was red for his impatience and intensity.

Gianna was not lifeless pale blue and white.

Black powder had been lightly fanned all over the filing cabinet, light switches, and desk. The evidence team had already left, but Detective Sanchez had waited to speak with Gianna. The files that the police had said had been all over the floor were gone, and the drawers of the filing cabinet were empty.

"The police took every file?" Gianna was stunned.

"Whoever broke in pulled every file out of the cabinet and dumped them on the floor. We took them for prints. Would you know what was missing from an inventory?"

"I have no idea. I can look, but there had to be at least forty files in there. Everything from appliance warranties to Violet's report cards from grade school."

"Can they pull prints off those paper files?" Chris asked.

"Yep. You'd be amazed what they can get prints off these days." Gianna nodded in agreement.

"Anything else look missing or out of place?" Sanchez asked.

"No," said Gianna after a long look. "The computer tower is gone, obviously, but everything else looks normal."

"Let's walk through the rest of the house."

They followed the detective. Gianna checked some cupboards in the kitchen and drawers in her bedroom but couldn't spot anything missing. She rooted through a box of jewelry, shaking her head. "I would have at least expected them to take these rings. They're pretty valuable."

"What about the walk-in closet?" Chris asked. "You'd said you leave that door closed." Again, black dust on the handle of the closet door.

Sanchez followed the two of them into the closet. Gianna appeared to have a weakness for bags and shoes. Two walls of the large closet were covered with shelves neatly displaying an obscene number of both. In contrast the section of clothing seemed quite small.

Gianna tapped her toe against a pink-striped shopping bag on the floor. "This shouldn't be empty. I just bought this stuff the other day, and it still had the price tags on it."

Chris glanced in the bag. A sheet of pink tissue paper lay in the bottom. "What was in it?"

"Lingerie. Two bras. Three pairs of panties," she stated.

Sanchez's cheeks reddened, and Chris's mouth suddenly went dry as he tried to look anywhere but at Gianna's chest. She wasn't top-heavy. He'd noticed early on that her proportions were perfect, but her description of the bag's contents suddenly seemed to shine a spotlight on her body. She stood there in his sister's rolled-up sweat pants with her long hair casually twisted and clipped on top of her head, and he realized he had no desire to look at another woman.

Gianna Trask was stunning even at her worst.

"Any other . . . lingerie missing?" Sanchez asked.

Gianna went back to the dresser and dug through two more drawers, a frown on her face. Chris looked away again. Bits of black and pink and lace and satin flew through her fingers. She shoved the drawers closed. "I don't think so. But frankly, I don't think I'd be able to tell. I have a lot of stuff."

Sanchez nodded and made a careful note on his pad.

"That's kinda creepy." Gianna wrinkled her nose. "Although maybe they'll just try to return it to the store for cash since it still had tags."

"Or someone has a girlfriend the right size," Sanchez said with a small grin.

"If they wanted something to sell for money, they would have taken the jewelry." Chris pointed out. "They took the computer tower but left your huge expensive monitor. You were targeted; they wanted the information on your computer."

Gianna stood perfectly still, holding his gaze. A small tremor flickered near one eye.

I rattled her.

"Do you know why someone would want your computer?" Sanchez asked.

"Identity theft," she said.

Her tone told Chris she didn't believe her own words.

"I can see the computer being stolen along with other items if these were thieves looking for a fast buck," stated Sanchez. "But they left the easy stuff. Unless you have all your passwords on an easily accessible Word document, they'll have to do some work to get anything useful. Most thieves are pretty lazy. I have to agree with Chris's suggestion on this one."

"Let me look around a little more." Gianna abruptly left the bedroom.

"What's she not telling me?" Sanchez asked Chris. He tapped his notepad with his pencil. "This will be a lot easier if I don't have to guess everything. I think she has an idea of what's going on."

"I don't think she knows," Chris said slowly. "I think she's stunned and a bit overwhelmed."

"Maybe she doesn't want to believe that someone she knows would do this to her."

"No one wants to believe that sort of thing. But I don't think Gianna's the type to sugarcoat things. If she knew of someone threatening in her life, I think she'd immediately speak up."

"Detective Sanchez?" Gianna called from down the hall.

The two men found her in a nook adjacent to her kitchen. She pointed at a small wooden side table that had a few glass figures and framed photos. "There's a photo missing."

"What's it a picture of?" Chris asked.

"Violet and me."

Sanchez pointed his pencil at the figurines. "Are those glass things valuable?"

"They're crystal, not glass."

"So, yes," stated Sanchez. "But our thief was interested only in a family photo."

Alarm shot through Chris. Even if Gianna had struggled to believe the break-in wasn't personal, she had to believe now. The thief hadn't just stolen information, he'd taken trophies for himself.

"I can't stay here tonight." Gianna shuddered as she stared at the empty spot. "I don't know if I can ever sleep in this house again."

★ ★ ★

Nora Hawes leaned against the wall of the autopsy suite, waiting for Dr. Rutledge to finish recording his notes. The stainless steel table in front of him held the burned remains of the man found in Gianna Trask's rented cabin. The suite was clean and orderly. Empty silver tables were lined up in a row beyond Dr.

Rutledge's current work site. Sprayers that appeared to belong in a small car wash hung behind the four tables. A scale dangled over each station, waiting to weigh organs. Nora wondered what the room sounded like when several autopsies were occurring at once. Right now it was very quiet except for the low hum of fans and the doctor's voice.

Autopsies didn't bother her, but she didn't have any desire to get up close and personal. Henry would rather pay for her Starbucks habit for a week than attend, so she'd made him a deal. He didn't realize she would have done it without the offer of free coffee. He was a solid partner, but knowing he had a weak stomach gave her something to harass him about.

Gianna Trask and Chris Jacobs entered the suite, and Nora held her position in a shallow alcove as she studied the couple. Drew Sanchez from the Portland Police Department had briefly updated her with a phone call and told her the couple were on their way. She'd spent the last few minutes processing Sanchez's findings. Especially the fact that all stolen items were personal and didn't appear to have been taken for their value on the street. Someone had wanted very specific items from Gianna's home.

But how does it tie to the deaths during the storm?

It was a big juicy riddle. She loved figuring out answers.

Especially with people as interesting as the two who'd just entered. She'd done her research last night. She'd noticed the scars on Chris's neck and the side of his face yesterday, but hadn't realized she was talking with a local legend. *The boy who survived.* He'd managed to stay out of the limelight for decades. Now Chris Jacobs had a new cause that was making him step forward.

Dr. Gianna Trask.

Chris had stood directly behind the petite medical examiner and scanned the room as if checking for hidden assassins; he'd spotted Nora within seconds, forcing her to step out of her lousy hiding spot and cross the floor to meet them. Gianna lifted one hand in greeting to Dr. Rutledge, who returned the wave but continued his monologue into the microphone over the burned remains, and then turned her attention to Nora. Gianna had a solid handshake.

"I hear you've had a busy day already," said Nora after shaking hands with Chris.

"Sanchez said he would call you," said Gianna. She glanced over at the work area, an eagerness in her gaze. "Was there identification on the body?"

She cuts to the chase.

"He didn't have ID on him," offered Nora. "I haven't had a chance to ask Dr. Rutledge about his findings, but I believe he's almost done."

"Yes, he is," Gianna said with confidence after a glance at Dr. Rutledge.

Nora figured Gianna experienced the same curiosity and desire for answers that she did when presented with a dead body. There was a reason the woman had become a forensic pathologist. The ones Nora had met all had a thirst for answers. Nora's primary motivations usually centered around making the perpetrators pay for their crimes, but she loved uncovering the science and evidence that paved the path to the suspect. And the more unusual the case the better. This case had all her neurons firing. A fire, a medical examiner with some missing memory, a local legend, and an unknown assassin and victim.

Am I wrong to be fascinated?

Dr. Rutledge removed some of his protective gear and crossed the suite to the group. "I'm glad to hear you're all right, Dr. Trask. I'm sorry your introduction to Oregon has started off on such a bad note." He jerked his head back at the corpse. "Not what you want to discover in your home."

Nora had dealt with Seth Rutledge several times and liked the sharp chief medical examiner. If she'd met him outside the ME's office, she would never have guessed that he spent his days with death. He was simply enjoyable to be around, witty and pleasant.

Too bad he's taken.

"What'd you find?" Nora asked.

"Dr. Trask was right that he was shot before the fire." He tipped his head at Gianna. "But before that he was hit twice in the head. Hard. First on the back of the head and then on the left temple. The blows were enough to eventually be the cause of death, but the two shots assured his death. I suspect he was lying down when he was shot . . . he probably fell after the blows to the head."

"I didn't see any evidence that he was shot in the cabin. There wasn't a blood pool," said Gianna. "Plus I believe Violet would have heard shots if it'd happened after we were out in my truck."

Dr. Rutledge looked at Nora. "Did you find bullet holes under him? The angle of the entry and exit wounds indicate a prone position to me."

Nora knew the body had been shot elsewhere. The lack of bullet holes in the floor and Dr. Rutledge's assessment of the gunshot angles backed it up. "No bullet holes were found in the floor near the body. No shells nearby either. But we recovered the slugs and shells from the shots at the forest ranger." She glanced at Chris Jacobs. Her research on him had indicated that he owned nearly a dozen weapons. Five of them rifles.

His face gave her no clue to his thoughts.

"You're welcome to compare my weapons," he stated.

Nora nodded. It was already on her list, but she had a hunch it wouldn't bear fruit.

"Then our John Doe was moved to his position in the cabin very soon after he was shot," Dr. Rutledge continued. "Lividity matches up with the photographs of the position he was found in."

"English, please," said Chris.

"Blood is prey to gravity immediately after death," said Gianna. "It settles in the tissues of the lowest point of the body and stays there, creating dark patterning in those tissues. He was on his left side when I saw him and Frisco took the first photos."

"Got it," said Chris. "But how do you know he took a blow to the back of the head before the temple?"

Nora saw Gianna start to speak, then defer to Dr. Rutledge, who grinned at her restraint. "Can I see your notebook?" he asked Nora. Her current small notebook was tucked under her arm. Her notes were organized and legible. Not scribbles on a wrinkled flimsy pad like some detectives'.

She flipped it to a blank page. A small twinge of vulnerability shot through her as she handed over her book. Her cases relied on what she wrote in that book, and her hands abruptly felt empty and useless.

Dr. Rutledge drew a large circle. "Here's the skull. The first blow was enough to send cracks from the point of impact. Think of the blow like a kid's drawing of a sun." He drew a tiny circle for the impact site and added a series of lines that shot out like rays from a sun. "These cracks follow the path of least resistance, creating a distinct pattern. Now the second blow over here doesn't have the freedom of expression that the first blow did." He drew a small impact site and started to give it the same sun rays. "The cracks from the second site will be blocked when they come to the first site's cracks." His lines stopped as they tried to cross the first set of lines. "We look for which site has the unblocked cracks. That's our first impact."

"Fascinating," Chris said softly. "I can't imagine what it looks like when someone has taken a dozen blows to the head with a hammer."

"That's a tougher puzzle to solve," admitted Gianna.

Nora watched Chris's hand creep up to touch the back of his own skull. He'd spent months in the hospital after he was found. Head trauma had been only one item on the long list of his injuries.

"There's a distinct muzzle stamp around both of the bullet entrances," added Dr. Rutledge. "Even with the burns from the fire, I can still see it. The gun was pressed against his skull when it was fired."

"Caliber?" asked Nora, knowing it would be only a guess from the medical examiner, since the bullets were still missing.

"Not small. Big enough to blow through his skull in a straight line. Unless the perpetrators dug up the floor or ground where they shot him, I imagine they're buried and waiting to be found."

"So we agree the cabin wasn't the murder scene for John Doe," Nora stated.

"Correct," said Dr. Rutledge. "Obviously it was for Francisco Green, but I haven't gotten to him yet."

"Why go through the trouble of dumping the body in an occupied cabin?" Chris asked. "Either Gianna and Violet were in the cabin when it was placed or it was put in there right after they got out."

"Wouldn't Violet have seen someone with a body when she was in your vehicle?" Nora asked.

"I know she slept part of the time," said Gianna. "But from what I understand, she was focused on me in the backseat and the windows steamed immediately. Under the cover of dark, it could have happened. I think it's more likely than someone doing it while I was sleeping on the main floor."

Chris shook his head. "It doesn't make sense. Is someone trying to make a point with his death?"

Nora agreed. "That's what I'm here to find out." She knew she'd be closer to the answer once she figured out the identity of the victim. "What do you have so far to help us identify him?" she asked the examiner.

Dr. Rutledge blew out a breath. "Caucasian male in his fifties or sixties. Gray hair, five foot ten, medium build, poor muscle tone. Extensive dental work. Implants have replaced three of his front teeth and he's had other cosmetic dental work done on his front teeth. Expensive work. I need to take a closer look at all his films, but right off I noticed old breaks in his right radius and ulna."

"Both bones?" Gianna asked. "Possibly from the same incident?"

"I'll take a closer look, but they're in the same location and demonstrated the same amount of repair. They're old, nearly smooth in their healing."

"Clothing?" asked Nora.

"Jeans, flannel shirt, long-underwear-type shirt, heavy winter jacket. All from Eddie Bauer. Same with the boots."

"All from the same store?" Gianna wrinkled her forehead. "That's odd. Right?" She looked at Chris and the medical examiner. "Or do some men do all their shopping in one store?"

"Whatever's fastest," stated Chris. Dr. Rutledge nodded in agreement.

"Must be a man thing," said Gianna, looking to Nora for confirmation.

She nodded, but found the fact as curious as Gianna. Had the victim suddenly needed winter clothing and bought it all at once? Did the fact that Eddie Bauer had a large mail-order business indicate that the victim avoided stores? Or was the victim from an area where clothing stores weren't readily available?

Or did it mean nothing at all . . . simply a man who shopped the fastest way he knew how?

"Do you have the medallion he was wearing?" Gianna asked.

"Yes." Dr. Rutledge walked back over to where his assistant was stitching up the long incisions the medical examiner had made during the autopsy. He grabbed a small silver tray from an adjacent table and brought it back to the group. The three of them leaned forward for a closer look.

The medallion's gold-colored chain was heavy and thick. It reminded Nora of an ancient foreign coin, and she wondered if it was real gold. She suspected so. Something about the quality of the piece told her that someone had spent a lot of money. With relief she noticed the jewelry hadn't been cleaned. Possibly she could find fingerprints that would reveal the victim's identity if he'd been arrested in the past. Maybe she'd get lucky and he'd be local. Swirling loops covered the medallion in a raised pattern. To Nora it looked like it'd been designed with one of the old Spirograph sets. She and her brothers had spent hours with the small plastic disks and colored pens, trying to outdo one another's designs.

"Can you turn it over?" Gianna asked.

Dr. Rutledge produced a pair of long-handled tweezers and the medallion clanged in the metal tray. More swirly patterns shone through the dusty ash that clung to the metal.

"Are those initials?" Chris muttered.

"Yes," whispered Gianna. "GDM."

Nora looked sharply at the petite doctor. She'd gone pale and Nora had the feeling that she'd fully expected to recognize the pattern when she'd asked Dr. Rutledge to flip it over. "You know who this belongs to?"

"It belongs to me," she said quietly.

CHAPTER THIRTEEN

"It's a very masculine-looking piece," said Detective Hawes. Her stare made Gianna feel like Gianna herself had pulled the trigger that had killed the man on the silver table. "Why didn't you say it was yours when you saw it in the pictures?"

"I didn't know," said Gianna. "I didn't recognize it then. I knew it felt familiar but didn't know why. It wasn't until sixty seconds ago that I remembered."

How did my necklace end up around the neck of a dead man?

The thought ricocheted through her head.

Who is he?

"Why?" asked Hawes, her green eyes as penetrating as lasers. "How could you not recognize your own jewelry? Was it missing from your break-in?"

"No." Gianna's heart pounded faster as she tried to unscramble her brain. Both Dr. Rutledge and Chris were watching her with the same intensity, and her mouth dried up. "I haven't seen it in ages. It was mine as a child. A gift from my maternal grandmother. I haven't seen it since . . . since my parents died. We'd always thought it'd been lost in the mess of clearing out their house after their deaths. I really don't remember it that well . . . I got to wear it or see it only on special occasions. My mother always kept it in her things and promised I'd have it once I was older."

"So you're not positive that this is the same medallion. It could just be something similar."

Gianna looked back in the metal tray. "This is it. I *know* it is."

Doubt raced across Detective Hawes's features.

"This man must have known you somehow," Hawes said. "And you know we need an identification on him as soon as possible. Nothing else about him prompts any memory?"

Gianna stepped closer to the table. In the cabin there'd been little to indicate his age without further investigation. The victim's face was half-gone, his hair burned away. His lips had curled back and burned away, exposing his teeth. His torso had been well protected from the flames by his clothing and seemed unnaturally white compared to what was left of his face.

Something has to be familiar.

Nothing about him stirred a memory.

"No."

Nothing.

"I'm sorry, I truly don't know who he is."

Hawes nodded in acceptance, her eyes slightly sad. "I'll start looking in other ways. We'll figure it out." She turned a curious gaze to the body. "I bet it's going to be a fascinating story."

Gianna felt like she'd let the detective down.

"The chain on the medallion is different," said Gianna, searching for something helpful to add. "I remember it being thinner . . . it was one of those square-shaped chains. A box chain. I remember running it between my fingers over and over, fascinated with the movement of the chain more than the medallion. I always thought the medallion was boring even though my initials were on it."

"Any chance you have a picture of it from back then?" Hawes asked.

Gianna took a deep breath. "I can't remember. Maybe at my uncle's house. He kept ninety percent of all the photos that belonged to my parents. He boxed them up and put them in storage, but he'd put together two nice albums of pictures for me, so I always had pictures of the three of us to look at." Tears threatened, creating burning sensations in her eyes.

Her parents had died over twenty-five years ago. *Why does it still hurt?*

It wasn't their deaths that ached today; it was what her parents had missed. Primarily it hurt that they'd never known Violet or seen the major accomplishments of Gianna's life. Her memories were so old, she often wasn't certain that they were accurate. When she looked through the albums, she believed she remembered the circumstances of each photo. Or were the photos creating the memories? Would she still remember riding the pony at the fair if her mother hadn't taken the photo?

Chris put an arm around her shoulders and gently pulled her against his side. "Pictures are important," he said. "When I look at old photos of Michael and me, it's like they're from someone else's life. That time period ended, and I went for a long time with nothing to remind me of that life. Michael and my mother put together some albums for me about a year ago. One is of the four of us Brodys together, and I have another one of their lives after I was gone. They weren't sure that they should do it, but I wanted to see how they'd lived without me, because every single day I ask what my life would have been like if one event hadn't shifted everything to a new course."

He'd nailed it.

Gianna understood perfectly. One event had changed her life and it still guided her current course. *But what if . . . ?*

She couldn't make an album that showed what could have been if her parents had lived. She had to rely on imagination.

The photos were both a curse and a blessing.

"You can't be certain this medallion is yours," Hawes stated.

"That's correct," admitted Gianna. "It could be one that simply looks like it and happens to have my initials. But I'm telling you, I remember that pattern. I remember tracing the swirls on the other side and wishing they formed a flower or a tiara instead of nothing. I remember—"

What did she remember?

Her teeth ached with a memory.

"I remember biting it as a child," she said slowly. "I'd seen people in cartoons bite gold coins to see if they were real. I bit it and it made marks. I was terrified my mother would notice and I'd get in trouble for damaging it, but she never said anything."

A childish recollection of fear swept through her. She'd been terrified for days that she'd be in trouble for ruining the precious present. She leaned closer to the medallion. Dr. Rutledge picked it up with his tweezers and peered closely.

Gianna saw two small dents on one side. So tiny. Barely remarkable within the pattern of swirls. He turned it over and she saw four more in an arc.

"I'm not an odontologist, but I'd say those are bite marks. Someone bit it at some point. No way to tell who did, but it lends some credence to your story," said Dr. Rutledge. He grinned at Gianna.

I knew it.

She wondered when her uncle Saul would arrive. She remembered discussing the lost jewelry with him after she'd moved into his home. He'd had his people search through all the belongings from her parents, but the necklace hadn't been found. She'd missed it, but not because she loved it. She'd missed it because it was a link to her maternal grandmother and it'd been created expressly for her. She truly hadn't thought about the piece since junior high.

"Did you find anything else at the cabin?" Chris asked. "Any trace of the shooter?"

Hawes smiled. "We found some interesting things that I'd like to ask both of you about." She glanced at Dr. Rutledge. "Are we done here for now?"

"Yes. I'm going to examine the forest ranger a little later. Did you want to observe?"

Hawes glanced at her watch. "Why don't you call me afterward with a briefing? Francisco Green's supervisor is in the waiting room with another of the ranger's coworkers. Why don't you let them know when you start? I don't think they want to come in, but they wanted to be here. I'm going to find a quiet place to talk with Chris and Gianna."

Her smile was kind. Gianna felt Detective Hawes genuinely cared about the case and would be ruthless in the hunt to find her answers. Her job in New York had required Gianna to interact with a lot of detectives, and Hawes was the exact type she wanted pursuing her case.

"How about we grab a bite of lunch?" Hawes suggested.

"I'm starved," agreed Gianna. Working at the examiner's office had never affected her appetite.

Chris gave a rueful shake of his head and touched his stomach. "I don't mind watching the two of you eat."

★ ★ ★

He ate three pieces of barbecued chicken pizza. After smelling the autopsy suite, Chris had believed he wouldn't eat for a few days. That idea had dissolved as soon as the three of them had stepped through the restaurant doors and the good food odors pushed away the memory of the burn victim's scent. The lunch rush had already cleared out and the restaurant was quiet. Hawes's partner, Henry Becker, had appeared within moments of their being seated.

Chris had never been inside a medical examiner's suite. He hoped he never had reason to go back. He'd never forget the sight of the victim under the bright autopsy lights. He didn't understand how Gianna and Seth Rutledge got up every morning and happily drove to do that job.

Doesn't it get to them?

He was thankful there were people in the world willing to deal with death. They sought answers to help others. He wondered how it'd felt today for Gianna to be on the other side of the autopsy table, unable to jump in and perform a job she was trained to do, find the answers to her questions. It must have felt like she had her hands tied behind her back. At least they knew Seth was thorough.

Chris had watched her face as she examined the gold medallion. She'd been careful not to speak until she'd seen the other side, but her face had told Chris she connected with it. When the medallion was first highlighted in a picture, she'd blinked several times, as if trying to clear something out of her view. When she'd seen it in person, she'd pressed her lips together, her eyes widening, and her hands quivering the tiniest bit. Once she'd stated that she believed it was hers, she'd relaxed, but until that moment Chris could have sworn he'd nearly seen a cloud of tension around her.

How the fuck did her necklace end up on a dead man?

He didn't like it. Someone was playing a fast and dangerous game, moving a murdered body into Gianna's cabin and setting the cabin on fire. Chris firmly expected the fire would be declared arson. Everything circled around Gianna. Her necklace, her rented cabin, her life under attack. Had she been intended to die in the fire? He also believed she'd been drugged. Now that he'd spent time with her, he knew she was nothing like the confused and awkward woman he'd woken in the Suburban. She'd ingested or inhaled something that affected her.

He hoped Nora Hawes would have some answers. And he hoped Gianna wasn't covering up something dangerous.

More dangerous than being drugged, caught in a fire, and shot at?

He watched her bite a slice of pizza and wipe the sauce from her lip. A dreamy look entered her eyes as she chewed, and he smiled. She was enjoying her food, but he was enjoying her company. She didn't intimidate him. "Intimidate" wasn't the right word . . . few people intimidated him, but there was an easy comfort to being in her presence that made him want to stay. Most people made him want to spend more time with Oro.

"You'll be happy to know we got an evidence team up to the cabin early this morning," Nora began. "Obviously we recovered the bodies and delivered them to the examiner. A fire investigator is scheduled to go up this afternoon or tomorrow."

Gianna set down her pizza. "Did the evidence team have any opinions on arson?"

"That's not their area of expertise," Henry said.

"But they've told you something," pushed Gianna.

Henry and Nora exchanged a look. "Several of them commented on the smell of an accelerant. But it could be from something else."

Right. Chris could see in their faces that they were certain the fire had been arson but were holding back on using that term until they had official word.

"What did you want to ask us about?" Chris questioned.

"First I'd like the two of you to take a look at some of the photos they took this morning." Nora glanced at his empty plate and then met his gaze. "They're of the forest ranger."

Chris nodded, steeling his stomach, wondering if it would have been better to look at them before he ate.

Probably not.

On a tablet, Nora pulled up a series of thumbnails and chose one, then held the screen out for him and Gianna to see. "The footprints with the blue markers . . . do you remember if they were there before you left?"

Chris was relieved to see Francisco wasn't in the first picture she'd picked.

Gianna scowled as she looked at the photo of the snowy and ashy porch of her rental cabin. She pointed at a large indentation in the snow. "That's where I landed when I dived away from the shot. You can see how I scrambled in the snow, and I assume this one is my boot print from when I ran. It looks like two or three inches of snow fell since I left . . . my boot mark isn't very clear. I don't know about the ones with the blue markers. They're definitely more clear than mine. They must not have been made until well after I left."

"We figured that one was yours. It matches the smaller ones in the ash in the cabin. But we have a mystery set. It appears someone walked up to the ranger's body after he was killed."

"Did he go in the cabin?" Chris asked.

"Yes. We're extremely lucky Francisco took pictures and Gianna managed to grab the camera," said Henry. "It's clear that someone visited the cabin and both bodies after you left. Take a look." He switched to a set of side-by-side photos. "Here's the one Francisco took and here's one an evidence tech took from the same location."

Tracks littered the ashy floor in the second photo.

"Francisco wouldn't let me walk in until he'd photographed the scene," Gianna said softly. "I wonder if the second person knew that we'd taken photos. Did he tamper with the bodies at all?"

"Our John Doe looks the same in the crime scene photos as the ones that Francisco took. Obviously we don't have a first set of photos of Francisco's death." Henry took a deep breath. "But you saw him immediately after the shooting, right? I want you to think back to that moment and fix in your head an image of Francisco. Then we'll look at our photos."

Gianna closed her eyes, her throat moving as she swallowed.

She sees death every day. She shouldn't have any problem with this. Chris realized he was holding his breath and quietly exhaled, knowing he shouldn't worry for the medical examiner in the chair next to him. But she'd talked to and interacted with Francisco in the moments before he was murdered. And been present for his death, the evidence splattered across her face and clothing.

Anyone would struggle.

She opened her eyes and nodded at Nora, who revealed a new photo.

Chris looked away, the image burned on his retinas. Francisco Green was spread-eagle in ashy snow. Half his head was gone, his blood staining the snow around him.

Gianna was quiet. Chris finally looked back, keeping his gaze on her, not the photo she was intently studying.

Her profile was perfectly still, her gaze darting over the photo. She tucked loose hair behind her ear, never looking away from the tablet.

"He fell on his right side when he was shot," she stated. "When I grabbed the camera, his right arm was stretched out above his head and his left arm was across his body, his left hand in the snow. Someone rolled him onto his back."

"Anything else?" Nora asked.

Gianna was quiet another second and then shook her head. Nora closed the photo.

"The team is still gathering evidence," said Henry, "but it was pretty clear when Nora and I were up there this morning that at least one other person walked through the scene inside the cabin."

"Did anyone else from the area report the fire or deaths? Perhaps it was someone from nearby who went inside," suggested Chris, searching for another explanation.

"No other calls. We've canvassed the other nearby cabins." Henry glanced at Nora. "There're not many."

Chris nodded in agreement. "But what about the footprints outside? Surely he left a trail coming in and going out."

Nora sighed. "Too much new snowfall. Right next to the cabin we can make out the prints because there was some protection from the walls. But as soon as we moved away, the tracks were lost. Even around Gianna's Suburban, it almost looks like nothing ever took place. Except for the fact that the window was broken out. We want the vehicle for evidence," she said, with an apologetic look at Gianna. "I arranged to have it brought back to town. We shouldn't keep it long."

"That's the least of my worries," said Gianna.

"Sanchez said the items that you're missing from your home are more personal than valuable," Henry said. "Obviously we're moving forward with the idea that it might be related to what happened up at the cabin."

"Both incidents seem very focused on Gianna," Chris pointed out. "I get that there are two men dead, but everything seems to be circling around Gianna. And her daughter."

The two cops looked at Gianna with thoughtful expressions and she visibly squirmed. "That's not news to anyone. But I'll say again, I have no idea who would want to harass me."

"I'd say this goes far beyond harassment," Nora said in a dry tone. "I'd like you to try to find some old photos with that medallion if possible. You said your uncle has them? Where does he live?"

"Southern California. But he's supposed to arrive in town today."

Disappointment crossed the detective's face. "Is there someone else who can look through them while he's gone?"

"I'm sure he can assign it to one of his assistants or staff."

"Staff?" Henry asked. "Wouldn't he ask a family member?"

"I'm it as far as family goes. And he has plenty of spare staff. That's his business. He owns WorkerBee, the temporary employment agency, and has offices all across the United States."

"That's who called you today?" Chris asked. WorkerBee was huge. A successful company built on a reputation of caring about its employees and always listed as one of the top one hundred places to work in the States.

"Yes."

Chris wondered if Michael had discovered that fact in his background check on Gianna.

"I didn't connect you with WorkerBee," Nora said with a frown. "It's not referenced anywhere in your history."

Gianna gave a small smile. "Uncle Saul has worked hard to protect my privacy. He's tried to eliminate any traceable connections between me and the business . . . with my blessing. I prefer people know me and like me for who I am, not whom I'm connected to."

Chris understood. In Oregon the Brody name was synonymous with politics. His real father had given decades of public service, working his way up through state and national politics.

"How big is this business?" Nora asked. "Would an angry former employee strike out at you to get back at your uncle? What about competitors? Are there any implications here in business competition?"

Gianna leaned back in the restaurant booth, surprise clear on her face. "There's no way. What would be the point of stealing some of my things to get back at my uncle? Or setting that fire? I don't see the connection. I don't have anything to do with his work."

"That's what I'm trying to feel out. Maybe it'd be a good idea for you to talk to your uncle while he's here. Perhaps he knows something that could shine a light on your situation." Nora tilted her head. "Is that like him, to immediately fly out when you're in trouble? Did you tell him everything that happened?"

Gianna silently stared at Henry and Nora, tension spiraling around her again. Chris fought an urge to tell Nora to ease up on the questions; the detective was right to explore the possibility. WorkerBee was huge and part of an extremely competitive industry.

But this feels personal. Not like a business dealing gone wrong . . .

"Why don't you arrange to talk to her uncle?" suggested Chris. "Like Gianna said, she keeps her connection to his company to a minimum. No doubt her uncle can tell you what you need to know."

Nora and Henry exchanged a look. Henry nodded.

Chris tensed as Nora leaned forward and paused to search for words. She pressed her lips together and held Gianna's gaze. "I told you we'd canvassed the other cabins. Our teams found another murdered man. He was in one of the cabins closest to where you were staying."

Chris's heart stopped. *Another one?*

"What?" Gianna sounded like she was choking. Chris saw her hands quiver, and she moved them under the table. "Who was it? Was there a fire?"

"No fire," said Henry. "This guy had two shots in the head just like the guy in your cabin. But his were through his forehead."

"Then this might not be about me," argued Gianna. "Something was going on up in the Cascades, and Violet and I got caught in the middle. You might be missing something if you're focusing solely on me."

"I think the medallion and the break-in at your home say this is about you," argued Nora. "As soon as we identify these two victims, I think we'll have a clear picture of what's happening."

"How old was the other guy? Was there any identification or vehicles at the cabin?" The questions spilled out of Gianna's mouth, and Nora held up a hand.

"I can tell you he looks to be in his early thirties or late twenties, with a stocky build. He appears to be Hispanic. Any vehicle tracks are gone under the snow."

Gianna stared out the window, and Chris knew she was searching her memory for a face.

"I don't know," she said slowly, tilting her head as she looked at the investigators. "I honestly can't give you any help off that description. I'll take a look when he arrives at the morgue."

"Three dead," commented Chris.

"Was nearly five," stated Gianna. She shuddered, but looked determined, not scared.

Nora met her gaze. "You need to be careful."

Chris straightened in his seat as Gianna blinked at the detective. "Of course," said Gianna.

"More careful than usual." Henry leaned on his arms, looking sternly at Gianna. "We both think someone tried to kill you. They did a lousy job and it makes us wonder if they'll be back to try again."

"Violet," whispered Gianna. The color drained from her face.

"She's with Michael," Chris interjected. "There's no one I'd rather have watching my kid. And we had the same theory this morning. He's already on high alert for anything odd around your daughter."

Gianna looked at him. "You two talked about us?"

Sensing he was on shaky ground, Chris chose his words carefully. "After seeing the break-in at your house, Michael and I decided that someone might come looking for the two of you. We agreed that one of us will be with both of you at all times."

"You didn't tell me that." Annoyance and gratitude flickered through her dark eyes.

"I was going to talk to you about it."

"Are you armed?" Nora asked, giving Chris a careful look.

"I have a concealed carry permit. Michael does, too."

She nodded, still holding his gaze.

"We shouldn't be staying in Michael's home," Gianna stated firmly. "I don't want anything to happen to him and Jamie. We'll find a different place to stay."

"We'll come up with something," said Chris.

But no chance in hell would he let them go somewhere on their own.

CHAPTER FOURTEEN

Each time Michael passed through his family room, Violet was curled up in a corner of the couch with Oro as her lightning-fast thumbs tapped out texts on her phone. She'd spent most of the previous hours talking with Jamie. He was glad there'd been no school that day because he suspected she'd want to attend with Jamie. And there was no way in hell he would let Violet head to a place with children if someone was targeting her or her mother. Here he could protect her.

When asked what she'd like to do, Violet claimed she was happy to simply rest. She hadn't put her phone down at all as a TV movie played, another post-apocalyptic teen film where the female lead discovered she was the source of secret powers to save her people. Michael couldn't keep them straight.

"Everything all right?" he asked.

An automatic smile appeared. "Yes, thank you. I appreciate you letting us stay here."

Michael grabbed the ottoman, slid it over in front of Violet, and took a seat. Since he'd met her, a depressed aura had hovered around Violet, and it connected with him in a very personal place. He sensed there was a fun-loving girl under her quiet exterior. He'd seen a spark in her yesterday, but she seemed to hide it most of the time.

He wanted to know why.

He put his elbows on his knees and waited until she met his gaze. She blinked nervously. "Is something wrong?" she asked.

"No. But I have the sense that you need to talk to someone. A person who's not your mom or a friend three thousand miles away."

She set her phone facedown on the couch. Either she didn't want to be disturbed during their talk, or she didn't want him to see texts pop up. He took a hard look at her face, searching for her true feelings.

"Which of your friends did you tell about the fire?" he asked kindly.

Violet ran a hand over Oro's golden fur and his tongue appeared. Michael swore the dog smiled.

"I told Marie and Grace. They're my closest friends."

"They live here? Or in New York?"

"New York." She kept her gaze on the dog as she petted him.

"Did they know you were going to be up at the cabin for a few days?"

"I looked at my old texts. Chris keeps asking me the same thing. 'Who knows where you were?' But none of my texts said where we were going. The most I told anyone was that we were going to the mountains for a few days. I assumed I'd be able to continue texting up there, but it turned out there was no Wi-Fi *or* cell signals. That should be illegal. What if someone got hurt and couldn't call out?" Her gaze met his, pleading her case.

He held back his laughter. "I hear you. But there're lots of places in the US like that. Sure it could be dangerous in an emergency. Some people like it that way. They like the thought that no one can find them."

"That's so lame."

Utter disdain shone on her face. This generation was so different from his. Constantly connected. Always craving stimulation. He'd searched for excitement and answers throughout his teens and twenties, but he hadn't done it from a computer. He'd physically gone looking for the entertainment. It didn't matter if he had to drive across the country in a vehicle with a duct-taped window or fly at thirty-five thousand feet while squeezed into the smallest economy seat possible. He had to see things, touch them, smell the food of different cultures, and sleep under the stars. He doubted Violet had those same needs. Or did she have them and was unable to exercise them due to her age and sex?

"Is there something you'd like to go do?" he asked.

"No, I'm good."

"Have you gotten to see much of the Portland area since you've been here?"

"Not really. I started school immediately and there hasn't been time to explore."

His doorbell rang. "Stay here," he ordered as he left the room.

With one finger he moved a curtain in the living room, giving himself a view of his front porch. Two men stood there. A town car and driver were parked at the curb. His tension level lowered, but his curiosity shot up.

He opened the door. "Can I help you?" Michael asked.

"I'm Saul Messina, Gianna's uncle. Is she staying here? I know she lost her phone, so I wasn't able to tell her I was here."

Michael remembered the phone call Gianna had made on Violet's cell phone that morning, but . . . "Did she give you this address?"

Saul jerked his head in annoyance. "Not exactly."

Michael waited. Saul Messina was as tall as he and used the power of the direct stare. Michael fed it right back to the older man. He reminded him a bit of Christopher Plummer . . . not from the *Sound of Music* era, but the later years, when he was gray-haired but still exuded haughty power. The man beside Saul was younger, dark-haired, and intense.

"Is she here?" Saul asked.

"Actually Dr. Trask is not here. She had a meeting with the police." He didn't invite the men in. Red flags rose right and left in his gut. "I thought you were staying downtown."

The younger man stepped forward and held out his hand, trying a different approach. "I'm Owen Thomas. Gianna and I are old friends. I came up with her uncle because we're both worried about her."

Michael shook his hand, sizing him up. To him 'old friends' meant old boyfriend. No-longer-current boyfriend . . . most people he knew didn't keep in touch when a relationship ended. Would Gianna call Owen an old friend?

"She seems like a very competent person."

"Of course she is," said Saul. "I raised her after her parents died."

"I heard." Michael knew exactly who Saul Messina was. Part of him was impressed by the businessman's history. The other part was highly annoyed that he'd shown up on his doorstep and tried to order him around. "You didn't say how you got this address."

"Grandpa?" Violet rushed past Michael and into Saul's giant hug.

The love on Saul Messina's face made Michael mentally kick himself for being an overprotective ass about a woman he barely knew. Clearly this was a loving little family . . . although Owen's fake smile spoke volumes as he watched the reunion.

Not easy dating a woman with a teenage daughter.

Saul buried his face in Violet's hair. "I'm glad you're safe."

Violet pulled back and beamed as she looked up at him. "Mom told you we were here?"

Saul met Michael's gaze and looked away. "I didn't ask her."

"You never answered my question about that either," Michael pointed out. He noticed Owen shifting his weight around, trying to look past Michael into the house. Violet hadn't looked his way at all.

Saul lifted his chin and swallowed. "Your phone is linked to my account," he told Violet. "I can track it."

Violet stepped back. "*You tracked me?* Have you done that before?"

"It's an important function to have in case something happens to you."

That wasn't a no in Michael's book, and he bit his tongue to not point it out. *Not my circus. Not my monkeys.*

"Does Mom know you can do that?"

"She's on the same account."

Michael was mildly impressed with Saul's subtle evasions of Violet's questions; Violet wasn't. A bit of Gianna's stubbornness shone in Violet's dark eyes and stiff shoulders.

"We're fine. You didn't need to do that."

"Now, Violet—"

"I'll tell Mom you're on your way to your hotel, Grandpa. Her new phone should be activated soon, and I'll make certain she calls you. Maybe we can get together for dinner tonight." She kissed him on the cheek to lessen the blow. Saul gave a nod to Michael and turned to leave. Owen simply left.

Violet shut the door behind the two men.

Michael's chest tightened at the hurt on her face. "I take it you've had to do something like that before."

"Mom has always warned me about how manipulative he is. They've had huge arguments about it. He immediately knew he'd stepped over the line but wasn't about to admit it. I'll bet you anything Mom doesn't know he can track us on our phones."

"How often do you see him?"

"Maybe four times a year. We'd go out to LA or he would come to New York pretty often. I've always thought of him as my grandfather."

"As you should, since he raised your mom."

Violet eyed him. "You know about that?"

"I love a good story ten times more than the next guy," admitted Michael. "You lost your real grandparents. It's not easy for a single guy to step in and raise a kid on his own."

"Mom doesn't like to talk about her parents' deaths."

"That's understandable." Michael held very still, his curiosity off the charts, worried that if he said the wrong thing or moved the wrong way, she would turn and run. Violet hadn't looked him in the eye when she mentioned her mother. He believed she needed someone to talk to, but was holding back. Michael was a stranger . . . but sometimes strangers were the best people to unload on.

From the other room, a small chime indicated Violet had received a text. "Excuse me."

She left.

The moment evaporated and disappointment swept through him. He liked Violet and Gianna. Their story fascinated him and he wanted to know more. Especially about the man who'd had the nerve to track his granddaughter's phone when he couldn't reach her mother. Was Saul Messina genuinely concerned or simply a controlling ass?

But this wasn't Michael's circus.

★ ★ ★

It was a phone call he didn't want to make.

Play it cool. Only I know what happened in the woods.

"Yes?" came the voice in his ear.

"It's me," he said unnecessarily. "I'm waiting for Gianna."

"The old man gave it to her?"

"He said he did. What else would they have done at their meeting?" he lied, keeping his voice calm.

"The word on the street is that there is a new unidentified body at the medical examiner's office. I assume he'll stay unidentified?"

"I have no doubt. How could they figure it out? None of his records exist." His tongue felt thick in his mouth with the lies, and he struggled to speak clearly.

"What is Rafael doing?"

Rafael had been assigned as his partner. He'd protested the necessity of help, but his father had overruled him. "If this is the meeting we've been waiting for, I don't want the old man slipping out of our hands. Another set of eyes will help."

He didn't see Rafael as help; he saw him as a spy. Someone to report back if he messed up. He'd dealt with Rafael before. The man rarely talked. He stared at you with dark eyes and then picked at his nails with a pocketknife. The habit was disgusting and intimidating.

"Rafael is outside by Gianna's vehicle, waiting," he lied again.

"How close are you to the Trask woman?"

"As close as possible," he said. "This should all be wrapped up soon."

"I wasn't happy about the forest ranger's death. What happened?"

He silently choked. His father's stating he wasn't happy was the equivalent of the anger of a thousand betrayed men. "I took the action I felt was needed at the time." The sensation of his previous panic in the snow washed over him and he pushed it aside. "It was necessary. The fire had blocked me from cleaning the scene and the ranger was about to alert others. Killing him bought us some time."

"Bought *you* some time." Disdain flowed through the phone. "No more impulse decisions."

"You sent me here to take action," he argued, his face growing hot. "I have to act as I see fit."

"You are there because you fucked up at home. Sending you there was not a result of your *brilliance*. You are standing on American soil to protect your own neck. I gave you this assignment because you were in the right place at the right time. Don't make me regret it."

Shame burned through him. *I will prove myself.*

"That old man had been a loose end for too long," his father muttered on the phone. "It's unbelievable that it's almost over. Are you certain it was him?"

"I have no doubt. As soon as he crossed my path, I knew he was the one you were looking for. He hovered around the woman's home and then followed her to the cabin. Clearly they were to meet."

His interrogation of the old man a few days ago flashed in his brain. Rafael had been silent, watching him threaten the old man. The suspect had been belligerent, unwilling to share his knowledge, and smirked when he threatened to kill him. "You can't kill me." He'd laughed. "If I die, your father's empire will collapse. I hold the key that protects his business." The disrespect in the old man's eyes had pushed him over the edge, and he'd swung the hammer at his head. The old man had collapsed, and he'd hit him again before realizing he needed to stop.

The man had stopped breathing.

He'd sat down and tried to calm his panicking brain.

Rafael had pressed his fingers against the neck of the suspect and turned a leering gaze his way. "His heart has stopped. You lost your temper before he could give us the information! I won't be blamed for this." He leered, an evil smile on his face. "Your father will kill you with his bare hands. Your ass is dead."

He shot Rafael twice in the forehead.

Shock had crossed Rafael's face as he raised the gun, but he'd fired before the man could say another word. Disposing of his body had taken a few minutes and given him time to plan his next step.

Yes, he'd fucked up, but if he could find the device in time, he could save face and protect his father's hard work. And his own neck.

His father would never forgive him if he knew he'd killed the old man before he'd told them where the thumb drive was.

His only lead was Gianna Trask.

Interrogating her would be a pleasure.

CHAPTER FIFTEEN

Nora knocked on the door to the suite. *The presidential suite.*

Many hotels had them, but actual presidents had stayed in this one, and now Gianna's uncle had commandeered it. Nora wondered if he would have deigned to stay in another room if the suite hadn't been available. From what she'd read about Saul Messina, his ego was legendary, but he cared about his employees and it had paid off. His company's dedication and public praise were all over the Internet. He'd created the business from the ground up, his finger in every aspect. She knew he was single, but not from lack of women vying for his attention. She wondered what it had been like for Gianna to grow up in his home. He'd been commended for taking in his brother's orphan and had been quick to crush all media attempts to interview the girl. He'd protected her like his own.

Nora had found one old public photo of Gianna Trask—back then Gianna Messina—taken immediately after her parents' deaths. It was an image of Saul Messina carrying the girl out of the hospital, her arms clasped around his neck, his angry eyes looking directly into the lens of the camera. Newspapers and magazines across the nation had printed the photo of the survivor. Gianna was in profile, terror apparent in her expression. Nora assumed she'd been scared of the masses of media that'd camped outside the hospital where she'd recovered after her harrowing accident. Nora had blown up the photo and studied the child's face, seeing the resemblance to the woman who'd survived another near-death experience in the Cascade Range.

Some people seemed to attract bad luck.

Or was Dr. Trask's survival an example of good luck?

Nora wasn't sure. What she did know was that three men were dead and Gianna Trask appeared to be a common denominator.

A man opened the suite door and Nora knew instantly it was Dr. Trask's old boyfriend, Owen Thomas. She'd already run a quick check on him and nothing had jumped out at her. Chris Jacobs had reported that Saul and Owen had shown up on his brother's doorstep, searching for Gianna, and been sent packing by her daughter.

Nora looked forward to meeting Violet Trask.

"Detective Hawes?" Owen asked.

Nora nodded and handed him her card as she stepped inside the suite, her boot heels sounding hollow on the marble floor. *Nice.*

Saul Messina came forward, shook her hand, and waved her toward a sofa in the living room. "Can I get you something to drink?"

She refused as she studied the man. His manners were impeccable. He was tall and moved with a deep-rooted confidence. She turned her gaze to Owen Thomas. What was his relationship to Saul Messina?

"Mr. Messina, I know you've built a successful business. Can you think of a reason someone would strike out at Dr. Trask to get back at you?"

A glimmer of respect crossed his face, annoying Nora. She didn't waste time when she had an interview to do. She got down to business and got her questions out of the way. She didn't have time to sip coffee and make pleasantries.

"The same thought occurred to me, Detective Hawes. I've tried to create a wall that separates my business from my family life. I've always protected Gianna's privacy." His face was fierce and Nora believed him. It was the exact same look she'd seen in the old photograph. "But I've come up empty. I have no enemies, Detective Hawes. At least none that I'm aware of. No threats have been made against WorkerBee or myself in over five years, and I'm proud of that fact. I run my company with the philosophy that we need to be good neighbors. It's always worked well for me."

"I've asked Dr. Trask if she can think of someone who would like to hurt her, and she can't, but often I've found that the people closest to victims have different opinions. So I'll ask both of you if you have any ideas." She included Owen with a glance. The tall man had perched on the arm of a chair and pulled out his phone, and was occasionally scrolling, telling Nora that he didn't feel the interview was worth his time. Saul had sat in a chair directly across from her and given her his full focus. Yes, the man knew how to win people over.

Owen needed lessons.

"Gianna doesn't make enemies," stated Saul. Owen nodded his agreement.

"Not intentionally, I assume, but sometimes things happen. Incidents with crabby neighbors. Road rage. Angry coworkers." She looked expectantly at the two men, who exchanged a look and shook their heads.

"Truly," said Saul, "I can't think of anything."

Nora let the silence linger a second longer. "Dr. Trask told me about a necklace with a gold medallion she had as a child. It was given to her by her maternal grandmother but has since been lost. Are you familiar with it?"

Saul's eyebrows rose. "Of course. Gianna was distraught over the loss of the necklace. I looked for it several times in the boxes from her old home but could never find it. She hasn't mentioned it in years until she emailed me about it this morning. Why are you asking about that now?"

His reaction appeared sincere. Owen stared at her with one brow raised, echoing Saul's question.

"It's turned up. It was around the neck of the man who was found dead in Gianna's rented cabin."

Both men simply stared at her, their body language frozen in place.

Saul reacted first. "Gianna didn't say anything about that in her email. How can that be? Are you sure it's the same? Perhaps it's only similar." Bushy gray brows formed a single line above his eyes.

"Dr. Trask is quite positive it is the same."

"She hasn't seen it in decades," said Saul. "She must be mistaken."

"Did you look for it?"

"I forwarded the request to an assistant. All her parents' things are in storage. It could take some time, but yes. I can tell him to put a few more people on it."

"Dr. Trask hasn't said much about how she came to live with you," Nora began, choosing her words carefully. "I've read the newspaper articles, but I'd like to hear your side of the story. I noticed you weren't quoted in any of the articles."

Saul's facial expression shut down. "I refused to feed their media frenzy."

"Understandable."

"Why are you asking about something that happened so long ago?" Owen asked.

Nora glanced at Owen, who'd lost interest in his phone and now listened intently. "The appearance of a long-lost necklace has me curious about her past. I'm exploring many areas. This is one that I assumed you'd describe best, Mr. Messina. Dr. Trask was a child at the time. I imagine her memories of the incident are cloudy."

"She doesn't remember the accident," Owen stated. "She's told me that several times. She recalls the bright lights of the house where she found help. That's it."

Several times? Why would Owen ask her about it more than once?

"I got a phone call early that morning," said Saul. "My brother's car had gone off the road and down the cliff to the ocean. I was told Gianna had crawled out of the car, up the steep cliff, and walked several miles to find help in the pitch dark." He swallowed hard. "They were on vacation in Southern California. Some of those roads along the coast are treacherous."

"You went there?"

"In a heartbeat. It wasn't that far from where I lived. She'd been transported to a hospital by helicopter. They were concerned with her head injuries."

"She didn't break any other bones," Nora commented.

"But her skull had a hairline fracture. The rest of her injuries were bruises and abrasions. The doctors thought some of the wounds came from her climb up the rocky slope to the road."

"The accident happened around midnight?" Nora asked, knowing the accident report placed the mother's death at that time.

"So they say."

"The car was partially submerged in the ocean."

Saul nodded. "When they looked at the tide levels and salt marks inside the vehicle, they estimated the car was almost fully submerged."

"She was a very lucky girl," said Nora. "I can't imagine how traumatic that must have been. And either she realized her parents were dead or she needed to get help." Pitch-dark sky, water, cold, a steep rocky bank to climb up. No wonder Gianna had blocked all memories of the accident.

"Since his body wasn't found at first, for three weeks people speculated that her father had sent the car over the bank to murder Gianna and her mother." Anger flooded Saul's face. "The media was brutal. But when his body washed up a few weeks later, they shut up. I'm thankful Gianna was in the hospital most of that time. I insulated her the best I could from the horrors of what was said during that time, but I assume when she was old enough, she did some research and read the articles for herself."

"I read them," Nora said simply. "Can you imagine what would be said if it'd happened in our Internet age? Every conspiracy theorist in the world would be commenting and creating their own evidence."

"People have no lives," interjected Owen.

Nora agreed completely. "When Gianna was interviewed about the accident back then, what did she say?" She directed the question to Saul.

"She didn't say anything until a few weeks after the accident. She'd been sedated a lot and the detectives at the time didn't bother to question her. To them the event was clear: a car wrecked and a child survived. I talked to her after she was weaned off the strong medications, and she remembered being wet and her feet hurting. She'd lost her shoes and walked barefoot for several miles along the road. Under sedation in the hospital, she often cried about pain in her feet. The skin on the bottom was in shreds."

They didn't interview the lone witness? "I'm shocked they didn't talk to her. Her father's missing body must have raised red flags at first."

"It did. But all the doors to the car were open and the ocean is extremely powerful. They had suspicions but didn't believe Gianna would be helpful. Once Richard's body appeared, they considered the case closed."

Nora had read the official reports, and Saul's recollections agreed with them. "Did Gianna have any counseling after her injuries healed?"

Saul scowled. "No. I didn't see the need for it. She adapted well to living with me. There were many nights when she cried for her parents but we got through it together. I lost my brother. She knew I was hurting, too."

"You and your brother were close?"

"Very. We came from a poor background, but we were both determined to make something of ourselves. He was fascinated with computers and was one of the first to make headway in cordless computer hardware technology. He wanted to build a better mouse," Saul said with a wry grin. "And he did. Several companies were exploring the option at that time and his company was one of them. If he'd lived, he would have seen the elements of a technology he'd created sold to an industry leader."

Nora froze. "These elements were sold after he died?"

"Yes, Gianna got her share. Richard's partner, Leo, knew full well that Richard was the engineering brain behind their success. He approached me first when he'd received an offer to buy the technology. Leo wanted Gianna to benefit."

Nora frowned. "I read her father and Leo Berg had formed Berssina Tech, but the company dissolved after his death, correct?"

Saul shook his head. "No. Leo simply renamed it BergTech. They're still a player in cordless innovations, and he continues to pay Gianna a portion of their profits."

How did I miss that? Nora penciled a note to herself to look into BergTech. *Could someone be tired of sharing profits?*

"I didn't know that either," said Owen. "Gianna never told me about her income from them or from her father's technology."

"What is the relationship between you two?" Nora asked pointedly, looking from Saul to Owen. She had Saul pegged as an intelligent man, but Owen had yet to impress her. How had Owen stayed in Saul's circle?

Saul looked surprised. "We've been golfing together for about ten years and have dinner occasionally when Owen is in town. I introduced Gianna to him years ago. I called him when I found out about Gianna's accident. I knew he'd be concerned, and he was in LA on business." He glanced at the younger man. "I thought Gianna would appreciate seeing supportive faces after her incident."

Golf. A game Nora didn't have the patience to try, but she knew it held a magic sway over a lot of men.

"You haven't seen Gianna yet, correct?"

"That's correct." Saul's expression indicated he was biting his tongue.

She glanced at her notes and decided to see if she could push his buttons. He'd answered her immediate questions, but now she felt like fishing. "I see you showed up on the doorstep of a friend of hers this morning."

He stiffened the slightest bit. "I was concerned."

"You tracked her daughter's phone to locate them?" Nora gave him her best "what the fuck?" expression.

"Yes. And I'd do it again. My daughter had been through a harrowing experience, and I wanted to see her."

Nora tilted her head a degree, holding his gaze, letting him know she was processing his answer. "Why didn't you simply ask where they were when you talked to Gianna on the phone earlier?"

Annoyance flashed in his eyes. "I didn't think of it."

She reined it in, feeling guilty for enjoying his discomfort. "I understand wanting to make certain they were safe."

He accepted her olive branch. "Yes," he replied with a nod. "Is it possible to see a photo of the man they found in her cabin?"

"I don't think that's a good idea."

"Why not? What if it's someone I know? Maybe I could solve your mystery in thirty seconds. It seems like a waste of time to not have me look."

Owen perked up, clearly interested in a look at the dead man.

Nora seethed at his disrespect. "He's been severely burned in the face. Recognizing him won't be a simple task."

"Do that reconstruction thing with a computer," Owen offered with the wave of a hand. "Create a face for us."

She stared at Owen. "This isn't some movie. You think we have the resources for something like that? I don't know if that even exists outside of books and TV. I'll talk to the medical examiner and see what's appropriate here, but unless you're aware of some missing acquaintances, I think we'd both be wasting our time. Maybe you should make some calls and take a head count of your friends." She gave him a toothy smile.

A quick glance at Saul revealed he hadn't been impressed with Owen's suggestion either. Saul met her gaze and raised one shoulder.

Nora knew she needed to meet with Gianna Trask again.

★ ★ ★

Gianna had thought long and hard before making the phone call, but she didn't know where else to turn. She took a deep breath and heard Chris's footsteps upstairs as he did a check of the house. She quickly dialed.

"You want me to do what?" Disbelief filled Lacey's voice over the phone.

"Please, Lacey. I know it's weird. But I don't know who else I can ask," Gianna pleaded quietly. "I left what you need in an envelope in my locker. It's unlocked."

"You need to talk to Dr. Rutledge," Lacey Campbell stated. "He should know about this. I don't think this is right."

Gianna heard the uncertainty in the forensic odontologist's tone. She and the dentist had hit it off when they worked together during Gianna's visitation in the medical examiner's office. She'd discovered a kindred spirit in the lively woman and they shared a point of view that only women shorter than five three could understand.

"I'll tell him if anything comes out of it. I don't want to make a big fuss if I'm wrong."

"This is crazy."

Gianna exhaled, knowing that was Lacey's way of agreeing. "They'll do it quickly?"

"I think so. Usually they ask for two days, but I have a favor to call in at this particular lab, so maybe I can get it sooner. I'll warn you, the cost is pretty steep."

"I don't care. I need to find out, and I'm not doing anything illegal."

"It's not illegal, but I think you're pushing ethical boundaries," Lacey said. "Dr. Rutledge isn't going to be happy. You understand you're risking your job?"

"I do, and I'll make sure no one finds out you helped me."

"I can plead ignorance if it comes back to me."

"It won't. I promise," swore Gianna. Her mind spun as she hung up the phone. *What have I just done?*

Gianna stood in the kitchen of her home, her words about not knowing if she could ever sleep in the house again echoing in her head. She was starting to feel back in control of her life. She had a cell phone and a rental car, and the police had released her home. Detective Sanchez had apologized for the black dust but hadn't offered to send anyone to clean it up.

If there was a chance she was being targeted, she couldn't stay under Michael's roof. She wouldn't lead a killer to his doorstep.

So I lead him to my own house? Where is the safest place for Violet?

Chris had neatly countered her arguments about removing Violet from under his brother's wing. If what he claimed about his brother's skills was true, then Violet was in good hands. But Gianna ached to be the one to protect her daughter. Being separated from Violet had increased her anxiety. She'd bitten the nails on her left hand down to the quick.

Questions bombarded her brain like birds attacking prey. Where could she find a safe place to sleep? A jail cell?

"Do you want to visit your uncle next?" Chris asked as he entered the kitchen. He'd insisted on following her home even though she had a vehicle, and she'd been grateful. She hadn't wanted to enter her home alone. Her nerves had been on high alert since they'd left lunch with the detectives.

The thought of dealing with her uncle instantly exhausted her. She loved the man, but he was intense. She had enough on her mind. "Not yet."

Chris was silent for a few seconds. "He's not easy, is he?"

She exhaled. "Exactly. I love him, but sometimes he's best in small doses. He means well, but he has a tendency to take over a situation when it's not necessary. I feel like I lose a bit of myself every time he swoops in. He started it when I was a child, and I allowed it to continue as I became an adult. You could say I enabled him."

"He loves you. He's probably being the best parent he knows how to be."

"I know. Which is why I let it go on for so long."

"It must have been a shock for him when your parents died and he suddenly inherited a child."

Gianna gave a sad smile. "I wish I'd been more aware back then. I really don't remember much of a transition. By the time I was healed and functioning, he was in full parenting mode and determined to do it right. He's not one to back down from a challenge."

"What do you remember from the accident?" Chris asked softly.

She looked at him. In his eyes she saw curiosity, but she also saw someone who cared. She'd grown very comfortable with Chris since he'd led her and Violet back to his cabin. She'd become accustomed to turning and discovering his face close by. His scars had faded from her notice; now she simply saw *him*. "I'm not sure which are memories and which are dreams," she admitted. Over the decades the images had jumbled in her mind, and she didn't share them with others because she was uncertain of their reliability. Even when Violet asked, she put her daughter off, saying she couldn't recall.

It'd become her mantra: *I don't remember anything.*

But at night her mind raced with bits and pieces of memories. Or were they creations of a young girl's imagination?

"I remember seeing a shocked man wearing a brown sweater standing in a doorway. This was at the house where I knocked on the door after the accident. He told everyone that I didn't say a word but just stood there bleeding on his doorstep, looking like I was about to collapse. I had gashes all over my legs and a deep cut on my forehead. I remember wiping at the blood several times as it ran down my face."

"He lived miles from the accident site," Chris stated. His eyes were cautious, and she knew that he of all people would understand the blurs between facts and a child's memory. "Do you remember walking there?"

She did. She remembered the pain in her feet and the dark trees against the darker sky. But she also remembered someone holding her hand. "I don't think I was alone," she said slowly. She'd never said it out loud before. The distinct feeling of someone gripping her hand had always been strong, but when she'd recovered enough to ask about it, she'd already been told a dozen times how she made the long trek alone. She'd doubted her memory and kept her mouth shut, choosing not to contradict the admirers of her survival skills.

His gaze narrowed and his head turned the slightest bit as if to hear her better. "Someone found you? Before you made it to the house? Did they give you a ride in a car?"

"I don't know." She took a deep breath and looked away. "This is where I don't know which part is true. I've had so many dreams about that night, I can't determine what is fantasy and what actually happened."

"Tell me what frequents your dreams the most."

She let her mind wander, allowing the most prominent recollection to pop up. "A voice telling me not to give up. A hand pulling me up the embankment. Someone carrying me at times."

Chris was silent a long moment. "Male or female?"

"Usually male. Sometimes female. When I try to see their face, it's one of my parents. Or my uncle Saul."

He nodded.

Of course a child would imagine her dead parents helping in a time of need. Some people believed the souls of loved ones were always near, and who would love a child more than a parent? Her face heated. She sounded like one of the crackpots on TV reality shows who talked to spirits.

But part of her always wondered. Had the soul of a parent helped her survive?

"You're not crazy," he said firmly. "You don't need to shape your memories to please other people or mold them into satisfactory explanations. *Weird shit happens every day.* Accept what you remember. There's nothing unusual about conflicting memories. You had a head injury, you were in a traumatic situation, and you were a *child*. I'm not telling you anything you don't know, but I don't think you need to hide your memories behind 'I don't recall.' Violet would probably love to hear your mixed-up images. I think you need to embrace them, not fight to straighten them out."

Her eyes burned as she heard the truth in his words. She *did* love that feeling of hope and safety that floated through some of her darker memories of the crash and walk. At times she'd felt protected and guided during her long ordeal. Real or not, those were the recollections to treasure. She shouldn't dwell on the terror and darkness and fear. She'd made it; she'd survived.

She looked directly into Chris's hazel eyes. "Thank you," she said simply.

"I've been there."

"I know. At least you were a bit older, so you must be able to separate reality from a child's dreams."

His jaw tightened and the muscles in his neck tensed. "I remember everything." Pain flashed across his eyes, and she regretted her words. Her child's brain had protected her in the best way it knew how. Chris's hadn't.

"I can't imagine what you went through." She looked down at his hands, stiff at his sides, and took one. It was rough and calloused. Not the hand she'd expected to feel on a man who claimed he sat at his computer all day. Images of him digging out the snow in front of the shed and tying the knots to secure the sleds flashed through her mind. There was a lot below the surface of Chris Jacobs. He was skilled at allowing people to see solely what he wanted them to see, but he'd allowed her glimpses that made her want to know more.

He didn't pull his hand away. Instead he looked down at the two clasped hands and she felt him struggle with a decision. He raised his gaze, and she caught her breath.

Old pain, grief, and torment. But also *need*.

She understood. Tension had simmered between them for days but had been held in check by their environment and their own insecurities. With one look, Chris Jacobs had laid it bare before her. He'd lowered his scarred and battle-hardened defenses and offered her a chance to touch, feel, and learn.

She knew the moment was fleeting. One wrong word and his defenses would be back in place and stronger than before. Possibly never to lower again.

What do I want?

She shut down her rational brain and stepped closer. Brief terror flashed in his gaze but it was immediately replaced with determination, and she knew it was difficult for him to allow her to see him exposed. All of her senses focused on him, she saw the dilation of his pupils and felt the small tremor in his hand. He stood deathly still, suddenly a hardened statue, and she knew one mistaken touch would make him shatter.

"I've seen things no person should ever see," he whispered. "I've seen the sickness that drives a human to hurt innocent people. And I've been on the receiving end of that pain."

Grief radiated from him, igniting a primitive need in her to heal him. But she knew he would never be whole.

Perhaps she could help a tiny bit.

She stepped closer, pressed her chest to his, and stretched up on tiptoe, sliding her other hand behind his neck. He froze under her touch, then seemed to explode with movement as he moved their clasped hands behind her back, pressing her closer, wrapped his other arm around her waist, and lifted her to his mouth. Her eyelids closed and heat shot through her from where his lips met hers.

They'd both been balancing on the edge of violent memories, and she'd saved them from a plunge to the bottom.

CHAPTER SIXTEEN

Chris's brain shot into fifth gear.

It had been at a full stop as he told Gianna that he remembered everything about his captivity with the Ghostman. He hadn't shared his memories with anyone since Brian's mother, Elena. His secrets had died with her. Early on, Michael and Jamie had asked a few leading questions, but he'd shut them down. He didn't want their minds polluted with images from his past. They had imaginations; they could use them.

But with Gianna it was different. She'd moved toward him when he alluded to the horrors that had been done to him. She hadn't run. She hadn't rejected him. For one terrifying, heart-stopping moment he'd thought she'd look away; instead she'd reached out.

He'd grabbed her offering and clamped on like a man dying of thirst.

As he kissed her, he acknowledged that he'd been closed off for years. Gianna had gently touched his surface, sending small waves across his senses. The waves had rippled over the black memories that'd risen to the surface and calmed them, buried them. He hadn't fought his usual internal struggle to make the images vanish; they'd simply dissolved.

He wasn't a fool. They weren't magically gone. But they'd never fallen away into the background with such ease.

Since he'd first seen her, Gianna had soothed his environment. Usually he escaped to his cabin to find that calm; yesterday he'd discovered it'd followed him back home on two legs. Two petite legs attached to one of the most gorgeous women he'd ever seen.

And she accepted him. She'd looked right into his nightmare and not shied away.

Her heart beat against his and he ran his hand up into her hair, cradling her skull. She felt so small under his fingertips. Her hand was still clutched in his, gripping like she was scared to let go, and he held their clasped hands against her back, feeling the soft give of her skin and the harder bumps of her spine. With her arm behind her she was open and vulnerable to him, but she didn't seem to care. He tightened his hold on her, causing her to exhale, and she turned her lips from his, her breath brushing over his cheek. He moved his lips up her face to her cheekbones and her eyelids, to her forehead. A soft scent of coconut shampoo entered his senses, and he abruptly wished they were alone on a tropical island, not standing in her violated home in a rainy city.

He went back to her lips and her doorbell rang.

"Holy crap," she uttered.

"We're not done here." He held her gaze, turning his statement into a question. Once again he placed the decision in her hands.

"Definitely not." She pulled back; her eyes were dark, but her lips curved in a promising smile that made his heart painfully contract. In a good way.

"I'll get the door." He let go of her, his hands suddenly feeling empty, and stepped to a window. A white van with the name of a security business on the side sat in her driveway. "Did you call a security company?"

She groaned. "My uncle said he would."

"Good." A glance at the wry expression on her face told him she didn't consider it good.

"Let's get your place secured." He let in the security company agent after a good look at his credentials and the van. He followed the tech through the house as the man took notes; he promised to have his supervisor call back with an estimate. Chris wished he could install the equipment immediately, but understood.

Gianna sighed after the tech left. "I still don't want to stay here, but I don't want to put your brother and Jamie in a bad situation."

He ached to ask her to stay with him, but it felt too soon; he didn't want to scare her off. And there was Violet to think of. "I think you need to check into the hotel with your uncle." He watched her face and quickly amended his statement. "Not stay with him, but stay there with someone else's name on the room. I really think that's best. We'll pick up Violet on the way. You said you need to see him at some point anyway, right?"

"I do." Resignation filled her features. "I love him and I know he's here because he's worried. A hotel makes sense over staying with your brother." She tilted her head. "Although I like the idea of an armed guard with Violet."

Again he backed away from asking her to stay at his home. It'd been right to take her to Michael's home the first time. He'd known Jamie would be there. He changed the topic. "Did you ask your uncle about old photos of the medallion?"

"I emailed him this morning. He forwarded it to his staff with a request for someone to get right on it, so I assume someone is digging through photos as we speak. When he asks for something, people move." A thoughtful look crossed her face. "I'd like to take another look at the medallion. I know we just saw it at the medical examiner's, but my mind was spinning so fast, it's all a blur."

"I have the photos."

"What photos?"

"The one's from Frisco's camera."

"And how did that happen?" she asked in an accusing voice.

He shrugged. "You plugged the memory card into my laptop. I copied them at that time."

"I don't know whether to be impressed or scared that you're that devious."

"Nothing devious about it. I believe in making immediate copies of everything. You'd be surprised how often things go missing or get changed."

"We tried so hard to keep track of evidence at my old place of work, but I swear gremlins would go through our stuff."

"People are generally dishonest."

Gianna took a step back and gave him a pointed look. "I don't agree with that at all. I've found most people to be forthright and helpful. Most have good intentions."

"Most," said Chris in a dry tone. "Apparently I've dealt with the underside of society for too long. I've learned to not believe a word anyone says."

She held his gaze. "That's sad."

"No, it keeps me from making mistakes. My work turns out best when I act as though everyone is out to lie to me."

"So why copy a memory card that I handed you?"

Chris tiptoed around the question. "It was for future issues. What if a key photo was suddenly missing?"

"Can we look at it again? I want to see the medallion pictures."

"When we get you checked into a hotel. Call your uncle and ask him to reserve you a room under his name."

She reluctantly agreed.

★ ★ ★

The Benson Hotel in downtown Portland was over a hundred years old, with one of the finest reputations in the city. Every president since Woodrow Wilson had stayed there, the bellman told Chris proudly. Chris wondered if the presidents had been disappointed.

He'd expected more.

The woodwork in the lobby had been impressive and the ceilings were stunning. But it felt and smelled old. Violet wrinkled her nose but didn't comment. Apparently he had the taste of a teenager.

It's one hundred years old. What did I expect?

Where was the presidential glamour? The Benson had a stellar reputation for service and quality. No doubt those factors made it worth the price. He'd heard about the Benson for years, and his father had recommended it to visiting senators all his life, but this was Chris's first step into the legend.

Maybe he simply preferred open spaces and modern looks.

There was a touch of a closed-in feeling that had made him feel itchy as they'd left the lobby. It'd intensified in the elevator.

I need space. Huge windows and long sight lines.

He had his first look at the presidential suite when Saul Messina opened the door and hugged Gianna like she'd been missing for months. In Saul's big suite he found old-fashioned living room and dining room furniture. Violet got the next hug from Saul, while Chris received a guarded and curious look over her shoulder. He returned the look as he shook Saul's hand and introductions were made. He felt a web of protection flow out of the older man and over Gianna and Violet, and he approved.

A man about Chris's own age appeared from another room. *This must be Owen Thomas.*

"Gianna. Thank God you're okay." The man enveloped her in a hug, which she returned.

Out of the corner of his eye, Chris noticed Violet take a step backward, her expression carefully blank. The dark-haired girl had been quiet since they picked her up from Michael's home. She'd been reluctant to leave, which Chris had attributed to Jamie's connection with the girl, but the entire ride to the hotel, she'd primarily asked about his brother. He understood. Michael was fascinating to many people, a bundle of energy who constantly moved and talked. After the fifth question about his brother, he'd raised a brow at Gianna, who bit back a smile. A small pang of envy touched his chest, surprising him.

I'm jealous of a kid's interest in my brother?

Impossible. He'd given up being jealous of Michael decades ago.

Or have I?

Michael had lived the life he'd been destined for while Chris had hid behind the name of a dead friend. Michael was outgoing and unscarred, and had the love of a beautiful woman. Chris waited for the jealousy to flow through him. It didn't.

He wouldn't trade *anything* in his past because that would mean he'd never have had his son.

It put a cork in all jealousy arguments.

He turned to look Violet directly in the eye as she tried not to scowl at Owen, and she gave him an embarrassed half smile. Chris suddenly realized that what he felt wasn't envy toward his brother, it was simply a desire to get to know Gianna's daughter better.

Owen held out his hand to Chris and did the usual gaze at and bounce away from his scars that always happened during introductions. "Thanks for looking out for Gianna. We were worried."

Chris simply smiled. "You're welcome."

Owen glanced at Violet. "Hey, kid. Good to see you." He turned and asked Saul about ordering dinner before Violet had a chance to reply. She met Chris's gaze and rolled her eyes.

Saul handed Gianna two key cards. "I got you a smaller suite on the next floor down." He frowned. "I tried to get something closer to me, but this is the best they could do on short notice. Are you sure you don't want to stay here with me?"

"I'm sure," she said. "And no one was told my name, correct?"

"That's correct. Can you stay and eat with us?" Saul asked.

The man pleaded with his gaze, but Gianna still declined. "We're beat. We might order some room service, but I plan to turn in as soon as possible. Brunch tomorrow?"

"That will do."

Pleasantries were exchanged, and Chris was relieved to be out of the suite.

"Who is Owen Thomas to you?" he asked as they took the elevator down a floor.

"He's a golfing buddy of my uncle's. We dated for a while. It's been over for months." She gave him a pointed look.

"Thank God," muttered Violet.

"Violet!"

"He's a creep."

Gianna was speechless. Chris looked from her open jaw to her daughter's matter-of-fact expression. "I take it you didn't know Violet's opinion?" he asked.

"No." Gianna stepped out of the elevator. "What was wrong with him?" she asked her daughter.

"He's rude. Condescending. He just wanted the prestige of dating you."

"Prestige?" Gianna wrinkled her nose.

"Yeah, because of Grandpa and who your dad was. And that you're an ME. Everyone thinks that's cool." Violet had yet to look her mother in the face. "And because of the accident," she added quietly.

"He said that to you?"

"No. I heard him talking about it with someone at Nana's funeral. He acted like it was no big deal and that you'd told him all about it. But I knew you hadn't, right?" Dark eyes turned toward her mother.

Gianna was quiet as she studied Violet. "You're right. I told him I preferred not to discuss it."

"I *knew* it. That asshole."

"Language!" Gianna slid the key card in a slot and opened the door, then entered and began flipping on light switches.

"Smells old," mumbled Violet as she tossed her bag on a bed.

"It is old."

Chris took a peek in the closet and checked the bathroom of the suite. All clear. "Do you want to look at those photos again now?" He'd grabbed a spare laptop at his brother's when they'd picked up Violet. He set it on the large desk and turned it on, then opened up the remote software he and Michael used. He remoted into his computer at home and accessed his private server, where Frisco's pictures had been automatically backed up. He pulled up the photos.

Gianna walked up behind him as he sat in the desk chair and placed a hand on his shoulder as she leaned over it. "I need to get into my email, too. I noticed on my phone that one of Saul's assistants sent me an attachment. It must be scans of the photos we asked for. Can we look at those first?"

He followed her instructions to access her email and downloaded the attachment, opening the photos in a viewer. Gianna gasped at the first one and leaned closer. He could smell her skin. If he turned his head, her chest would be inches away. He stared forward, not seeing the screen for a few moments as he got control of his thoughts.

Us alone in a hotel room.

Violet is here.

He waffled between being thankful for Violet's presence and resenting it. He blinked and the photo in front of him came into focus. A huge Christmas tree with a small girl standing alone in front of it, her feet buried in ripped-open wrapping paper. She was dressed in a Winnie-the-Pooh nightgown and had a broad smile that showed missing front teeth. She wore a gold necklace that looked like it belonged on a rapper, not a child.

The original photo was quite old and had yellowed slightly. Chris enlarged the image.

Gianna laughed at what appeared. "I remember that necklace. I loved it."

The gold necklace featured a Barbie head.

"Didn't they look closely at the photos?" Chris asked.

"I think Saul told them to send any pictures of a large gold necklace. He wasn't specific."

Chris moved to the next and moved on after a quick glance. The next several photos showed Gianna or her mother wearing jewelry, but none were of the large pendant they wanted to see. Gianna stopped him on several photos, her dark gaze drinking in the pictures of her mother. More than once she commented that she didn't remember a photo. Violet silently watched from the other side of Chris.

"Why did he keep these from you?" Chris asked. The photos were a wealth of history. Frozen moments of two people who'd been cruelly ripped from the world.

"I don't think my uncle thought of it that way." Gianna didn't look away from an image in which her parents were dressed up, clearly about to head out for some important social event. Her mother had the long skinny curls and huge poofy bangs that were a fixture of eighties fashion. Gianna's father wore a skinny tie and looked like a younger version of Saul. "I think he was worried I'd be overwhelmed by all these pictures if he'd given them to me when I was a child."

"You didn't ask for them later?"

She grimaced and a shot of pain flashed in her eyes. "I did. He told me where they were stored, but I never made the effort to go look. It's my own fault."

"Are there other things that belonged to your parents stored away?"

"I think so. I don't know what exactly. I should go sort through them. Seeing these photos makes me excited to do it." She smiled at the screen, and he understood her need to connect to her past.

"Your dad looks a lot like your uncle. What's the age difference?"

"Two years."

"I wonder if resemblance made it harder or easier for you to adapt to him in your life," Chris mused out loud.

Gianna reached over and enlarged her father's face. "Good question. I really don't remember. I never thought they looked alike when I was a kid. I see it clearly now that I'm an adult." She continued to stare at her father's face.

"Ready?" Chris's finger was poised over the touch pad.

Gianna nodded. He tapped.

"Ohhhh!" Violet and Gianna leaned closer.

"Is that your grandmother?" Chris asked. A regal-looking woman with a sixties hairdo held a very young Gianna close to her face. Broad smiles shone from both of them, and even with the large age difference, it was apparent that Gianna resembled her grandmother. A large medallion hung around Gianna's neck.

"Yes," she said simply.

"Mom, you look just like her!" Violet breathed. "I wonder how old she was in this picture."

"There's the necklace," Gianna whispered. "I think this is when she gave it to me. I faintly remember seeing this picture before. Or maybe I just remember the occasion."

Pride sparkled in the eyes of both figures in the photo.

"I miss her," Gianna said softly. "I miss all of them. I can barely remember anything." Violet put an arm around her mother and rested her head on her shoulder.

Chris watched their reflection in his computer screen. He was simultaneously happy and sad for them. He zoomed in on the necklace, but couldn't make out any details. The size looked right, but the photo was too old and fuzzy to show the gentle swirls. "Let's ask them to overnight the actual picture."

A quick look through the other photos didn't show any more views of the medallion. "Are you ready to look at Frisco's photos again?" He hated to switch gears. Something about looking through Gianna's history had brought a sweet and tender atmosphere to the room. He didn't want it to end.

Gianna nodded.

"I'm done. I don't want to see them," Violet said. "Mind if I watch TV in the other room?"

"Go ahead," Gianna told her.

"At least now you can look at those old pictures whenever you want," Chris said, as he switched to a different folder on his screen.

As her daughter left the room, Gianna wiped at her tears with a shaking hand. She'd managed to hold it together while looking at the photos, but as soon as Violet was out of hearing, the dam had broken. Guilt swamped him.

"Sit down." Chris stood and guided her into the desk chair. "I don't know why I sat in the chair."

She leaned back in the chair with a sigh. "You know part of the reason I moved was to get Violet away from some of the influences in New York, but most of all I simply wanted our connection back. It's been just the two of us for a long time, and she's the other half of my heart. I've desperately missed her. Since the fire, I've felt her slowly crawling back to me. I hate that it took something so drastic to bring her back, but I'll take it."

"She's a great kid."

"The exhaustion crept up on me. I think I've been running on adrenaline and suddenly I hit a wall. But it was so wonderful to see those pictures. I've forgotten so much."

"I bet the police lab can do something with the actual photo to get a better look at the medallion," Chris said.

"It won't be a priority. Proving the pendant is the same as one as I had as a child doesn't get them any closer to finding out who murdered Frisco and the other two men."

"Assuming it is the same one, why was he wearing it?"

"I've asked the same question over and over." She pressed her hands against her eyes. "I'm done for today. Can we look at them tomorrow? I just want to crawl in bed."

Chris closed the lid to the laptop. "Absolutely. Reach out to me in the morning."

She moved her hands. Her eyes were red-rimmed and bloodshot, and her exhaustion filled the room. A loud television laugh track sounded from the bedroom, and Gianna gave him a weak smile.

If Violet weren't here . . .

Tension hummed between them. The good kind. The kind where his body ached to touch her. He lifted a hand to touch her hair, knowing that Violet's presence would keep him in line. Her hair was pulled back tight in a ponytail, but small wisps hung around her face. They were soft to the touch, and she closed her eyes as his fingertips touched the skin of her cheek. He ran a finger over the wet track from the corner of her eye and pulled back.

"I should go."

Her eyes opened and she said nothing. Her gaze told him she was fully aware of what could have happened if they'd been alone.

"Tomorrow," she said softly.

He nodded, bent to kiss her lightly on the lips, and left the hotel room.

Her single word raced through his brain.

★ ★ ★

In the dark of the hotel room, Violet studied the tiny screen of her phone. Ever since Jamie had shared bits and pieces about Chris's past, Violet had wanted to find out more. In the other bed in the room, her mother breathed steadily in sleep. After Chris had left, her mom had kissed her good night and fallen asleep almost instantly. Violet had read every article she could find about Chris Jacobs, and now she couldn't sleep.

At the age of twelve, he'd been kidnapped along with a small group of other schoolchildren. They'd been held underground in a large tank of some sort by a sexual predator called the Ghostman.

Violet's skin crawled.

Her best friend had been attacked by a man with his mind set on rape. If a passerby hadn't intervened, Grace would have been violated and possibly killed. Her friend still had nightmares and refused to go anywhere alone. Violet suspected Grace's attack had been part of Gianna's abrupt decision to move. Part of her understood her mom's fear, but couldn't that happen anywhere?

Two years after Chris and the other children had vanished, Chris walked out of the forest half-dead, claiming no memory of what had happened to him.

Stunned, Violet set down her phone, remembering how Jamie had said that after he returned, Chris had spent most of his life pretending to be someone he was not . . . to protect the Brody family.

He was a boy at the time.

How did a child make and endure that choice? He'd purposefully stayed away from a family who loved him to keep a killer from seeking revenge. What had happened in that bunker that'd driven him to turn his back on his loved ones?

He was scared. Terrified.

Could she have sustained a lie like that? Chosen to no longer see her mother?

She shuddered.

Violet enlarged twelve-year-old Chris's school photo on her phone. He looked eager and ready to take on the world. She had briefly seen that happiness when his brother had met them on the mountain. She had a hard time thinking of him as a scared child; he was the most fearless person she'd ever met. He was always calm, almost eerily so. When she and her mother had been worried and shaken, Chris had been a rock.

Or was that just how he looked on the outside?

CHAPTER SEVENTEEN

"Another day, another autopsy," Nora mumbled under her breath.

Actually she was simply getting summaries from Dr. Rutledge today, but Henry had still declined to accompany her. He'd pointed out that they could read the emailed summaries instead of going in person, but Nora liked talking to people face-to-face. It gave her a chance to get immediate answers to her questions and pick their brains, possibly stimulating something they hadn't included in the summary, instead of waiting for an email reply. There was plenty about this case to keep Henry working the phone and computer, so she'd hit the Starbucks drive-through and driven to the medical examiner's.

Dr. Rutledge walked her back to his office from the lobby. "What I found on Francisco Green fits exactly with what Dr. Trask saw happen. He was shot in the head. The damage is what I expected from the type of round that was recovered from the site."

"It could have been Dr. Trask on your table," Nora pointed out. "She said that if she hadn't moved at the right time, the bullet might have hit her."

"So perhaps she was the target, not the ranger?" He shook his head. "I don't know how I would have handled that. I'd have had to bring in someone from one of our satellite offices to do the autopsy. Everyone has been very fond of her since she worked here for a couple of weeks on a visitation. I was thrilled when she applied for the new opening. She's a good fit personality-wise and is very thorough."

"What about the body found in the other cabin?" Nora asked.

"Hispanic male in his late twenties," recited Dr. Rutledge from memory. "Five foot ten, one hundred sixty pounds. Healthy. No tattoos. His only scars were on his hands and lower arms. Either he got in a lot of fights or he did some sort of manual labor that banged up his skin. He has an old break in his left foot, but outside of that there aren't any strong identifiers." He sat at his desk and pulled up his preliminary report. "No lab results back yet, of course. The angles indicate he was shot once in the face and then again once he fell. I believe that corresponds to the locations of the rounds found at the scene."

Nora thought back to the photos from the man's crime scene. He'd been dressed for the outdoors in a thick coat, hat, and boots. All his clothing had appeared well worn but ill-fitting to her. As if he'd collected it from friends or the bargain bin at Goodwill. "Do you still have his effects?"

"Yes, they haven't been picked up yet. I know there was no wallet, no jewelry, and no cell phone."

"I'd like to look over them when we're done." *No cell phone?* No cell service on that part of the mountain. But had someone removed a cell phone or had he simply never had one?

"Do the shots appear to be from the same gun that killed the older man?" she asked, feeling the need to needle the medical examiner a tiny bit.

Dr. Rutledge's eyebrows shot up. "Seriously? Did you just ask me that?"

"Sorry, it slipped out."

"Rookies ask me shit like that," he muttered. "Not you." He took a closer look at her. "You're screwing with me, aren't you?"

She grinned at him. "How about . . . do the entry and exit wounds seem similar in size to the wounds on the other man?"

He smiled. "That's better. And yes, they are *similar* in size and damage."

She appreciated his opinion. That was all he could offer on wounds like that and it wasn't something she could take to a district attorney. Forensics on the rounds could determine if they had come from the same weapon—but they hadn't found the rounds from the old man's death. All Dr. Rutledge's suggestions could do was guide her instinct and investigation, and most of her information suggested the same person had shot the Hispanic man as had shot the burned man from Gianna Trask's cabin.

"What about time of death? Who died first?"

Dr. Rutledge's expression shifted into lecture mode, and she held up a hand. "I don't need to hear the details behind your results right now. Give me the big picture."

"You take all the fun out of it, but I can't tell who died first between your burn victim and the Hispanic victim. With the crazy temperatures and the fact the burn victim was moved from where he was originally killed, there are too many factors going on."

"Shit. So it's possible that the Hispanic man could have killed Frisco Green and our burn victim."

"That is a possibility. But you still have someone walking around who killed the Hispanic victim."

"You've fingerprinted the bodies?"

"Yes. And sent them over."

"Anything else I should know about our mystery bodies?"

"You *will* read my reports, right?" His gaze bored into her.

"Of course. I just like getting the highlights first." *And I have Henry for reading reports.*

"Not that I can think of."

She excused herself and left the office. In her car she called Henry. "Have comparisons been done on the fingerprints from the John Does and the break-in at Gianna Trask's place?"

"Jeez. Hello to you, too."

"Doc Rutledge wanted to know why you never come see him."

"Bullshit."

"I told him you prefer keyboards to weighing organs."

"Damn right. Like any normal person would."

"So . . . fingerprints?"

"Let me check."

Nora listened to him tap keys. "I bought my own coffee this morning, so you owe me an extra day this month."

"That's not how it works. I only have to buy when we're together."

"Then you should have come with me."

"One of us had to actually get some work done. Here it is." The tapping stopped, and she heard him mumble under his breath as he scanned the document. Not only did Henry move his lips when he read, he mumbled. She'd learned to tune it out.

"No match from either to Gianna's break-in."

"Damn it!"

"But there was a match to the Hispanic John Doe inside the burned cabin. They found it on the underside of the refrigerator handle."

"I'm stunned they were able to lift anything in that place. It was covered in ash."

"They know where to look. But why would he get into the fridge? Was he hungry after dumping a dead body in there?"

"The fire started in the kitchen area. Maybe he did that while starting it."

"Could he have been in their place before starting the fire? Maybe before they even arrived?"

Nora let her brain travel down the new thread Henry had started. "Crap. Gianna speculated that she'd been drugged. But we never had her tested and now I'm kicking myself for it. I wonder if she still has some sort of drug in her system. He could have entered their place at any time and slipped something into her food."

"But the daughter didn't have any effects."

"She might have eaten or drunk something the daughter didn't. Did we pull the fridge's contents for testing?"

"We will now. But discovering what type of drug she ingested doesn't find us our killer."

"Very true." Nora grimaced, knowing the testing would be a low priority. "But it offers an explanation for why his prints are on the fridge."

"Someone had this planned for a while," said Henry. "That shows some forethought."

"But it's so sloppy," Nora pointed out. "Dr. Trask is fine. Her daughter is fine. We've got a fire that didn't hurt anyone and two dead bodies left behind for us to investigate. It doesn't add up."

"Are you arguing that criminals are supposed to be smart?"

She snorted. "No. But usually there's a bit of logic to their madness. I'm not seeing it with this guy yet."

"This guy . . . you think we're looking for a single person?"

Nora was quiet. "I don't know. My gut says the Hispanic John Doe was kicked off the team for some reason. His manner of death suggests someone was pissed off."

"Can we call him Juan Doe to keep them straight?"

She rolled her eyes. "No."

"By that logic, the older John Doe could have been part of a team focused on one of the Trask women. He was eliminated in the same way. Maybe the leader of the group has little patience for people who screw up."

"So someone targeted the Trask women and hired some people to go after them? Their hiring standards suck. Two of their team are dead and the women are fine."

"Could someone be looking out for the women?"

"A double-crosser inside their group?" She enjoyed her brainstorming sessions with Henry, but wondered if this suggestion had just gone over the top. She didn't shoot down his idea; it could lead to something worth investigating. She and Henry made a good team. Their brains fed off each other's ideas, taking the two of them in directions they wouldn't have come up with on their own.

"Maybe someone on the inside doesn't want them dead. He's taken it upon himself to make certain they survive."

"Then he has to answer to someone about losing two of his group. And explain why the women are still alive."

"That's assuming anyone else knows. We've managed to keep most of this out of the media. They've been totally wrapped up with the snow-and-ice stories. A cabin fire and a break-in haven't caught their notice."

"Good. But if someone from a newspaper or news station decides to look into Gianna's or Chris's background because this story caught their eye, we'll have a media circus on our hands. Individually these two are ratings grabbers. Together they're a media hot fudge sundae. With whipped cream."

"Warm peach pie," Henry countered. "With vanilla ice cream."

"You win," Nora admitted. "We need to keep this as low-key as possible. At least both of their personal stories are pretty old. I don't think their names will trigger any immediate attention. Although Chris Jacobs's story was refreshed in the media when the remains of the other victims were discovered two years ago."

"I think it'll stay quiet."

Nora said a silent prayer that the media would stay away. Chris's brother would do what he could in that area. Michael Brody had no interest in putting his family in the media spotlight. Again.

"No identifications from the fingerprints?"

"They've been entered into the major data banks with no luck. I can start trying some of the smaller ones."

Nora wished there were one primary data bank that held *all* fingerprints, but the truth was that there were dozens of them. And that was just in the United States. The systems had greatly improved over the last decade, but they still had a long way to go.

It wasn't as simple as scanning prints into a computer and having it search everywhere for a perfect match. For some data banks a person had to physically *mail* a copy of the prints along with a letter of request that they be run for comparison. The funds to computerize simply weren't available in all communities. "See if there are any small databases we can submit to in the area where Gianna grew up. The fact that this guy had a necklace she lost long ago makes me suspect he's connected to her past."

"I will. I feel like the necklace is an important factor, but we can't figure out what to do with it."

"I agree. I think it could crack this whole case wide open, but the damn thing doesn't talk," said Nora. "Anything back on the photos from the crime scenes? Did the photography techs see anything we didn't?"

"Nothing has come back yet. I'll call the lab. It's a bit soon to ask," he said pointedly.

"I know. But poking them will make them want us off their backs and get the job done sooner."

"Or piss them off and they decide to take their time."

"Don't talk about our lab guys like that. They love me. I send them cookies at Christmas."

"They see right through that, you know."

"Did you dig up anything on that Sullivan autopsy case Dr. Trask mentioned?" The case had flitted through Nora's mind several times. Could a Sullivan relative be angry enough to harm Gianna over her stand on a case?

"I did. The family tried to file some sort of lawsuit against the New York medical examiner's office and named Dr. Trask specifically, but it was thrown out before it got anywhere. Basically she classified it as a suicide and the Sullivan family took exception to that."

"She seemed very positive about her results when she mentioned it to us."

"It went through some sort of peer review with the other medical examiners. They agreed with her findings."

"Any issues after that?"

"Dr. Trask reported receiving threatening letters to the police, but the letters all went to her office. Nothing came to her home, so I don't think they knew where she lived, and as far as I can tell all the remaining relatives are over seventy. The letter writer was an aunt who rarely leaves her home in New York . . . she's also known for writing threatening letters to the president and several members of the Senate. I don't think these are people who can create the type of destruction we've seen over the last few days."

"Are they from money? Could they have hired someone? Our first John Doe was older. Could he have been a Sullivan?"

"Yes, there is a lot of money in the family," said Henry. "But they aren't spenders. They have these huge bank accounts and investments but live off almost nothing. I have a mental picture of a bunch of old people who wear darned socks and drink weak tea while they're wrapped up in patchwork quilts because they don't want to turn on the heat in their million-dollar homes."

The older John Doe's new clothing and the Hispanic victim's old clothing spun in Nora's mind. *Could they have been hired by the Sullivans? Or was one of them part of the family?* She was liking the theory more and more. "Let's find out if any family members are missing and request their bank records. Maybe we'll get lucky with a suspiciously large payout."

"Will do. But I'll warn you, these people are the type who also hide cash in their mattresses."

"Any other people with an ax to grind against Gianna Trask? Or her daughter?" asked Nora.

"I'm looking into some of the daughter's friends. I'm waiting for my calls to be returned."

"Good. I'm headed in. See you in a few."

"Pick me up an Americano with half-and-half," Henry begged.

She hit End on her phone without replying, but grinned as she put her car into gear.

★ ★ ★

It'd been easy to slip the new tracker onto Gianna's rental car.

Now he knew where she was at all times. While her car was parked in the garage at the hotel downtown, he'd taken the time to review the last few days.

So much to cover up.

Looking back, he could see each mistake. His father didn't need to know about them. So far he'd managed to keep them from leaking out, but if he didn't recover the thumb drive soon, his father's questions would become more persistent.

He had to find the storage device.

She and her daughter had not been meant to survive the flames and smoke. After prematurely killing the old man, he'd panicked, worried his father would find out he'd lost their primary lead to the thumb drive.

He'd thought the fire would be a perfect way to eliminate all evidence and cover his ass. If both the old man and Gianna Trask had died in a fire, there would have been no way his father could blame him for not finding the thumb drive first. He'd hauled the man's body through the snow to the other cabin, berating himself every step for acting in haste and not thinking. He'd been wrong to hit the old man. He'd been wrong to shoot Rafael. He'd made too many moves without thinking first. The hike through the woods with a dead body had been an exhausting trek, but his fears over his father's anger had driven every step.

He'd cautiously entered the cabin, but once inside he'd realized Rafael's drugs had put the women to sleep. Gianna Trask was passed out on a sofa, and he'd assumed the daughter was above in the loft. He'd been fully prepared to shoot if confronted by one of the women. The need had never arisen.

He'd touched Gianna's hair and considered taking advantage of her drugged state, but the thought of taking her in the same room as a dead man repulsed him.

He'd regretted passing up that chance a dozen times.

He'd set the fire and left, believing he'd solved his problems.

The fire had been another wrong decision.

When he'd returned the next day, he'd gone to a window and peered in, hesitant to enter the smoking, crumbling cabin. The couch where Gianna had lain was empty. Tracks went between the cabin and her Suburban. He'd checked the vehicle and found it empty, smashing the driver's door glass in his fury.

Where had they gone?

Then he'd heard the snowmobile and dashed back into the woods.

Hidden, he'd watched her and the other man, his mind unable to plan his next move.

He'd fired, simply wanting them both dead.

So many mistakes.

All his life he'd reacted before thinking.

It was one of the reasons he'd been sent to the States.

But he was still in the clear. When someone asked what happened to Rafael, he would play innocent and claim he had failed to show up one day. As long as he was able to get the thumb drive to his father, everything would work out.

He took a deep breath.

I can make this work.

The old man had claimed he hadn't given it to Gianna. He didn't believe that now; he'd searched every place the old man could have hidden it. The woman had it somewhere, and what was on it could destroy his father.

Should I ask for more money once I have it?

He let his thoughts go down that path, imagining dangling the precious information over his father's head. He didn't know what the information was; he knew only that his father wanted it desperately.

Could it be worth millions?

His father had expected him to climb the company ladder. He'd seen it as a waste of time. Why should he have to work when his father had already done all the work? He should be able to enjoy the perks of his father's success. *I am the only son. Why do I have to prove anything?*

But now he was in a situation where he had access to something his father desperately wanted.

How much would he pay to have the thumb drive returned?

He backed away from that train of thought. His father would send other men to take the thumb drive away. And they wouldn't be gentle about it. His best chance to redeem himself was to hand it over as soon as he had it.

He swallowed hard, noticing his lower back had started to sweat, stunned that he'd even considered going against his father. *At least I thought that idea through first.*

He eyed Gianna's tracker on his cell phone. He'd watched from the home behind hers as she discovered the break-in, and wasn't surprised that she'd refused to sleep in the house the last two nights. That's where he'd first seen the scarred man; he'd soon discovered he'd rescued the women from the fire. Some sort of self-appointed protector. Now he went everywhere Gianna went, hovering at her side, studying her surroundings like he expected an assassin to leap out.

Chris Jacobs.

He didn't know where Jacobs stood in relation to Gianna, but he knew he didn't like it. Not only did the man create a barrier he had to cross to get the thumb drive, he was pissing him off. Jacobs kept touching Gianna. The small of her back. Her upper arm. Her hand, to get her attention. It was setting him on edge.

He wanted to touch her. She'd consumed most of his thoughts during the night. Her long dark hair, her eyes, her hands. He loved her hands. Some men were into feet, but he liked hands, and Gianna's were spectacular. She talked with her hands, looking extremely Italian when she passionately discussed something. They arched and fluttered, and he imagined them stroking his chest and shoulders. Would there be an opportunity for him to see her in the lingerie he'd grabbed in her home? *I must make that happen.*

She and Jacobs didn't appear to be a couple. There was no apparent intimacy between them. But he knew the look of a man who felt possessive about a woman, and Jacobs was dead serious when he stood next to Gianna.

Stay back.

Either they didn't care to demonstrate their relationship in public or Gianna wasn't aware of how Jacobs felt.

To him Jacobs might as well be wearing a sign staking his claim.

He knew how to tell when a man had claimed a woman. He'd picked up the skill in the nightclubs of South Africa. The men were like sentinels standing next to the women they'd chosen for the night. The women would chatter with their girlfriends, often ignoring the man at their side, but the men were always looking around them, making eye contact with the other men. *Hunt somewhere else.*

He'd been bored in the nightclubs, their novelty having worn off within months. His father's business didn't hold his interest and his father had given up hope that he would take over one day. He'd tried attending the university and failed. He'd worked a half-dozen different jobs for his father's huge corporation, seeking a position or division he found interesting. It didn't exist. He shared a last name with one of the biggest businesses in the country, and he hated it. So he'd looked for entertainment, hanging out with his peers. Other bored young men. Some of them had successful careers, while others preferred to live on their fathers' dime. Like him.

Politics. He wasn't interested in politics but his closest friend believed he'd discovered a path to a new future. And it was violent. His birth country had a brutal past that it'd tried to overcome for decades. His friend believed that violence was the only way to continue, and his friend's vivid passion had held his attention.

Something new. A different direction in which to try his hand.

He didn't care about the fringe group's politics or its focus on skin color, but he was excited by its techniques.

It believed in using pain to convince and punish, a concept that excited him.

The group's primary purpose was to be a thorn in the side of the current political regime, but he'd focused on the physical havoc the group created, not the beliefs. Essentially he'd been given a license to destroy. Instead of telling him to hold back and think before he acted, now people encouraged his anger. And it felt good.

For his first assignment, he'd worked with two other men who'd already proven themselves to the organization. Their target had been another young man; he didn't know who or why and he didn't care. Electricity had rocketed through his limbs as they waited for the man to leave his friend's house. The prey had strolled down the street, a cigarette in his hand, appearing more cocky than anyone had the right to be. They'd pounced. The first swing of the bat to the target's knees had knocked him to the ground. Adrenaline flowing, he'd stepped forward and swung his bat straight down into the man's belly. The victim had gasped and heaved.

"In the head! Hit him in the head!" the others screamed at him.

He brought his bat up for another swing and met the gaze of the terrified man on the ground. He was on his side, his knees pulled up to protect his gut, but for one long second his eyes were visible between his hands clasped over his face. He swung at his skull and the shock of the impact shot up through the bat to his arms, jolting his shoulders. A split second later, the sound of the blow reached his ears—a muffled wet crack.

The other men cheered and the bats swung faster. Blood flew from their ends. He swung two more times and then stepped back, panting like he'd been sprinting. Power surged through him and slammed into his brain, an addicting high.

He needed more.

He stepped back into the circle, but the body on the ground had gone silent, its arms and legs no longer moving in reaction to their swings. A foul smell filled the air and the other men stepped back.

"What the fuck is that smell?" muttered one.

"Death," said the other. "Let's get out of here."

He froze, his gaze locked on the still body as the smell assaulted his nose. He spun around and vomited away from the dead man.

"Pussy!" The other men laughed. "Let's go!"

He wiped at his mouth with his shirt and tasted blood. He stared at his expensive shirt. Trails of blood had been flung across his chest from the swinging bats and he hadn't even noticed. He looked at his friends and saw they were covered in the same. For a brief second terror replaced his exaltation. *What if we get caught?* The other men started to run, and he ran after them.

Days later he'd stopped looking over his shoulder, his worry replaced by an overwhelming need to feel that rush of power again.

Over the next two years, he'd had a hand in four more deaths. Each time, the exhilarating high had raced through his nerves. To give that level of pain. To watch. To destroy the life essence of another. It became an addiction.

He'd found success. With this group he was someone. His ability to act fast and not overanalyze made him a perfect addition. And he'd done it on his own. His father's wealth and name hadn't come into play; he'd risen in their ranks on his own skills.

Then the police got too close. His closest associate was taken in for questioning, and he realized he had to ask for help. Fighting every fiber of his new independence, he went to the most powerful man he knew. His father.

His father found out everything. About the women, his friends, their politics, and every beating he'd participated in.

What he'd believed were secrets among friends were immediately revealed once his father waved his money around.

He took note; money buys anything and *everyone* has their price.

He'd had to sit and listen to his father rant and rave. *Ungrateful, social pariah, sadist.* The tone and utter disappointment more powerful than the words.

His father immediately sent him to the States. His words burning in his son's ears. "Because you are my only son, I won't turn you over to the police. I got you a job with a respectable company. This man owes me a favor. Don't blow it, because no one will bail you out next time."

Now he felt his body surge, craving the power.

He needed it again.

CHAPTER EIGHTEEN

At home Chris enlarged Frisco's photos on his big monitor. He'd loaded them into software that allowed him to examine every pixel in detail. Since four a.m. he'd studied a dozen photos, and he still hadn't found anything at the scene that would help figure out who'd targeted Gianna. He agreed that the criminals had been sloppy, but they hadn't left any clues behind that had been caught in Frisco's pictures.

Not that I've found yet.

He still had several more to look through.

He hadn't slept well. Gianna had been on his mind all night. Walking out of the hotel and driving home had been two of the hardest tasks he'd done in years. He'd wanted to sleep in the hallway outside her door. Something evil was circling around her and every cell in his body screamed at him for leaving her alone.

She's behind a bolted door. In a hotel.

But he couldn't sit still.

How early is too early to call?

He decided to wait another twenty minutes until nine a.m. He felt like a teenager wondering when to call the pretty girl he'd met the night before. But this was different. He needed to hear her voice to know she was still safe. He didn't want to wake her if she'd had the same trouble sleeping that he'd had. So instead he looked at the clock every ten minutes and made himself wait.

His phone vibrated on his desk and he jumped in his seat. He grabbed it and answered, not recognizing the local number. *Did something happen to Gianna?*

"Is this Chris Jacobs?" a female voice asked.

"Yes. Violet?" The voice was young.

"No, are you asking about Violet Trask?"

"Who is this?"

"This is Cynthia James, with *Channel Six News*. I wanted to ask you some questions about the fire near your cabin in the Cascades a few days ago."

"No comment." The air pressure in the room abruptly increased.

"You were seen leaving the medical examiner's office, where they have an unidentified body from that fire. Is this related to your captivity several years ago? Or is it related to Gianna Trask?"

Chris hung up, instant sweat beading his forehead.

He hated reporters. *Hated.*

Call Michael. Have him handle it.

He didn't want to run to his big brother, even though this was Michael's area of expertise. He blew out a lungful of air and focused on breathing evenly as his brain picked apart the quick phone call.

The reporter had his phone number.

She was aware of Violet and Gianna.

She knew about the fire, John Doe, and Chris's background.

He pressed the palms of his hands against his eyes, fighting back the headache that had started tapping on the inside of his skull.

What are the positives?

His son would be out of town for a few more days.

No one was knocking on his door. *Yet.*

He breathed hard, mentally getting his feet back under him. The reporter had neatly cut him off at the knees with a few questions; he'd been caught unprepared.

She's fishing for information.

He'd revealed that he knew Violet, so no doubt the reporter would assume he knew Gianna, too. In the news world, it was enough to keep someone digging.

He dialed Gianna, no longer concerned with the time.

Her groggy voice answered. "Have you heard from any news reporters today?" he asked, without identifying himself.

"No. Why?" she asked in a sharper voice.

"I just heard from one. She knows about the fire, you, your daughter, and that I'm involved somehow. I think she was fishing for more information, and my hanging up on her might have made her more curious."

"Shit."

"Yes."

Violet's voice sounded in the background. "What? Did you open the door?" Gianna asked, speaking away from the phone.

"What's going on?" Chris asked. He shoved his wallet in his pocket and grabbed his keys, the phone pressed against his ear.

"Violet says there're some reporters at our door. She didn't open it, but they held up their ID to the peephole when she asked."

"Call the front desk. Have security remove them. Now."

Gianna relayed his order to Violet. "I can't believe they had the balls to knock on my door," she said to Chris. "How did they find us?"

Owen's face flashed in Chris's mind. "The only people who know you're in that hotel are Owen and your uncle."

"My uncle wouldn't tell anyone."

"And Owen?"

Gianna didn't answer. Chris let the silence linger. "Is there bad blood between you two? Would he try to strike out at you for something? You'd be amazed how fragile the male ego is."

"We ended on a good note."

Chris wondered if Owen would agree with that statement.

"We both agreed we were on different paths that really weren't going to coincide anytime soon. He's been friends with my uncle Saul for a long time, and he encouraged us to date, but Owen's mind-set is still like a college guy's. He wanted to have fun and be seen together, not look down the road five years."

"You were looking down the road?" Chris asked carefully. He was in foreign territory. He rarely posed personal questions. He seldom got to know anyone well enough to do so and was uncomfortable when people asked them of him.

"I have a teen daughter," Gianna stated. "It's not just about me. Owen understood."

Chris wondered how true that was, but he couldn't see how Owen could benefit by giving Gianna's personal information to reporters. Except through spite.

"I can hear voices in the hall," Gianna said. "Security is asking them to leave."

"Good. But we need to find you another hotel or place to stay. And this time I don't think your uncle should know where you're staying."

"I disabled the tracking on our phones," Gianna said dryly. "I wasn't happy about that stunt. I know he meant well, but it was too overbearing for my comfort. I'll figure out another hotel."

★ ★ ★

Gianna hung up and turned around to find Violet listening carefully. "The reporters are gone?"

"Yes," said Violet. "Was that Chris?" The teen was dressed in pink plaid fleece pajama pants and a matching long-sleeved top. Her hair was pulled to the back of her neck in a messy bun. She would have had a just-woke-up look if not for the sharp curiosity in her eyes.

"Yes, he had a reporter call him this morning. Some sort of word has gotten out about the fire and deaths."

"Have you read about Chris?" Violet asked abruptly. "Beyond what his sister told us?"

Caution settled on Gianna's shoulders. "No, why?"

"I have. I Googled him. I swear there are thousands of articles about him and those other kids who disappeared so long ago."

"That doesn't surprise me," said Gianna, watching her daughter carefully. "It was a tragedy."

"There were a million more articles published when he came back two years later."

"Also what I would expect. It was amazing that someone suddenly reappeared."

"He nearly died," said Violet. "He had severe injuries when he came back."

"Jamie told us that."

"Horrible things happened to him while he was held captive." Violet's eyes dampened.

Aha. "I know, honey." She pulled her daughter into her arms. Violet was an empathetic girl. Nearly to the point of feeling things too deeply. Injured animals, friends with bruised feelings, people with sad stories on the Internet. Violet longed to comfort them all. Gianna had known she had a sensitive daughter when four-year-old Violet had begged her mother to find the injured kitten from a newspaper picture. "Look at her sad face. I just want to make her *happy*," she'd cried. Violet hadn't said, "I want a kitten." Her primary goal wasn't about herself; it had been the kitten's happiness.

Chris Jacobs was now the kitten.

"What do you think he went through?" Violet whispered into Gianna's hair. "How does he get up every morning? I also read about the adults the Ghostman killed. He had victims of all ages. I can't think about all those children . . . and his burns. Did the other children watch while he burned Chris? Did Chris see him do it to others?"

Gianna was silent. *How much does it influence the person he is today? Does he suffer from PTSD? How many scars does he have that I can't see?*

Could he have a normal relationship?

She held her breath. Was she getting involved with a man who could be dangerous? It wasn't often that people came out of that type of situation and went on to have normal healthy lives. There was baggage. Usually lots of it. Is that what she would find if she moved forward with Chris?

He seemed in control, but she'd seen his shields briefly drop. His eyes had reminded her of a wounded animal's. Feral, ready to run at the slightest movement, self-preserving. Then the look had vanished.

"I think he's had a long time to put it behind him. He's not fully healed, of course," amended Gianna. "I don't think anyone can fully recover from what he went through. But he appears very grounded to me."

"What do you think his son is like?"

"Brian? From the pictures and what Jamie said about him, he seems like a bright kid."

"Do you think he knows what happened to his father?"

"I imagine he knows some version of the story. I suspect the only person who will ever know everything is Chris, and he doesn't seem the type to share his burdens."

"He likes you," Violet said softly. "I've seen him watching you when he thinks no one else will notice. It's like he's looking at a movie star."

"Oh." Gianna couldn't find a coherent reply.

"Be careful, Mom. I like him, but he's been through a lot."

"I like him, too. I think he's a good man."

"He is. He's like a guy in a movie who steps in front of the bullet for his friend without an ounce of regret."

"Selfless."

"Yes, in an old-fashioned type of way."

CHAPTER NINETEEN

"Hi, Lacey." Gianna answered her phone, her hands shaking. Her heart had nearly leaped out of her chest when she saw the odontologist's phone number on her screen. She sat down on the hotel bed, thankful Violet had been picked up by Jamie and wouldn't hear the conversation. Gianna had just finished packing, planning to switch hotels to avoid any more reporters.

"You were right," Lacey blurted. "It's a match."

Gianna sucked in a breath, her vision darkening. *Daddy?*

"Gianna, are you okay?"

"Yes," she answered automatically, her mind racing. *Daddy?* The image of the burned corpse on the metal table in the medical examiner's office was stuck in her mind, and her stomach heaved.

"Oh, my God, Gianna. Your father was alive all those years. How can that be possible?"

"I don't know," Gianna whispered. She lowered her head between her knees, pressing her cell phone against her ear until it hurt. *Why? Why?*

Why didn't you contact me?

"What made you ask for the DNA comparison?"

She strained to hear Lacey's voice over the ringing in her ears. "I don't know. It was just a hunch."

"If he was alive, then why—"

"I don't know why," Gianna said harshly. She wanted to throw her phone against the wall and scream.

Why?

Lacey was quiet for a few seconds. "I know this is a huge shock, but you must have had some sort of inkling, since you asked me to run a test for you. It was more than a hunch."

"It was the medallion," she choked out.

"Just the medallion? Nothing else?"

"I didn't know," Gianna whispered. "'Hunch' isn't the right word. It's more like I was questioning a dream . . . a fantasy that I'd set aside a long time ago but that has been at the forefront of my mind since the autopsy. Something about the body made me think of my uncle, and I remembered how much my father resembled him. And every child who's lost a parent dreams of discovering it was a mistake. It's all I've been thinking about. I had to run the test so I'd have some peace of mind."

Now she knew, but there was no peace.

My father isn't alive. He died a few days ago and was left for me to find in that cabin.

Sounds and images cluttered her brain, and she fought to stay focused.

He never talked to me.

Or did he? Her brain leaped from memory to memory as she tried to recall every time she'd talked with an older man.

Would he have reached out to her? In some obscure way?

"I'm so sorry, Gianna. This is horrible news. It must be like losing him twice."

Yes, yes it is.

She'd already grieved her father once. Now she had to do it again?

Mom? Her knees shook.

"Your mother—" said Lacey.

"My mother . . . is she . . . oh, my God, Lacey. I don't know what to think now." She rubbed her temple, her brain spinning around thoughts of her mother. *Is my mother still alive?* Every childhood dream and wish and prayer had been about her parents' surviving that car accident. That one day they'd knock on her uncle's door, laughing and saying it'd all been a big mistake. Gianna had learned early on to stop wishing.

Death was final. People don't come back. No matter how much you love them and miss them. She'd never been the child who lied to her friends and said her parents were traveling or international spies. It'd been tempting to say something like that several times, but she'd never been a liar.

Someone's been lying to me for years.

Uncle Saul.

Did he know? All of a sudden every word he'd ever said to her felt false. His expression when he'd seen the image of the necklace . . . his words when he talked about her father . . .

Had he hidden the truth from her? Her limbs grew numb.

"I need to go, Lacey." She struggled to form the words.

"Gianna. Wait. You shouldn't be alone right now. Is Violet with you?"

"No, Jamie picked her up for the day. I have to go to the police station and back to the ME's office. I didn't want her tagging along."

"Then sit tight. I'll be right there."

"I need you to call Becker and Hawes for me. Tell them what you found out, please. I don't think I can have that conversation right now. I'm fine, but I—"

"I'll call for you, but you are not *fine*. No one can be fine after getting news like this."

"My uncle is here in the hotel. I'll head up to his room." *We need to talk.* Anger replaced her shock, clearing her mind as she focused on Saul.

"Are you sure? Is that what you want to do?"

"It's what I need to do, Lacey. If anyone knew my father was alive, it would have been his brother."

"How could they have hidden this from you?"

"That's what I plan to find out."

★ ★ ★

The door to Gianna's suite opened as Chris raised his fist to knock.

Gianna looked ready to strangle someone. Anger flushed her face, and he stumbled back a half step.

"What happened?" he asked, alarm pulsating through his veins.

"The man in my cabin was my father."

He couldn't speak. He held her gaze as he moved into the suite. "What do you mean?"

"The first John Doe. He's my father." Heat flushed her face. "He was alive all those years and never *contacted me!*"

Chris put his hands on her shoulders, looking into her brown eyes. "Tell me how you know this." He didn't doubt she believed it. Every ounce of her energy hummed with the truth of her words.

She exhaled. "I had a private lab run an immediate DNA comparison between the two of us. It cost me an arm and a leg and Lacey Campbell called in a big favor at the lab, but I needed to know. The results came back and it's him. I knew it."

"You never said a thing. At the medical examiner's you said you had no idea who it was."

"I didn't, but something about seeing Uncle Saul put the idea in my brain. I hadn't seen him in quite a while and for the first time I noticed how much he'd aged recently. It made me wonder what my father would have looked like. Suddenly I *knew.*"

"Why did you keep it to yourself? You could have mentioned it to Detective Hawes or me."

She laughed harshly. "Don't you see how ridiculous that would sound? 'I think this is my long-dead father.' Everyone would have thought I was hanging on to childhood delusions." She put her hands over her eyes. "I feel like I'm going crazy."

He pulled her to him, trying to stop the shudders he felt shooting through her body. "You're not crazy. You're sure about the lab work?"

"Absolutely."

"Someone had to know he was still alive."

"I think Uncle Saul knew," she whispered into his chest. "He must have known."

"And never told you? Why would he keep that a secret? How could a father go all these years without getting in touch with you?"

"I was about to go ask him those questions." She pulled back and lifted her gaze to his. "Will you go with me?"

Her red eyes didn't plead with him. This was her battle and she was fully prepared to face her uncle on her own. But she'd asked, and he wanted to be there for her.

"Yes."

★ ★ ★

Uncle Saul seemed to shrink in his chair.

"It's true?" Gianna asked. "You've known all this time and didn't tell me?" On the way to Saul's suite she'd nearly convinced herself that he hadn't known about her father. She'd started to believe that her father had hidden from everyone, but when she told her uncle about the DNA tests, she knew by his face that he'd lied to her for most of her life.

"That was him?" Saul's voice cracked. "Richard was killed in that fire?"

"He was shot first," Chris pointed out. "What in the hell was he doing there?"

"I don't know," said Saul.

"I don't believe you!" Gianna shouted. "How could you lie to me for years and years? You lied to a child about her parents! Is my mother alive, too?"

Saul shook his head. "No, she was killed in the car accident."

"That's what you said about both my parents! I don't know what to believe now!" Aware her legs were about to let her down, Gianna dropped into a chair across from Saul. She wanted to scream at her uncle and then crawl into his lap as if she were a child again. She gripped her hands in her lap; she wanted to pummel her uncle as hard as she could and then hug him and beg him to tell

her that it wasn't true. Chris's hand squeezed her shoulder. Not a pansy-assed, gentle squeeze like he'd give to a damsel in distress. It was a painful grip; he was pissed.

"Start talking," he said to Saul. "Start at the beginning. You knew it could have been Richard who died when the medallion was revealed, didn't you?"

Gianna froze. *Did Saul know yesterday?*

"No!" Saul said. "I never connected the medallion with Richard. I didn't know he had it. I assumed it would be found in one of the storage units with their things."

His eyes pleaded with Gianna. "It never occurred to me. I figured Richard had vanished into Mexico again. I'm as shocked as you that he was here."

She wanted to believe him.

Saul sighed. "I need a drink." He stood and walked over to the wet bar in the suite. "Anyone else?"

Gianna was strongly tempted. "No. Is Owen here?" She didn't want him intruding on something so personal. While they'd dated, she'd never discussed her parents with him, and she wasn't about to start now.

Glass clinked behind the bar. "No. He isn't staying here. He has his own room." He met Gianna's gaze. "Do you want him here for this?"

"Lord, no."

"What happened to Gianna's parents?" Chris asked.

Saul looked at Chris. "Do you want something to drink? You might as well pull up a chair, son."

"No, thank you." Chris grabbed a chair from the dining set and set it close to Gianna's. She suspected he'd bitten back a retort to Saul's "son" comment. That was Chris. Polite. But extremely direct.

Saul sat down and looked at Gianna. His face sagged, and he appeared to have aged ten years since he'd opened his suite's door. "I love you, you know. You couldn't be my daughter any more than if I'd fathered you myself." His gaze was sincere.

"I love you, too," she said from between clenched teeth. "But right now I want to hit something. And cry. I might do both."

Saul took a drink and stared into his glass, swirling the ice in the alcohol. "Your parents wanted the best for you. My brother Richard was a fucking genius when it came to electronics."

"I know." She did know. Even before her parents died . . . disappeared . . . she'd been constantly told how smart her father was.

"He was a straight arrow. He couldn't tell a lie to save his soul."

Gianna made a choking sound, pain welling up in her chest. "You're killing me, Saul."

"He nearly died in that car accident, Gianna. He should have died. Instead he carried you for some of those miles to that house for help."

Truth. All the dreams about someone helping her in the dark had been true. And it hadn't been her uncle; it'd been her father.

"He did?" Her voice cracked.

"Yes," said Saul simply.

"But the man at that house said Gianna was alone," interjected Chris. Gianna glanced at him; his focus was on her uncle, but she wondered if he'd researched her past, as Violet had read up on his.

"Richard essentially left her on the doorstep," agreed Saul.

"Why?" begged Gianna. *Why would my father abandon me?*

"He was protecting you the only way he knew how. They'd killed his wife and nearly killed him and you. Even with a severe head injury, he'd managed to do what he thought was right at the time."

"A head injury?" Gianna thought hard, remembering the blood on her hands from that long walk in the night. Had some of it been her father's? She'd had her own lacerations and blow to the head, which doctors referenced to explain away her odd recollections and the gaps in her memory.

"Are you saying the family was targeted?" asked Chris. "That the car accident wasn't an accident?"

"That's exactly what we believe happened."

"We?" asked Gianna.

"Yes, your father and I." Saul held her gaze. "I'm sorry, honey. But your father got mixed up with some very bad people."

"Who?" Chris asked sharply. "Who would try to kill a family?"

Chris's face was calm, but Gianna knew this revelation must have brought an overwhelming rush of memories and stress. He'd hid behind a false identity for years to protect his family from a killer. No one knew evil better than Chris.

"None of what I'm about to tell you has been proven. These are deductions your father and I came to over the years." Saul reached over and touched Gianna's knee. "Everything we did was out of love for you. It was for your own protection."

She couldn't move. His words didn't comfort. She saw her uncle's fingers on her knee, but she couldn't feel them. She'd shut down her peripheral nerves as she tried to keep her head above the sucking black water of confusion and lies. All of her energy focused on staying upright in the chair and not screaming. She didn't want to hear about love; she wanted to know *why*.

"Your father and his partner Leo Berg were making big strides in cordless technology in the early eighties with Berssina Tech and competing with the big guys on certain levels in the industry. Your father called it 'a race to build a better mouse.'"

"They sold their cordless mouse technology to one of the biggest computer hardware developers of the times," Gianna said for Chris's benefit. "It was an enormous deal for Berssina Tech. It was the cornerstone that funded all their other technologies. If it hadn't happened, I don't know if the business would have survived, let alone have paid Leo and me all these years."

"Did Berssina make other big strides in technology?" Chris asked.

"Not like that one," answered Saul. "Gianna's father was the engineer and Leo was the business side. Once Richard was gone, there never was another brain quite like his."

"Who were the people Richard shouldn't have gotten involved with?" Chris asked.

"Leo had been approached by a South African company who wanted to invest in Berssina. Richard had a problem with this company's politics and refused to agree to accept their money, but Leo felt that money was money."

"You're talking about apartheid," Gianna said slowly. "You're saying my father would never have accepted money from a company that actively supported racial segregation. Or worse."

"Yes, your parents were both very outspoken in their politics. It was a hot topic of the times."

Gianna tucked that new fact away in her memory banks for safekeeping. She hadn't known her parents were passionate about politics. Her childhood memories didn't include politics. Why would they?

"So what happened?" asked Chris.

"Leo accepted the money. A lot of money. Your father didn't know about it at the time because he left the business details to Leo. All your father knew was that he was able to continue his research and design in peace and earn a good living from their company. He didn't realize this company's investment was keeping them afloat."

"Wait. I thought the sale of their cordless technology made them successful." Chris's tone was sharp.

"It was. But Richard would never have been able to finalize the design without this company's money first keeping their doors open for several years. After the sale he found out about their silent backer, who'd naturally received the lion's share of the money."

"What did my father do?" whispered Gianna.

"Threatened to expose a dirtier side of this South African company if Leo didn't cut ties. Once he was aware of the deal Leo had made with them, he started digging. One side of this company's profits came from arms dealing. You can imagine what sort of mess that was back then. There'd been a United Nations voluntary arms embargo against South Africa since the early sixties."

"So you're saying Leo managed to tie Berssina Tech to arms dealers?" It sounded like a Cold War spy novel to Gianna. It was unreal and hit home simultaneously, causing her stomach to churn and her head to throb.

"The car accident happened within a week of Richard taking his complaints to Leo."

"But how did he decide the wreck was deliberate? Maybe it was *just an accident*," Gianna pleaded. "What if he was wrong? He stayed away from me all these years based on a guess?"

"It was the fourth attempt on his and his family's lives in five days," Saul said gently.

Gianna's lungs struggled to work. She couldn't speak. Or breathe.

"One of the first attempts was with the gas line in your home. If your mother hadn't seen someone outside the house and immediately investigated one morning, the two of you might have died. Your father had already left for work."

"Is that why we abruptly went on vacation?" Gianna whispered. She remembered being pulled out of school, her parents telling her they wanted to take a trip. She'd been excited, convinced they were returning to their carefree, globe-trotting ways. Instead it'd been a car trip across the country. She hadn't cared; it'd been the three of them alone and on an adventure for the first time in months.

"Yes. There'd also been an incident with your father's vehicle and an attempted mugging outside his office. But when he realized that someone might have tried to blow up his home with his family, he took action."

"He told you of his suspicions?" Chris asked.

"Not until after. He called me in the middle of the night after the car accident. He'd gotten you"—he nodded at Gianna—"to safety and he needed his own medical help. I left immediately. He begged me for silence, hoping the killers would accept his and your mother's deaths as sufficient and leave you alone."

"But . . . there was a body . . . it washed up on shore a few weeks later . . ." Her voice trailed off at the sad expression on her uncle's face. "Who was he?" she whispered.

"I don't know for certain. Just know that man died of natural causes and no one had claimed his body."

"You placed him there?" she squeaked.

"Not me personally. But it was the last bit needed to take those men off your family's trail."

I've been pushed into a movie. A horror film.

This wasn't her life.

"Where was my father all this time?"

Her uncle moved his gaze to look out the window at the gray skies and buildings. "He was never the same man after that night."

"Who would be?" Chris pointed out.

Saul met his gaze. "No, I mean with his head injury. I got him to a different hospital than the one Gianna was taken to that night and checked him in under a false name. He almost didn't survive."

"But he walked several miles with me."

"He did. And to this day I don't know how he did it. It must have taken every ounce of his will and determination to get you to safety, because the man who called me that night was near death. He'd cracked his skull and suffered a horrible blow to his brain from the accident."

"The car did go over the cliff, right? I remember the ocean and the rocks, and climbing back up to the road."

"It did. The tide later covered the front end of the car. Your mother was dead on impact, your father said. He'd left the vehicle's doors open before he left with you, hoping to confuse whoever had run him off the road. You probably wouldn't have survived if you hadn't been in the backseat."

She closed her eyes. "I don't remember how the accident happened. I remember the feeling of flying . . . of being weightless and hurtling through the dark and then an explosion of sound and being jerked against my seat belt. I think I must have been asleep in the back of the car and woken up as we went over the edge." She put her hands over her ears as an echo of screams rang in her head.

Were they real? Or imagined?

"I stayed with you in the hospital," Saul told her. "I had my closest assistant watching over your father in the other hospital. I was afraid to go near him, fearing I'd lead your mother's killers to him. The press responded immediately to your story, and I was in the limelight every minute."

"The other hospital didn't wonder about the man with the head injury in their care?" Chris asked.

"I don't think so. We checked him in under the name of a trusted friend of mine and used his medical insurance. His bills were paid, so they didn't look too closely. It wasn't like today where you have to show photo ID at every doctor's appointment.

"Your father had a serious brain injury, Gianna. He wasn't the same person when he could finally form a coherent thought." Saul looked deadly serious. "There were months when he didn't even remember that he had a daughter. Or a wife."

Her heart cracked in half.

"He didn't recognize me half the time. I swear an angel was sitting on his shoulder the night that he managed to get you to safety and call me, because he wasn't capable of doing anything like that for the next year. He was lucky that the accident happened not far from my city. He'd been afraid to fly out to see me, worried they'd track his name if he bought tickets. He told me that he and your mother had argued about where to go. She didn't want to involve me, but he'd thought I could help. Another hour of driving and you would have been in my home."

A wet warmth touched her lips and she blinked hard, wiping the tears with the back of her hand.

"Richard's never been the same. The official diagnosis was a TBI. A traumatic brain injury. All that did was slap a label on what he suffered. It offered no prognosis or glimpse of his path to health. Everyone suffers differently and many are never the same."

"He didn't know me?" Gianna asked softly.

"Some days he did. On those days he knew that he had to stay away from you. The one logical conclusion that he managed to maintain from the first day of the injury was that any interaction he had with you could lead to your death and his. That fact he *always* remembered. Even on the days he forgot how to tie his shoes, he knew he needed to stay hidden."

Chris took her hand and squeezed it. She felt a subtle tremor shoot through his grip. *How much of this story does he identify with?*

"Where has he been living?"

"Here and there. He's been in and out of a few rehabilitation centers for people with brain injuries. I made certain he was financially taken care of. He even managed to marry a woman for a few years down in Baja. It was good for him. He lived a very simple life by the ocean, and she helped take care of him. I thought he was getting much better, but she died about five years ago. He had a bit of a setback after her death, but he was able to function almost normally in society by then."

"Did he visit you? At the house?"

"No, I always went to him. I didn't want him to see where you'd grown up. The more you stayed out of his mind, the better he functioned."

Her cheeks flamed like she'd been slapped.

"It was for the best, Gianna," Saul said gently. "Emotions were very hard for him to process."

"Why was he here?" Gianna asked. "How did he come to be in my cabin?"

"That's where I get a bit confused," answered Saul. "I hadn't heard from him for several months. The last few times I talked with him, he seemed obsessed with Leo Berg. After years of not caring, suddenly he was upset that Leo had changed the name from Berssina to BergTech. He worried that you weren't getting any money from the company, even though I assured him Leo always paid."

"He did. Leo has always been nothing but wonderful to me."

"Your father didn't think so. Several times he ranted on the phone to me that he thought Leo wanted you dead so he no longer had to share the company's profits. Other times he'd claim that the South African company had hired someone to make that happen, so they'd have more profits, too."

Ice formed in Gianna's throat. "He thought someone wanted to kill me?"

"Why didn't you warn her? Or call the police?" Chris interjected. "Christ. She's got a daughter."

Saul held up a hand. "You don't understand. You don't know what Richard was like."

"No, I don't, because the two of you decided to keep him from me and Violet for the rest of our lives!"

"Richard didn't think rationally. His brain was never the same. People who suffer TBIs often have anxiety and panic attacks. They're easily overstimulated and can't deal with everyday tasks like a trip to the grocery store. I was used to hearing Richard's crazy stories. He never got over the feeling of being hunted. He thought people were following him almost every day of his life." Saul's gaze went from her to Chris, pleading for understanding. "I'd learned to never take what he said at face value."

"It almost got Gianna and Violet killed! Maybe if they'd been warned, they wouldn't have been alone in a cabin in the middle of the woods!" Chris's grip on her hand tightened.

"You did what you could," Gianna said slowly, looking at her uncle. "That's why you had the tracking on our phones. That's why you came immediately when you heard I had a close call." Small pieces slipped into place in her brain. Her uncle always wanted to know where she was going and what she was doing. Even when he lived three thousand miles away.

"What else could I do? Tell you to look over your shoulder for assassins?"

"Wait a minute. So who killed Richard?" Chris asked. "And tried to kill Gianna? Who did Richard believe was after him? And why would anyone kill Richard after he'd been in hiding all these years?"

Saul leaned forward. "I'll make some calls and get his apartment searched. The last time I visited him, he was living in a place outside of Palm Desert. Maybe there's something there that will indicate what he thought was going on."

"I'll want to go see it." Every cell in Gianna's body wanted to see where her father had lived. After the crushing news of the last hour, her heart had finally found something to latch on to. "Don't let them throw out anything."

"I'll be right back." Saul pulled out his cell phone as he vanished into the bedroom.

"This is crazy," Chris stated. He didn't let go of her hand. It was a small tether keeping her grounded after the events of the morning. She clung to it.

"My father was murdered for something he knew," Gianna said. She had no proof; it was simply what her heart and head told her.

"I think you're right," said Chris. "And I believe it's connected to his old company or that South African business. Why would they kill your father now? What threat could he pose to them? It sounds like he was a very confused man."

Her heart ached for the years with her father she'd missed. She didn't care how messed up his brain had been; she'd deserved to know him. Violet had deserved to know her grandfather. "It must have been big. My father hid for all that time, believing they'd kill him if they knew he lived."

"Somehow he got on their radar."

"What did he do?" whispered Gianna. "They killed him and came after me and Violet. *Violet!*" She whirled to face him. "We need to tell her. No! Wait. Don't tell her. Tell Jamie and Michael. Maybe they should take her to the police."

Chris already had his phone out and was tapping a text. "I'm reaching out to Michael. But really, Gianna." He stopped and a serious hazel gaze held hers. "I'd want Michael watching over Brian instead of any cops. He'd give his life for your daughter."

Gianna stared back at him. "He doesn't know her . . . or me . . . why would he do that?"

"That's who he is," Chris said simply as he finished his text.

I believe him. Calm settled over her. Her daughter would be safe with Chris's brother.

"He says he's heading home immediately. He'll call Jamie right now and let us know promptly if anything is wrong."

"The landlord will give a key to one of my assistants," said Saul as he stepped back in the room. "I'll arrange for someone to drive out to Palm Desert. The landlord said he'd been about to enter the apartment because the rent was a few days overdue, and Richard hadn't returned his phone calls. He says he can't remember seeing him for the past several weeks."

"We need to call Detective Hawes," said Gianna. "She needs to hear all of this."

CHAPTER TWENTY

Chris held Gianna's hotel room door open for her. She looked shell-shocked as she passed by him.

Who wouldn't?

She'd discovered the father she'd believed was dead had been avoiding her for decades, and now he'd been brutally murdered.

Chris wanted to wave a magic wand and fix it all. Her father would be alive and an active part of her life.

But then she wouldn't have been in the cabin near his.

He wouldn't have met her.

A wave of selfishness plowed through him, and he fought it back. He could be thankful fate had crossed their paths without feeling guilty about the events that'd made it happen. Gianna pulled off her sweater and tossed it on a chair. Her movements were those of someone who'd been on her feet for a twelve-hour shift, but when he looked at her, he saw the most beautiful woman he'd ever seen. She carried her burdens with grace. She pushed her hair over a shoulder and turned toward him, a question faltering on her lips. "Did . . ."

He waited for her to finish. She didn't. Instead she simply looked at him.

"What's wrong?" he asked after a long moment. No alarm had shown in her eyes. Instead she studied him, waiting for something.

Silence filled the room. She pressed her lips together and moved closer. Reaching out, she ran a hand down his upper arm, her gaze following her hand. "You're very dependable, did you know that?"

Denial ripped through him. "Only to my family. I don't care about anyone else."

"I think you're lying to yourself when you say that. You wouldn't let anyone down."

"If they're relying on me for something, then no, I wouldn't."

"You've been here for Violet and me since that morning." She lifted her gaze from her hand on his arm. Her dark eyes heavy with an emotion that made his muscles instantly tighten.

"You needed someone. Only an ass would have left you two out there."

"You've had plenty of chances to leave and go back to your own life. Every time I need you, you're there when I turn around."

Who needs whom?

He slid a hand around to her back and pressed her to him as he ran his other hand up the back of her scalp, tilting her head back so she had to look up to him. Her neck was exposed and his mouth was on it before he could think. *Gianna.* Kissing her last night had fueled a fire he hadn't experienced in a decade. He ran his lips up her neck; her skin was warm and smooth, making him ache to taste more of her. His tongue traced the edge of her jaw and she moved her head so he could touch her better, her mouth opening slightly as she drew in shallow breaths.

"Chris."

He'd wanted her since the first moment he'd seen her in the snow.

He finally admitted it to himself. He'd kept his attraction buried deep, unable to acknowledge that this woman was someone he would risk being with. For too many years he'd avoided the opposite sex, believing they wouldn't have anything to do with him, and chosen to focus on his son.

Now every wall he'd built to protect himself came crashing down.

Will she run?

Her hand slid up his chest, and her fingertips lightly touched the scars that disappeared below the collar of his shirt. Moving up his neck, her fingers traced the small ridge of bone that'd formed on the side of his jaw. The bone had knitted together unevenly after the Ghostman had broken it. Self-consciousness punched him in the stomach and he set it aside. In her job she saw destruction inflicted on bodies every day. The fact that she'd stepped forward and accepted his defects kept him from shutting down and running out of the room.

Part of him hungered to have her see every bit of him. Her accepting gaze could wipe out the decades of self-loathing from studying his own body in the mirror. Constant daily reminders of hell.

Her hands drifted back down and tugged at the hem of his shirt, lifting it and pressing their palms against his abdomen. Heat raced from her hands and exploded in his brain. Every muscle in his body tensed. He cupped her face in his hands, and his mouth insisted she open for him. His tongue slid into her warm silkiness, and he pressed forward until she was backed up against the wall of her hotel room.

She turned her head to the side, taking deep breaths, and pulled his shirt over his head. Chris briefly moved back as he ripped the shirt off, and she stopped him from moving back to her with a hand to his chest. Her gaze traced his chest, moving down the side of his neck to the round scars on his pecs.

"Oh, Chris," she whispered.

He watched her eyes, and the familiar fear of rejection prickled in the back of his brain. She touched one scar and then another and raised her gaze to meet his. "I hate him."

His mouth twitched. "I did, too."

She touched the long scar on the left side of his torso that arced around almost to his back. "I know this type of scar. You gave a kidney?" she asked, her voice cracking. Her dark eyes looked up at him, and he felt like he could fall into them.

"Yes. My mother . . . and Michael's mother."

"Like I said. You don't let anyone down, do you?"

"She's my mother."

Gianna looked back to where her fingers lightly traced the surgical scar. It was the one defect he didn't mind. She leaned forward and pressed her lips against one of the cigarette burns on his chest.

His knees shook.

She lightly traced it with her tongue, and he thought his brain would explode. He bit his lip to keep from swearing out loud and sunk his hands into her hair. Long silky strands threaded through his fingers. He held her head against his chest, wanting to never let her pull away. She moved to two more scars and his breathing got louder.

His fingers trailed down her back. Her mouth found his, and the skin of her stomach pressed against his bare skin. Heat flared where they connected.

"I need you in that bed in the other room, Gianna," he muttered against her mouth. If he wasn't inside her soon, he'd explode.

"That makes two of us."

He spun her around and pressed his chest against her smooth back, pinning her against the wall. Her hair draped over his chest, tickling and driving him crazy. He pushed her hair out of his way and kissed the back of her neck, tracing a path to her ear. "Maybe not the bed." His groin nestled against her, the two layers of denim between them making her seem miles away.

"I don't care where," she panted, her cheek pressed against the wall. "Just soon. Now."

Chris froze. "I don't . . ."

"Crap."

He couldn't move. His brain stuttered to a stop. He didn't do casual sex. He wasn't the type to keep condoms handy and accessible. "I'm so sorry, Gianna." He stepped back, his stomach instantly cold where he no longer touched her.

"Wait. I think I have an answer."

Breathing heavily, she pushed away from the wall and disappeared into the bedroom. Chris waited a moment and then followed.

★ ★ ★

Gianna's face flamed as she dug in Violet's school backpack.

Please, please still be here.

She'd stumbled across the condoms months ago while snooping. They'd shocked the hell out of her and created an uncomfortable but necessary conversation with her daughter during which she'd learned a female friend had given them to Violet as a gag birthday gift. Still, Gianna had checked back several times to see if the tiny box had ever been opened. It hadn't.

Her fingertips touched the box, still tucked inside a rarely used pocket of the backpack. It was sealed shut.

How will I explain the disappearance to Violet?

She shoved the thought out of her head and turned around to hold the box up triumphantly to Chris. He frowned.

"Violet's?"

"No. Well, yes. But a friend gave them to her as a joke. They've never been opened."

He stood still, his gaze on the small box. "Is that what you want to do?"

Gianna's grip tightened on the box. "You don't?" The tendons on his neck stood out, but she didn't think it was from the intensity of the hormones in the room. Chris was pure lean muscle. With his shirt off, he was carved and cut and could have posed in a men's magazine. His scars were a testament to his perseverance. He was a true warrior who'd fought mental and physical battles and survived.

"Fuck yes, I want to." He moved across the room and tore open the box in one swift movement. "Your jeans are in the way, Dr. Trask." His gaze pinned her, and relief made her sit on the edge of the bed.

"Oh, thank God. I was afraid—"

"Stop talking."

He went down on a knee, tossing the opened box on the night-stand, small packets spilling out, and kissed her as he unsnapped the top button of her jeans.

She melted. He was taking control, which was exactly what she needed. She didn't seduce men; it wasn't her nature. And she knew Chris wasn't into sleeping around. Everything she'd learned about him over the last few days told her he never stepped over that line.

This was different.

He pushed her back against the pillows and slipped off her jeans. Wonder lit up his face as he ran a finger down her stomach and hooked it in the lace of her panties. "You're perfect," he muttered.

She touched a scar on his cheek and looked into his eyes. "So are you."

He held her gaze and she stared right back. He might not believe her; she doubted he would after his years of hiding, but over time he'd learn she meant what she said. "I don't speak lightly," she said.

He moved over her, kissing her deeply as her head sank into the pillow. That finger tugged, and she felt her panties slide down her thighs. She lifted her hips and he moaned into her mouth. He removed her bra, and then they wrestled to get the blankets folded back. The cool sheets made her skin pebble, increasing her sensitivity. His jeans were rough against her legs. She removed them.

Hot skin burned against hers. He was male skin and exploring hands and heat. She ached for his touch on every piece of her. Opening her legs, she grabbed one of his hands and guided it to her center. He hissed as he found her wet silkiness, and she felt him instantly grow and harden against her thigh. He stroked her with a light touch, and she pressed against his hand. "Harder."

He obliged, teasing for a long moment. She closed her eyes, giving him the chance to openly watch her without her scrutiny. Opening them, she met his hazel gaze. Desire flashed in their depths, and he broke away to grab a condom. There was a moment of cold while he pulled back to roll it on. As they lay beside each other on their backs, she ran a hand down his stomach, feeling the small hairs part under her fingers. He groaned as she touched him. With one abrupt movement, he was back on her and buried deep.

Her gasp filled the room. Pain. Good pain. A rush of pleasure and heat spiraled through her and she moved against him, needing him to give her more.

He did.

★ ★ ★

Chris set the bottle of water on the nightstand and looked down at the dark head nestled against his side. Gianna had positioned herself so that one entire side of her body touched his from her cheek against his chest to her toes against his calf.

He didn't want to move. Ever.

He'd uncovered every bit of himself and she hadn't run away. She'd pressed forward. Eager in bed, Gianna had surprised him with her forwardness. Condom wrappers dotted the floor. He'd had a lot of missed time to make up for and apparently she had, too. He watched the black silk of her hair fall through his fingers. How many women had he turned away from, preferring to be alone rather than risk being rejected?

Not that many.

He'd avoided women. Never letting a conversation get beyond, "Black coffee, please," or, "I'd like the steak."

It was simpler that way. It'd been just he and Brian for so long; it was how he preferred it.

What will Brian say?

Every now and then Brian would ask him about women. Usually after he'd spent time at a friend's house. Brian liked being mothered and Chris was thankful he had Jamie in his life to occasionally fill the role.

Sheesh. One time in bed and you've already got her mothering Brian.

He could dream.

"I don't sleep around," she said.

He looked down and found her studying his face. "I'm not surprised."

"You were frowning. Like you were thinking of regrets." She lifted her head. "No regrets here."

"None here. I was thinking about Brian."

She relaxed, resting her chin on his chest, and smiled. "I can't wait to meet him. Jamie talked nonstop about him."

Relief flowed through him. "He's a good kid."

"Violet is, too. It's just been rough for her since her grand-mother died. I really relied on my mother-in-law to help me raise Violet once my husband passed. Sometimes . . ."

Chris waited, not liking the way her eyes had saddened. "Sometimes what?"

"I often worry that I blew it with Violet by concentrating on my career. Kids have only one childhood. Maybe Violet and I would be closer, and she wouldn't have had the issues she did if I had been there more for her."

"She adores you."

"She's my heart. But I feel that I let her down by always being gone. There was always school or tests or work to be done. I couldn't have done it without help."

"Did her grandmother love her? And give her attention?"

"Absolutely. They were quite the pair. Sometimes I was jealous of their relationship."

"Then she had a terrific childhood. There's nothing wrong in doing what you need for yourself. Kids are resilient."

The room was thick with silence.

"Were you?"

"Resilient?"

"Yes."

Deep inside his memories a small door slowly opened. He kept it closed at all times, not wanting to face the pain that rushed out when he peeked inside. He held his breath, waiting for the anxiety to sweep through him. Nothing happened.

He looked closer, feeling a layer of invisible armor, a detachment that allowed him to analyze and tell Gianna the truth.

"It ripped me to pieces. It was only because I had the other kids to talk to that I managed to put myself back together. The real Chris and I were the oldest. We took it upon ourselves to console the other children. But once they were gone, it was only Chris and me. Dozens of times we dragged each other back from a very dark abyss. Luckily, when one of us was down, the other was usually sane enough to talk him back up."

"I think that's one of the saddest things I've ever heard."

"Don't pity me." He said it gently, but steel laced his words.

"I pity the child you once were."

He laughed harshly. "I'm not certain I ever was a child."

"Then I mourn that lost child."

"I do, too."

They lay in silence for a few minutes, and he waited for her to say she needed to leave. Instead she stroked his chest, her eyelashes occasionally tickling him as she blinked. Tension slowly seeped out of him. A fork had appeared in his path and he stood at it, studying both directions. His feet were fastened to the ground; it wasn't his decision. He already knew which path he wanted, but he wouldn't take that first step until she said so.

"My life flipped upside down today," Gianna said slowly. "I should be in a ball with the covers over my head." She lifted her head and planted her chin in his chest to look at him. "I'm not."

"Maybe it hasn't sunk in yet."

"Maybe."

His phone started to vibrate, and he crawled out of bed to grab his jeans off the floor, sliding the phone out of his pocket. Michael. He grinned at the screen, briefly wishing he were the type of guy who didn't mind sharing details of his sex life. "Hey."

"Chris? Holy fuck, he shot Jamie!"

"What?" Chris stiffened. *Jamie?*

"Violet's gone," Michael blurted. "Oh, my God. He took Violet!" Multiple voices shouted in the background.

Chris froze, his stomach dropping to his toes.

"What?" Vomit soured in the back of his throat.

"I don't know if Jamie's going to make it." His brother's voice cracked. "And Violet . . . they don't know *anything!*"

Gianna.

Chris slowly turned back to the bed as Michael kept talking in his ear. Gianna met his gaze and sat up.

"What happened?"

Chris couldn't speak.

CHAPTER TWENTY-ONE

Gianna couldn't focus. Her mind skittered and bounced from one terrifying image to another. Inside, her thoughts wouldn't stop spinning, but on the outside she couldn't move. She sat frozen, staring at a blank wall in Michael's home.

Violet.

She found a small crack in the wall paint and focused on it, pushing all other thoughts out of her mind. It lasted for two seconds before her mind rebelled and sprinted down a terror-filled path again.

Violet.

Jamie had been carjacked three blocks from her home. She'd crawled to the nearest house and barely managed to ring the doorbell before passing out on the doorstep. She'd gained consciousness in the emergency room and told the staff her name and that her car had been stolen with Violet inside.

Michael had been waiting in an empty house, wondering why Jamie hadn't returned his phone calls.

A fellow reporter from the *Oregonian* had overheard Jamie's name at the hospital and called him with the news just as the police arrived at his home.

Two hours had passed between the abduction and Michael's notification by the police.

Somehow Chris had helped Gianna dress and practically carried her to his car to drive her to his brother's home. She could still see the fury in his eyes. His face had lost all color as he'd stared at her, his phone pressed to his ear. She could faintly hear Michael yelling through the phone.

She'd known instantly that it was about Violet.

And Jamie. She glanced at Chris as he paced Michael's dining room and spoke urgently into his cell phone. *He must be going crazy.* The latest reports on Jamie's condition were optimistic. She'd lost a lot of blood, but a guardian angel had been watching over her. The residence where she'd rung the doorbell should have been empty, but the owner had stayed home sick from work. EMTs had responded rapidly to the scene. They got her stabilized, to the ER, and quickly into surgery to repair the artery the bullet had nicked.

Every police department in the state had been notified of the make and model of Jamie's missing car. Jamie's and Violet's cell phones had been turned off. Officers were knocking on doors where the abduction had happened, searching for someone who'd seen *something*.

Gianna sat motionless in a chair, petrified that if she moved, she'd shatter. She'd already cracked into a million pieces, and they were barely sticking together. One wrong move or word could cause her to permanently fall apart. And then who would help Violet?

Was her daughter scared? Was she hurt?

Hurt her and I will kill you.

"We'll get her back," Chris said, stopping in front of Gianna's chair. "No one knows how to find things better than Michael and me."

"There might be nothing you can do," Gianna said, staring over his shoulder as the hollow-sounding words floated out of her mouth. The voice didn't belong to her. "There might be nothing *anyone* can do." The sentences were worthless air. "You were missing for years. No one could do anything."

Who was speaking?

She clasped her hands over her mouth and looked at Chris's stricken face. If she'd taken out a knife and stabbed him, she couldn't have hurt him worse. "I'm sorry," she whispered. "Violet . . ."

"I know." He dropped to a knee and took both her hands. The chill of his skin bled into hers. "*I know what you're feeling.* She'll be okay. We'll find her. I know how weak that sounds right now, but we'll look under every damn rock. We won't give up." He stood and looked out the window. "Hawes and Becker are here."

"They're good people," she forced out.

Chris didn't say anything but strode to the door to let the detectives in. Gianna knew they'd already talked to Michael and examined the crime scene. If you could call it a crime scene. From what she'd overheard from Michael, it was simply a trail of Jamie's blood from a spot on the street to the front door of a home.

Is it the same person who killed my father?

What could he want with Violet?

★ ★ ★

He'd made the girl drive five blocks to where he'd parked his car. He'd left it out of sight behind a big shed that hid the dumpsters behind a strip mall. His plan had worked exactly as he'd seen it play out in his head. The woman had stopped the car at a stop sign, and he'd jerked the driver's door open before she'd realized what had happened. He'd crammed his gun against her neck, thrown her car into park, and unbuckled the seat belt in less than two seconds. Then he'd ripped her out of the car and flung her to the pavement. Fire had flared in her eyes, and she'd scrambled to her feet to come after him.

He hadn't wanted to shoot her.

The noise only drew attention, but he'd had no choice. In one way it'd worked in his favor. Seeing her friend shot had made the girl immediately follow his orders to move. She'd slid into the driver's seat as he'd walked around the front of the car, his eyes and weapon on her at all times. For a brief second he'd felt vulnerable in front of the car. If the girl had had her head on straight, she could have thrown the car into drive and plowed him over. Luckily she'd been terrified. He'd gotten in the passenger seat and told her to drive. She had.

He didn't give her enough time to get brave. If she'd driven any farther, he knew she could have driven into a wall or fence or another car to stop him. Behind the building he tied her hands and ankles and placed her in the backseat of the new vehicle. She'd kicked at the door, trying to hook her foot on the handle and open it as they drove. He'd shook his head. That might have worked in an older car.

When she rolled onto her back and kicked at the window, he'd halted the vehicle and pointed his weapon at her. "Do you ever want to see your mother again?"

She'd stopped.

Feeling invisible in the different vehicle, he drove out of the city in silence, ticking off the points of his plan. His father had come down on him, demanding results, and he'd had to act drastically. Kidnapping wasn't in his playbook, but now that he'd done it, it'd gone amazingly easily. Planning. That was the key: prepare for all problems. Confidence rocked through him, and he wished his associates back home could see him now. They'd never stopped harassing him after the first death. Vomit-Boy, they'd called him. No matter how well he'd performed after that first time, the name had stuck. Now he was a machine. Blood, guts, gore. He'd learned how to hide his emotions during the events. Shootings, stabbings, hangings. He could do it all. Even kidnapping.

He glanced at the girl in his backseat. Brown eyes burned as she glared at him. She looked exactly like her mother, he realized. The lingerie he'd stolen from Gianna's closet popped into his mind. His chance to get her alone hadn't presented itself yet.

He needed to create a situation for just the two of them.

Could the daughter be bait?

★ ★ ★

"The homeowner couldn't figure out what'd happened," Hawes told Chris and Gianna.

Chris felt the restrained energy behind the detective's calm voice. Detective Nora Hawes wanted Violet back nearly as bad as he and Gianna did. Next to him, stress rolled off Gianna. Even though she sat utterly still, he felt her hang on every word from the detectives. He reached for her hand and she held it in a death grip.

"He opened the door and there was an unconscious bleeding woman on his doorstep. He called nine-one-one and pressed a towel into the wound, expecting a crazed gunman to turn up at any minute. He had no idea who she was."

"No reports on the vehicle?" Chris asked. He wished Michael were there. He knew how to ask the right questions. Chris was calm, but he didn't know the ins and outs of police procedure like his brother did. Instead Michael was at the hospital waiting for Jamie to wake up after her surgery and working Violet's disappearance with his phone.

"Not yet. The weather is still keeping a lot of people at home, so at least there're fewer vehicles on the roads to watch for."

No shit. Twice Chris had almost slid off the slushy roads while driving Gianna from the hotel. "That probably means fewer cops on the roads, too. We can't wait for someone to report a vehicle. We need to know *where* he would take her."

Detective Becker nodded, eying him carefully. "We're giving a lot of weight to the lead that the same guy broke into Gianna's home and caused the fire at the cabin, but we're not ruling out anything else." He paused. "We got an ID on the prints of the second John Doe who was murdered in the Cascades."

Chris waited, and Gianna gripped his hand tighter.

"Rafael Jones. Age twenty-eight. He's local. Pretty long history of theft and moving violations. Has spent some time in the county jail, but nothing big-time."

"Family?" Gianna burst out. "Where's he work? Where's he live?"

Detective Hawes held up her hands. "Slow down. We're looking at all that. As far as we can tell he's been unemployed for the past two years, but he's been doing something to pay the bills. No immediate family in the area."

"Why was he up in the mountains?" asked Chris.

Becker grimaced. "Don't know yet. Haven't found anyone who can tell us."

"This is the guy whose fingerprints turned up on the fridge at the cabin I rented, right?" Gianna asked. "But his prints weren't found in my home?"

"Correct."

"He was shot in the head. Almost the same way that my father was. There might be two more people involved that we're looking for. The shooter and whoever broke into my house."

She didn't say it out loud, but Chris knew she worried the shooter had Violet.

"What other leads are you following?" Chris asked. Rafael Jones's background was a good place to start. It was possible that he was an associate of whoever had Violet.

"We're still trying to identify some of the other prints from your house. We're expanding to include more databases, but it can be very slow."

Detectives Hawes and Becker exchanged a glance. "Once Lacey Campbell from the ME's office notified us about the DNA match on the first body, we immediately started digging into everything we could find," said Hawes. She sat down next to Gianna, meeting her gaze. "So far we've been able to confirm that your father's been living under an assumed identity for a long time. One your uncle appears to have helped him create."

"He thought he was doing the right thing," Gianna whispered, strain filling her tone.

"I talked to your uncle. He told me the whole story and gave us a few leads to track what your father's been doing the last few months. He also told me that your father believed he'd been followed lately. Enough to make him go dark when it came to keeping in touch with his brother. There's a good chance someone tried to hurt you and Violet simply because he is your father."

Gianna nodded. "Uncle Saul had suggested that. But it makes no sense. I've never been in touch with my father. Why try to hurt us simply because of who we are?"

"People have died for a lot less," said Hawes. "It doesn't matter what the truth is. If someone believes that you are a danger to them, they'll do what it takes to eliminate that danger."

Violet.

Her hand twitched in Chris's, her fingers ice-cold. Her gaze didn't leave the detective. "So we need to know exactly who was after my father. Because apparently they believe Violet and I present some sort of threat."

"That's exactly what we're thinking. Following the trail left by your father also might help us find whoever took Violet. From what we've been able to track, your father moved to the Portland area about a month ago."

"*What?*" Gianna rose halfway out of her seat. "He moved here just after I did? Where did he live before that?"

"Here and there," said the detective. "We're going off address changes and some scattered utility records. He doesn't appear to have stayed in any area for very long."

"Do you think he moved here because I was here?" Gianna murmured.

"I suspect your uncle is the only one who can speculate on that."

"Saul said my father rarely remembered he even had a daughter."

"Right. Saul told me of his brain injury. Perhaps he was finally able to keep you straight in his head."

Two tears rolled down Gianna's cheeks, and Chris wanted to murder someone. Anyone.

"Do you have a local address for her father?" Chris asked.

"Yes, that's our next stop."

"We're coming," stated Gianna.

★ ★ ★

Chris pulled into the apartment parking lot behind the detectives and the truck rocked as he hit two potholes. "Nice," he muttered.

It wasn't nice, Gianna observed. She wouldn't let an enemy live in her father's apartment building. Snow still covered the roof, but the parking lot and tiny patch of lawn were covered with deep puddles. The 1970s-style building housed eight apartments with tiny windows. Even with the snow, Gianna could see where the roof line sagged at the center. A drain spout had detached from the gutter and stuck out at an awkward angle, water dripping from the end. Two overflowing dumpsters blocked a few of the parking spaces, and the cars in the lot looked like they were from an auto parts salvage yard.

She wanted to cry.

Misery pummeled her heart and her brain. Between losing Violet and learning about her father, she was ready to crumble. Accompanying the detectives was a distraction from her thoughts, but every time she realized she wasn't thinking about Violet, guilt swamped her.

She was being torn in two.

Detective Hawes had initially stated Gianna and Chris couldn't accompany her and Becker to her father's old apartment, but the detective hadn't sounded convinced. Gianna pressed the issue, suspecting Hawes was just going through the motions. Compassion shone in the detective's eyes, and she'd given in to Gianna's insistence. Becker had stiffened when Hawes agreed but kept his mouth shut. Gianna suspected there had been words between the partners on the way to the apartment.

Hawes had laid down the rules. They weren't to touch anything. The landlord had already opened the apartment for the police. Officers had secured the scene and one was waiting for the two detectives.

"Is there a crime scene unit there?" Chris had asked.

"Not yet. We want to look through it first. According to the officers who did the initial check of the apartment, it's practically empty. No crime happened there."

"But he's been murdered," Gianna had interjected. "Shouldn't someone be collecting evidence?"

"We'll make a decision when we get there." Hawes had the final word.

A uniformed officer stepped out of the bottom-floor apartment closest to the dumpsters, his face resigned. "Done with me?" he asked Hawes as she stepped out of Becker's car. The detective asked him a few questions that Gianna couldn't hear and held her hand out for the key. She dismissed the officer, who made an immediate beeline for his patrol car, glad to be done with apartment babysitting.

The four of them stepped under the stairs that led to the upper apartments. "He said it's unlocked." Hawes looked at Gianna and Chris. "Give us a minute to take a quick look." Gianna nodded as she and Becker stepped inside. They closed the door, and Gianna was left to look at the blistered, peeling paint on the door.

Will something inside lead us to Violet's abductor?

"I can't stand this," she whispered. Chris said nothing but wrapped an arm around her shoulders. Images of her father swimming in the ocean off Spain and skiing in Colorado flashed in her head. How had he lived *here*?

She wanted to scream at the detectives to hurry up. Her daughter was waiting.

The door opened. Becker's face was grim. "Okay. Once again. Touch nothing. Look all you want, but there's not a heck of a lot to see."

The light in the apartment was dim. A single bulb burned in the center of the kitchen ceiling, the light cover missing. The carpet in the living area had matted spots where furniture must have sat at one time. Now there was a single chair and a television tray table. No television. The kitchen revealed a glass by the sink and a tiny white coffee maker with dirty yellow stains.

One of her father's habits hadn't changed: a box of organic bran cereal, a plastic bag of bulk quinoa, three avocados, and two tomatoes huddled in a corner on the counter. Gianna paused, studying the food, remembering how her uncle had called her parents "health nuts" and how she'd once received an Easter basket filled with fresh fruit. She'd been crushed.

Looking around the apartment, she was stunned at the emptiness. "It's so plain and tiny," Gianna whispered.

"One bedroom, one bath," answered Hawes. "There's more in the bedroom. Looks like all he did was eat and sleep here."

"But Uncle Saul was sending him money," said Gianna. "I had the impression he didn't want for anything."

"What I gathered from my conversation with your uncle was that your father didn't think like the rest of us. Maybe this is all he wanted."

Who was my father?

Clearly he hadn't been completely the man she remembered. She recalled nice cars and furniture and tons of clothing during her childhood. Her father had collected valuable books and art. So far this apartment didn't have art or books. Saul had told her he was a different man, but seeing his living space drove the point home.

They moved down a narrow hall, stopping briefly to glance at an immaculate but tired-looking bathroom. One emerald-green towel hung perfectly centered on the towel rack. She looked away from the rust stains in the tub and sink. The entire apartment smelled like old dust, as if the carpet hadn't been vacuumed thoroughly for the last decade.

Becker moved out of the way to let her into the bedroom.

Here was where her father had *lived.*

A double mattress lay on the floor; two new-looking sleeping bags covered it, clearly used as blankets. Two pillows, no pillowcases. Magazines and newspapers were scattered across the floor. Right next to the mattress was a footstool used as a nightstand. It held a tiny alarm clock, a school box filled with number-two pencils, and two Darth Vader PEZ dispensers.

He always loved Star Wars.

Did he see the new movies?

She'd never know.

Design sketches covered the walls. Some as big as movie posters, while others were on small sticky notes. She spotted two that had been drawn on napkins. Her father's mind had never stopped figuring and creating. His ideas and computations on display. She looked at the closest sketch, unable to read her father's cramped handwriting. The design made no sense to her.

"What is this?" She looked at Chris, who stepped closer and frowned at the drawing.

"I have no idea." He looked at several of the drawings. "I don't know what any of this is. Either your father was brilliant or . . ."

Absolutely nuts.

Gianna took a deep breath and studied the rest of the room. The small closet door was open and she spotted two suitcases. New. She moved to the open door and reached to push aside some of the clothing.

"Please let me look through things first," instructed Hawes.

She jerked her hand back. "There's not much here, but it looks brand-new." Gianna stepped closer. "Eddie Bauer. All winter clothing. Just like he was wearing . . ."

"Saul said he was living in Palm Desert, so he would have needed new clothes for the cooler weather," offered Chris. "I suspect your uncle was right when he said your father doesn't think like most people. Clearly he had the funds to buy clothing and suitcases." He pointed at the sleeping bags. "Those are expensive bags. I think he purposefully chose to live here. I think he simply needed four walls and a roof and didn't see the point in paying a lot for it."

Gianna nodded. She couldn't look away from the mess on the floor. It wasn't garbage; it was his work. Did he feel the need for a desk or computer? Or did he simply sit on the mattress and write? She could recall a computer in his home office. It'd been a rarity back then, and she hadn't been allowed to touch it. "No laptop?" she asked.

"Maybe he took it with him," Hawes suggested. "But I don't see anything computer-related here." She pushed aside a journal on the floor with her toe. "Your uncle called him a 'freaking genius who could no longer remember to check his bank account balance before he spent money.'" She bent over and flipped open a notebook with a pen from her pocket.

The pages were packed with her father's writing. Gianna knelt beside the detective and tried to read the cramped hand-writing. The date at the top of the page was from three months ago. Her father had listed what he'd eaten that day, that he'd gone to the drugstore, and an account of everything he'd seen. Physical descriptions of people, clothing, cars, weather. The page blurred and Gianna wiped her eyes. Farther down the page he'd made a to-do list that included getting a haircut and researching the benefits of eating kale.

Looking closer, she realized there were stacks of notebooks mixed in with the newspapers and magazines. "Did he write in all of those?"

"Yep," said Becker. "I looked. They're like diaries. I noticed one is about four years old. I wonder if he has older ones stored somewhere."

"So he's probably written a description or names of who he thinks was following him. It looks like he wrote down *every-thing*," said Gianna.

"That's what Becker and I were thinking," admitted Hawes.

"Then what are you waiting for? Someone should be going through these!" Gianna grabbed the closest notebook. *Fuck fingerprints.* She opened it to the first page and squinted. Computer stuff. A technical language that made no sense to her and made her eyes hurt. She tried to scan a few pages, searching for something—anything—that seemed related to her father's fears for his safety. She couldn't do it. The cramped and messy handwriting had to be read word by word. "This will take forever."

"I agree," said Hawes, studying the pages. "Let's try to find the most recent notebooks and focus on those. We can take them with us. I'm not going to sit in this dark room and try to make out the words."

"What about collecting evidence?"

"No crime has happened here. I think anything of use will be in these journals, and the more eyes we have on them the better."

"Gianna," Chris said.

She looked up from her place on the floor. Chris was standing by the closet, studying some of the sketches on the wall. He'd lifted the edge of one to expose another beneath it.

"Is this you?" he asked.

Her gaze locked on the drawing; she stood; her flesh seemed to grow heavy. As she drew closer, she saw a drawing of a little girl's face. It was her. She was still a toddler.

"Yes," she whispered.

"Here's another." Chris lifted another odd sketch to show a drawing of an older child. She figured she was about eight. "He had some memories," Chris said. "He didn't forget you completely." Becker and Hawes started lifting other sketches, searching for more images of a young Gianna.

"How old were you when that car accident happened?" Becker asked.

"Eight."

"Then how did he do this one?" Becker moved aside to display an image near a pillow on the bed.

Gianna caught her breath at the sight of the teenage face. "That's not me. That's Violet." Her heart seized at the image of her daughter. Tears flowed.

Hang on, honey.

Hawes frowned. "She looks exactly like you. How can you be sure?"

"The collar of the shirt. It's hanging in Violet's closet right now."

Hawes smiled. "He's been watching you guys."

Gianna moved closer, staring at her daughter, aching to touch her hair and her face again.

Her father had perfectly captured Violet, although she'd understood how Becker had believed it was Gianna. The sketch made her chest burst with love and pain at the same time.

He knew us.

And we never knew him. "Violet will never know my father."

"Clearly he had a soft spot for her. There's four more of her wearing the same shirt right here." Becker shuffled through a stack of papers next to the mattress.

"That's lovely," said Hawes.

Gianna felt like she was shrinking, becoming a fraction of her former self. She'd been unaware that her father had hovered outside her and Violet's life. But he'd been there. Now her guilt filled the room, berating her for giving up on him. "I didn't know," she whispered. "If I'd known he was still alive, I would have tried."

"He set the boundaries," Chris said. "It's no fault of your own. Saul and your father thought it was best this way. For all we know, someone would have attacked you much earlier. You might not have seen your tenth birthday if your father had come forward."

"He could have reached out later!" Gianna wanted to punch someone. *"I would have understood!"*

"You have every right to be angry," Hawes started.

"Damn right I do!"

Detective Hawes closed her mouth, smartly recognizing that Gianna was in no mood for platitudes.

"Let's get the notebooks packed up so we can start going through them," said Becker. "We can come back for the personal drawings." He scooped a stack into his arms and disappeared out the door.

Hawes and Chris started to assemble more stacks to carry out.

Gianna watched them for a second, feeling helpless and completely disconnected from the man who'd lived in this apartment. Her gaze traveled the room, searching for something to connect to the father she remembered. She couldn't leave without *something*. She grabbed one of the Darth Vader PEZ dispensers and ripped a sketch of Violet off the wall. She folded it carefully and slid both items into a pocket. Hawes wisely said nothing.

Two painfully small mementos.

Gianna grabbed a stack of notebooks and followed Becker.

CHAPTER TWENTY-TWO

"They found Jamie's car," Becker reported, stepping into the small police station conference room where they'd gathered to look through Gianna's father's notebooks. Chris's chest contracted at his words; then he remembered that Jamie was already safe. Michael had recently reported that she'd woken from surgery. Her first question had been about Violet.

Michael had told her the truth.

Next to him Gianna sucked in her breath. "Violet?"

"No one's there. The car was abandoned in the rear parking lot of a furniture store only a few minutes away from where it was taken." Becker paused. "The car's clean inside."

No blood.

"But the police have been searching for that make of vehicle," Chris said. "He swapped it for something else or someone was waiting for him. We've been looking for the wrong vehicle for hours. *Goddamn it!*" He swung out of his seat and paced around the table. "Hours! It's been hours!"

Gianna covered her eyes, her arms propped up on the table. Her stillness alarmed him.

"The store owner reported that he noticed a strange vehicle parked behind the dumpsters earlier in the day. He didn't think much of it, assuming one of his employees had borrowed the vehicle. But now the police have checked with all the employees and it didn't belong to any of them."

"What was it?" asked Hawes.

"A newer Escalade. Black with blacked-out windows. Flashy rims," said Becker.

"Easier to spot than Jamie's sedan," Hawes pointed out, looking at Chris.

"They could be halfway through Washington State by now." Chris clenched his teeth, attempting to keep his emotions in check. Every minute counted in an abduction. The more time went by, the less likely they were to find Violet.

Don't let her vanish.

Hawes glanced briefly at Gianna's covered face and then gave him a death stare. "We'll find them. He's driving a pimp-mobile. That vehicle will catch the eye of every cop it passes. They'll remember it if they've seen it, and the best news is that the security camera behind the store caught an image of someone who could be the driver."

"Could be?" asked Chris.

"The camera's view catches just a glimpse of a bumper, but you can see a vehicle shadow cross the screen and then moments later a man walks through the frame."

"You've watched it?" Gianna asked. "Does it show when they return with Jamie's car?"

"I'll show you what we have." Becker opened a laptop and tapped on the keyboard. Chris and Gianna moved to look over the detective's shoulders as Hawes stepped back. Her face gave nothing away. If Hawes was excited about this new lead, she was keeping it to herself. Or she knew that the video clip was a disappointment. He envied her control. His gut was a swirling mess of emotion and acid. Violet's abduction was resurrecting memories he'd fought long and hard to bury.

We have to get her back.

Becker opened an attachment and a grainy black-and-white image of a parking lot filled the screen. The camera was positioned to cover the rear entrance to the store. Two small sedans and a covered dumpster area were close to the door. As Chris watched, a flash of black tire and bumper and then a long shadow crossed the upper third of the screen behind the two cars. He held his breath. Ten seconds later a man strolled across the screen, his head up. He swaggered, confidence rolling off him. Becker pressed the touch pad and froze the screen.

"Know him?" He enlarged the image, increasing the graininess.

Gianna leaned closer. "He's huge."

She was right. Even if there hadn't been any cars in the image to compare the man to, Chris would have picked up on his wide chest and large upper arms through his coat. But as he passed by the cars, it became apparent that he was large everywhere.

"I don't recognize him," said Chris. "I think I'd remember this guy." The thought of Violet in the large man's hands made his heart crack. He battled against a surge of memories.

Underground. Children. Pain.

Gianna stared a little longer. "I haven't seen him before."

"You sure?" Becker asked.

"Yes," she snapped, dark eyes flashing at him. "He might have my daughter. You better believe I'd tell you if I thought I knew him."

"Is there another image when he returns?" asked Chris.

"No," said Hawes. "The vehicle swap takes place off camera. We don't see Jamie's car at all, and there's a shadow as the Escalade leaves, but it's even smaller than before."

"What if this guy was just a customer?" Chris asked, striving to keep his voice even.

"The manager and employees were shown this clip. None of them had seen him. Like you said, he's huge. He'd be memorable."

"He's got to be pushing six foot five," said Gianna. "And maybe two eighty."

Becker raised a brow at her.

"I guess at the height and weight of people on my table all the time before weighing and measuring. I'm pretty accurate."

"Well, at least we have a possible description of the driver to add to the vehicle. Everyone will be looking for him."

"They fucking better," Chris muttered. He was ready to burst out of his skin. He knew the statistics. Every hour Violet was gone, her chances of survival dropped. He flopped back into his chair next to Gianna, exhausted from the deluge of flashbacks. "I'm sorry," he muttered.

This isn't about me.

He slid an arm around her shoulders and leaned his head against hers. She shuddered and relaxed into him. He inhaled her stillness, knowing it was odd that for once she was the one who was calm while he was ready to climb the walls. "Calm" wasn't the right word. He suspected she was simply too drained to vocalize.

She needed someone to lead.

He kissed her forehead and straightened up, pulling the closest notebook of Richard's in front of him. "Okay, Richard. Give us a clue about that huge beast who took Violet." He flipped it open and started to read. Next to him Gianna took a deep breath and opened another.

Somewhere in these notebooks was an answer.

★ ★ ★

The jumbled notes made Gianna want to scream. Her father had been focused on minutiae from everyday life. The detail part of his brain that had once made him a brilliant developer had taken over his life; unable to find focus, it had focused on *everything.* Had he vocalized the constant thoughts? Had he used the notebooks as therapy so he could function in the world? What kind of woman had been able to live with her father, whose brain constantly vibrated and expanded with useless details?

I hope she loved him. And that he was happy.

Her own brain constantly accelerated in a million directions. She couldn't stop thinking about Violet. Tension and anxiety sped along her nerves, making her skin feel like it'd been stretched rigidly over her bones.

Is she hurt? Is she scared? If he touches her . . .

She stomped on the brakes for that direction of thought.

Her father's notes offered a partial distraction. She refused for the hundredth time to look at the clock, and she felt the waves of impatience rolling off Chris as he flipped pages next to her.

How much longer?

Her phone buzzed. Saul. She gathered the energy to speak with her uncle. They'd parted on uncertain terms. She hadn't known whether to be furious with him or feel sorry about the burden he'd carried for decades. She still didn't know.

"Saul?"

"Gianna." His regularly booming voice was weak. "Any word?"

"Not really. They found Jamie's car not far from the location. It looks like they switched vehicles and they believe he's driving a black Escalade. There's an image of a man who might be the driver, but they're not one hundred percent certain. It's a start."

"Damn it. What can I do?"

She had no answer for him. "Keep praying."

"I need to *do* something. I can make some calls, get some private agencies searching."

Gianna understood his impatience. That same need to take action burned in her chest. Instead she scanned handwritten pages, searching for a needle in a haystack, fighting every second to keep from climbing the walls or dissolving into a puddle of tears.

Violet.

"Do what you need to do. No one will stop you." She glanced through the room's window at Hawes and Becker as she said the words. The detectives were deep in a discussion in an adjoining room. Maps had appeared on a wall there. Pins with flags marking the morning's incidents. A huge whiteboard was already covered with time stamps, and Gianna read Violet's name at the top. The investigation was taking shape, but it felt like a slow crawl along a dry riverbed.

I feel like I'm in a movie and Violet might stroll in at any moment.

"What are you doing?" Saul asked.

"We're at the police station. We found a ton of notebooks in my father's apartment. They needed every pair of eyes to help read through them. We're hoping he made a notation about who he thought was following him recently. He wrote down *everything* else," she added bitterly.

"Ahhh," Saul said in a knowing tone. "The notebooks. Yes, a few years after the accident he started making daily entries. I think one of his therapists told him to do it, to help him feel more in control. We talked about it a few times. He said that the world kept moving forward and that memories weren't being noted and they were dissolving into the air. He felt he needed to make records so that everything would be acknowledged."

"I don't understand."

"I think he felt that if it wasn't written down, then it didn't happen."

"He'd appointed himself some sort of universal record keeper?"

"Only the record keeper of what he could see."

Gianna was silent. How had her father stayed sane? "Is that why he lived removed from everyone most of the time? Less to take in?"

"I believe so. I have some of his notebooks in storage and a few at the house. He'd always give me some for safekeeping when we met. He'd beg me to keep them in a safe place. I have letters from him for you and Violet, too."

"What?" Her voice cracked. "He wrote to us?"

"Oh, yes. There were times when his brain knew exactly what had happened."

"Why didn't you give them to me?" she whispered. "I have to see them."

"We both agreed it was best you didn't know he was alive. It was hard at first. Later it was simply the easiest thing to do. Every time I saw him, I walked away thankful you didn't know what kind of person he'd turned into. Your father died that day, Gianna. In every sense of the word. There was a different person walking around in his body after that."

"I had the right to choose. The two of you took that away from me."

"We chose while you were still a child, and I have no doubt in my mind we did the right thing. Someone tried to kill you and your family. They succeeded on one count."

"Two counts," she said, thinking of her father. "You should have told me as I got older. I would have understood."

"I thought about it a million times. I'm not proud that I chose to perpetuate the lie. You have every right to be angry with me. But honestly"—he paused—"I'd do the exact same thing again. Especially because of what's happened in the last few days. Something isn't right."

"Maybe if I'd known my father was alive, he wouldn't be dead now. Maybe knowing me would have put him on a different path."

"Maybe you'd all be gone," he said sharply.

Violet is gone. No! I will get her back! She forced her brain to focus. "Leo Berg didn't know my father survived, right?"

"No, he didn't. Your father didn't want any word getting back to the South African company. He was afraid they'd come after him and you again. That meant Leo had to stay out of the loop, too."

"If the same man who killed my father now has Violet, then he could be linked to that company, right?"

"It's been years, Gianna. Surely too much time has gone by."

"But you said earlier that Dad was paranoid about Leo recently. That he'd implied that the investment company could have hired someone to kill me so Leo no longer had to share the company's profits, right?"

"I also told you that Richard had a *brain injury*. He didn't think straight, Gianna. He often talked about things that didn't make sense. You ever listen to conspiracy theorists? It was like talking with the crazy ones."

"I think we need to tell the detectives to talk to Leo."

"Let me reach out to Leo first."

"Why?"

"Because he'll answer the phone if I call. Anyone else is going to be put through three layers of secretaries or sent to voice mail even if they say they're from the police department. A call from me will get through immediately."

"I'll give you five minutes."

She hung up the phone as Hawes opened the door, her face flushed. Gianna leaped to her feet, her heart beating in double time.

"We've got a sighting of the vehicle. It was seen less than two blocks away from your home."

"Did they see Violet?" asked Gianna.

"Only the vehicle. Once the new report went out, a local patrol officer immediately let us know he'd seen that type of vehicle. He didn't have more information."

"Was it parked? Or moving?" Chris asked. He'd risen out of his chair in unison with Gianna, his body tense, ready to respond.

"Moving. More patrol cars are flooding the area. They'll find it."

"How long ago?" Gianna asked, her heart sinking.

"He estimated he saw it about an hour ago."

"Shit." Chris vocalized Gianna's thoughts.

"Becker and I are heading over to that area. Find anything in the notebooks yet?"

Gianna glanced at Chris, who shook his head. "Not yet. We'll keep looking." The last thing she wanted to do was sit and stare at pages. Her energy had returned in a burst at Hawes's announcement. She wanted to go with them.

"They're sending us some more bodies to assist wherever we need them. You'll have some more help to look through the notebooks soon." She left.

The energy drained out of the room, and Gianna sank back into her chair. "I hate this." She pushed away the notebook she'd been scanning. "Every word tells me how dysfunctional he was, and I can't stop thinking about Violet."

"Me too," said Chris.

Gianna turned toward him, studying his face. "What else is going through your mind?"

"I swear my brain is about as scattered as these notebooks indicate your father's brain was. It's taking every ounce of control for me to stay focused on the present." His hazel eyes clouded. "Trust me. The past keeps popping up and threatening to take over."

"Maybe you shouldn't be here."

His face lost all emotion.

Wrong thing to say. "I mean—"

"I know what you meant. You think you're trying to make this easier for me. But that won't do it. I won't go sit at home and wonder what's happening to your daughter. And I'd like to think that you need me here," he ended softly. His gaze held hers.

Again he'd laid himself bare in front of her, opening himself up for rejection.

"I need you," she whispered. "I'd be in pieces on the floor if you hadn't been here to hold me together."

He shook his head. "You're way too strong for that. You always land on your feet, don't you?"

"This time would have been different. I don't want to go forward without you beside me."

He reached out and gripped both her hands. "Not going anywhere."

"When does your son get back?"

"Tomorrow evening."

"Maybe this will all be over by then." *Over.* It could mean two different things, but she refused to acknowledge one of them. A commotion in the adjoining room caught her attention. Through the window she saw two patrol officers and a plain-clothes detective having a discussion and pointing at a spot on the map.

"Something's up." Gianna dashed out of their room and into the next. The officers looked up in surprise as she burst through the door. "What happened?"

"Another sighting of an Escalade," one of the patrol officers said as Chris stepped into the room behind her.

"Where?" asked Chris.

The plainclothes detective tapped the map. "Here. In a totally different area than the first sighting. It could be another vehicle or else it's simply traveled that far. I'll put my money on it being a similar vehicle. It's too far away from our prime location. That first sighting was near your home, right?"

Gianna nodded silently, her gaze locked where he'd just touched the map.

She turned to look at Chris. He nodded at her, his lips pressed together in a white line.

The second sighting had been on the highway a few miles from the burned-out cabin where her father's body had been found.

The detective had it wrong: her home wasn't the prime location—the cabin was.

★ ★ ★

Chris was silent as they sped out of town toward the Cascades and the cabin. Next to him in the cab of his truck, Gianna fidgeted.

"I'm glad Hawes and Becker had already left," said Gianna. "Hawes would have known exactly where we were going."

He didn't mention that Gianna had repeated the observation three times. He understood. She was stressed.

After seeing the location of the second Escalade spotting, Chris had explained to the detective that the vehicle was within miles of where Francisco Green had been murdered. He'd suggested the county police check the burned cabin and the cabin where Rafael's body had been found. The detective was aware of the case, but hadn't realized the Escalade was so close to those locations, and immediately called Becker and Hawes.

Feeling they'd done their duty to highlight the obvious, they'd immediately left the police station, claiming they needed something to eat, knowing Hawes would ask the county sheriff to send units to the two cabins.

Deep in his gut, Chris knew the killer was returning to the original scene of the crime. And hopefully he had Violet with him. The notebooks had suddenly become less important. One look at Gianna's expression in the police station, and he'd known she suspected the same.

"We need to tell them what we're doing," Gianna muttered. "We should tell Hawes that we're going up there. Although I know the county sheriff will get there first and won't let us get near the cabins until they decide it's safe."

Her phone vibrated. "It's Leo," she said with surprise. "Saul must have asked him to call me."

She answered and was quiet for ten seconds. "Hang on, Leo. I'm going to put you on speaker, and I want Chris to hear all of this." She tapped her screen and held the phone out so Chris could hear.

"I can't believe this is going on," continued Leo. "When Saul called me and told me about Violet, I thought I was going to lose it. I told him I had no idea this could go so far."

Chris looked at Gianna. Her lips were pressed together in a tight line, her gaze on the phone.

"What could go so far?" she asked.

"Richard showed up at my house a while back."

"*What?* You knew he was still alive?" asked Chris. *Did everyone know but Gianna?*

"No! It shocked the hell out of me. I thought it was some sort of prank at first."

"Why didn't you contact me?" begged Gianna.

A deep sigh sounded through the phone. "I thought I was doing the right thing. Your father convinced me that you shouldn't know about him yet, but he had plans to come forward once the danger was gone. Your father believed that if you knew he was alive, it'd lead your mother's killers to you."

"I think that happened anyway," stated Chris.

"Richard had a lot of questions about what had happened decades ago. He was clearly confused, Gianna. I didn't see the harm in respecting the time Richard wanted before he let you know he was still alive. I knew something was wrong with him, and your uncle Saul just explained his old head injury to me."

"My father was going to contact me?" whispered Gianna.

Leo continued speaking. "I think our South African investor hired someone to murder Richard. The investor had been irate when I tried to back out of the original funding deal. I really didn't want to give up on the money, but Richard was adamant."

"Of course he was," Gianna snapped. "The company was dealing in illegal arms."

"I know, I know." Leo paused. "But you don't know how badly we needed those funds. We were on the brink of going under. I told Richard it was too late to back out. He was furious. I didn't know he went to the investor on his own and tried to get us out of it, but I've always had my suspicions about his car accident," Leo said quietly. He broke into sobs. "Oh Lord. Your mother, Gianna . . . and nearly you and Richard. I didn't know . . . and now Violet. What did I do?"

"You should have said something to Saul or me as soon as he showed up," stated Gianna.

Anger washed over Chris and he tightened his grip on the steering wheel. Leo was lucky he wasn't standing in front of him.

"Richard was convinced the threat was still relevant. He wasn't making a lot of sense the day he came to see me. He seemed to think you were still a child."

"You could have done the right thing all those years ago and not taken the money!" Gianna steamed.

"I didn't know if the rumors about the illegal arms were true back then," Leo argued.

Gianna laughed in an eerie way that made Chris's skin crawl. "That was so typical of you, Leo. Unless you saw it with your own eyes, you didn't believe it. No wonder my father went to see you in person. You would never have believed he was alive if he'd simply called."

"What did Richard say when he showed up?" Chris asked.

"He told me he had proof of some murders ordered by the owner of the South African company."

Silence filled the cab of the truck.

"You're talking about decades-old crimes?" Gianna asked. "That happened on another continent?"

"No. Murders here in the States. Starting with your mother."

Gianna sucked in her breath.

"Wait," Chris said. "You said murders . . . plural. More than Gianna's mother?"

"Yes," Leo said. "It appears this company tried investing in several up-and-coming businesses in the States around the same time as they invested in Berssina Tech. Some of the owners were resistant like Richard had been. It appears this investor has one solution for getting his own way: eliminate the issue."

"He had other people killed?" blurted Gianna. "Because they didn't want to do business with him? What century was this?" she said bitterly.

"Last century," Leo replied with irony. "But it appears it has continued into the twenty-first. I reached out to my South African partner after Richard visited me. He laughed off my questions about Richard's car accident. I tried to find Richard to ask for the proof of the murders, but he'd crawled back under one of his rocks. I wrote him off and assumed all of Richard's ramblings could be attributed to mental illness and did nothing. Today was the first I'd heard of Richard again."

"My father went to you with evidence of murders and you did *nothing about it*?"

"I have no defense, Gianna, but your father no longer had any credibility. And he didn't show me this evidence . . . he only claimed it existed. The man who came to talk to me looked like a beggar. He hadn't shaved or had a haircut and I don't think he'd showered in a week. I thought he was nuts."

Tears streaked Gianna's face. "I would have taken care of him," she whispered.

Chris saw wetness drip onto her shirt.

"He had no one," she said softly.

"According to Saul, he liked it that way," said Leo. "He said your father preferred to be alone. He wasn't lonely. He chose to live that way."

"Saul let him hide away because he was ashamed of him. And you were no better, Leo." Her words whipped through the air.

No one spoke for ten seconds.

"Right now my main concern is helping you find Violet," Leo said slowly. "Over the last two decades, I've hired some employees that were *strongly* recommended by my foreign investor. Some of them have been great engineers or salespeople, but I suspect others were trying to get out of the country."

The hair rose on the back of Chris's neck. Gianna met his gaze.

"Why did you think that?" she asked.

"They rarely came into the office to sit behind a desk, and I wasn't allowed to fire them," Leo said grimly. "Their employment was a sham. I swear he's started using me as a halfway house to get rid of some of his problems."

Gianna gasped. "Leo, the police just showed us an image of the Escalade driver," she said. "He's enormous. He's a younger blond guy with a cocky walk."

"Damn it," muttered Leo.

"What?" asked Gianna.

"I think I know who that is," said Leo. "I was ordered to hire him a while ago. He's the son of the South African owner, so I've had no control over him. I heard that the guy can be brutal when pushed, and I believe he *had* to leave the country."

"What's his name?" Gianna asked.

"Reid Kruger."

"I'm going to give you Detective Hawes's phone number," said Gianna. "Tell her everything you just told us."

CHAPTER TWENTY-THREE

Her uncle's and Leo's descriptions of her father wouldn't go away. Gianna kept seeing a pathetic, lost old man. Someone who stumbled around through life, confused by the world around him. Sometimes aware of his past and other times living in a haze.

She didn't know if she could ever forgive Saul for keeping them apart. He should have overruled her father.

The right to choose to be involved in her father's life should have been hers, and hers alone.

The snow grew deeper on the sides of the road as they gained elevation, but the pavement was wet and clear as they pushed on toward the national forest. Slushy bits of snow mixed with the rain on the windshield. It was a different world from a few days ago when they'd struggled to get out of the forest. Now they were rushing back in.

Where's Violet?

She prayed the county sheriff would find her at one of the cabins.

But why would Reid Kruger take Violet up there?

It made no sense. Her phone buzzed and she paused before answering the blocked number.

"Is this Gianna?" asked a male in an accented voice.

Shock raced through her nerves. "Yes." *It's him.*

"I have your daughter. Where is the thumb drive?"

"Who is this?" She turned to meet Chris's questioning gaze. She pulled the phone away from her ear and turned on the speaker with shaking hands.

"That doesn't matter. Where is your father's thumb drive? Where did he hide it?" The connection crackled in and out.

"I don't know what you're talking about," she said. "Let me talk to Violet."

The phone went silent. She stared at the time ticking on the screen; the call was still connected.

Violet screamed, and Gianna dropped the phone in her lap. She snatched it back up, holding it in a death grip, terrified she'd lose the connection to her daughter. Blood pounded in her ears and the scream abruptly stopped.

Along with Gianna's heart.

"Violet?"

"That's her polite way of asking you to tell me where it is. Would you like to hear it impolitely?"

His voice curdled the liquid in her stomach. "Don't hurt her."

"Too late."

Gianna felt the truck surge as Chris pressed on the gas, recklessly passing a car on a curve. His hands were white on the steering wheel, and the tendons in his neck bulged as he clenched his teeth.

"Don't hurt my daughter," she whispered, not taking her gaze from Chris. "I don't know anything about a thumb drive. My father didn't give anything to me or tell me anything about it. *You killed him before he could.*"

A harsh laugh came over the line. "That old man. All he did was piss me off. He was like a greased pig trying to hide and sneak around. I knew if I watched you long enough he'd come crawling out of his hiding place at some point. At first I thought I'd missed him, so I went through your house looking for it."

This slime was in my house? She thought of the missing lingerie and shuddered.

"I finally spotted him when I followed you to the mountain. He was so fucking easy to catch." He snorted. "Old useless man."

Gianna winced, remembering the skinny burned body in the morgue. Her father had had no muscle mass or strength left.

"But he was stubborn. So fucking stubborn. He admitted he had the documentation but wouldn't tell us what he'd done with the thumb drive. It only makes sense that he passed it to you or put it somewhere for you to find. *Where is it?*"

"I don't know!" she shouted at the phone.

"Your daughter looks just like you," the voice whispered. "I took a few things from your closet, planning to see you in them one day. But maybe your—"

"She's a child!" Bile heaved in her stomach. Chris looked ready to explode, but Gianna knew he would stay silent, letting the asshole believe only she could hear him.

"She doesn't look like a child. Bring me the thumb drive and we'll talk."

She exchanged a glance with Chris. "Where are you?"

He laughed. "Think about where your father had gone."

"He was an old man," she whispered. "You killed him too soon and now you're scrambling to save your own ass."

"Didn't matter. I had my orders. Killing him was a mistake, but he *made me angry*! I need that thumb drive!"

"You knew he was alive all these years?" she whispered.

"Hell no. Shocked us all when Leo said Richard showed up at his house. We might have let it go, but the information Richard claimed he had could destroy my father's life work. We won't let one man take us down."

Gianna closed her eyes. Her father's pursuit of justice had gotten him killed. Whatever was on this thumb drive clearly threatened the South African investor. "Maybe it doesn't exist," she whispered. "Maybe my father made up the information. *No one has seen this drive you're looking for!*"

The killer was silent for a moment. "Richard knew things. He told Leo facts that only my father knows. He has the information hidden *somewhere*! I told my father I'd already collected it!"

"You fucked up!" Gianna shouted at the phone. "What if there is no thumb drive?"

"It exists! I *will* have it!"

"Hurting my daughter won't make it show up!"

"We'll see. I'll give you fifteen minutes." He ended the call.

"Fifteen minutes until what?" Empty air filled her ears.

She wanted to shove Chris out of the driver's seat and slam the accelerator into the floor.

They were still forty minutes away.

★ ★ ★

Violet's leg burned.

The tall blond man had pulled off the highway and climbed into the backseat with her, saying he had to make a phone call and that she was to be silent or he'd slash her throat. She'd eyed the blade in his hand and obeyed.

Until he'd jammed it into her thigh and twisted.

His eyes had lit up as he held his cell phone forward to catch her screams. Then he'd yanked the blade out and she'd collapsed. No one had ever purposefully hurt her before. The shock of the abrupt attack burned as much as the pain. She couldn't focus on his phone call, but knew he was talking to her mother. He'd stepped out of the vehicle, keeping his side of the conversation from her hearing, and let her bleed on the seat.

He ended the call and returned, grinding his palm into the place on her leg. She shrieked.

"Where's the thumb drive?"

"I don't know what you're talking about. What thumb drive?" Violet spit out. He'd asked her the same question four times but didn't answer any of hers. He'd simply glared when she said her school thumb drive was in her backpack. If he wanted her reports and project for school, he could have them. "You seem to think I have something that *I don't have.*"

"The one from your grandfather."

Finally. A clarification.

"My grandfather's never given me one." She gasped, trying to ignore the pain and think of presents that Saul had given her over the years. "He gave me an iPod a few years ago, but you can only save music and movies on it."

Now the man looked confused. "He's been with you for years?"

His accent puzzled her. She didn't think he was British or Australian. His eyes were a piercing blue, and he looked as if he could have been a body double for Arnold Schwarzenegger in the first *Terminator* movie. He was one of the biggest men she'd ever seen and he'd tossed her into his SUV as if she were a doll. His bulk filled the backseat.

Violet hated him.

She eyed the gun in his shoulder holster. If she was blessed with the chance, she wouldn't hesitate to use it on him. She'd frozen when he'd shot Jamie and leaped to obey when he'd turned the weapon on her and barked orders at her to move and drive. By the time she'd lost some of her terror and been ready to drive the car into a building, he'd ordered her to stop, and they'd changed vehicles. It felt like they'd driven for hours with her in the backseat of the SUV, but she had no concept of time. She'd slept briefly at one point and woken up stunned that she could sleep when she was terrified out of her mind.

Did Jamie die?

Bitter cold had greeted her when he opened the door to climb into the backseat. She'd stared in surprise at snowy fir trees and scrambled to sit up, scanning outside the vehicle. They were back in the woods. He gave a final blow to her thigh and moved back to the driver's seat as she curled up in pain. She didn't care where he was taking her. A few minutes later he stopped and she looked out at the narrow driveway where she'd spent that horrible night in their Suburban, terrified her mother would never stop vomiting. The vehicle was gone, towed by the police, and the road to the cabin was plowed, completely clear of snow and ice.

The difference a few days could make.

He slashed her bindings with a knife and dragged her into the burned shell, ripping down the yellow police tape that blocked the door. Violet stared up at the ceiling in horror, frozen in fear and balancing on her one good leg. She could see the gray sky and trees through the holes in the ceiling and remembered Chris's concerns that the roof could collapse. He shoved her onto a soot-covered couch and started the questions about the thumb drive again. "My mom hasn't lived with Grandpa since she went to college," Violet replied. "But he's always been part of my family."

Comprehension crossed his face, quickly replaced by anger. "Not Saul Messina. His brother Richard."

"Richard? My real grandfather died years ago," Violet said slowly. *He's crazy. Does he think I'm someone else?* "Before I was born. My mother was just a child when her parents died."

"Bullshit. Richard has been hiding for years."

The floor seemed to fall away beneath Violet.

"You all tried to keep it a secret. Richard was scared shitless that Leo Berg knew about the attempts on his life."

Leo? Violet knew the man only as the owner of the company created by her real grandfather.

"Leo's always been good to us," Violet said slowly. Her mother always had high praise for the man who'd honored her grandfather's role in founding the technology company. According to her mother, most of their income came from a portion of the company's profits even though her grandfather had died decades ago.

The man laughed. "Leo's walked the line for a long time, but he's not the one calling the shots. My father kept that company from drowning years ago. Leo owes everything to us. Richard had to have hidden the thumb drive here," her kidnapper said.

304 • KENDRA ELLIOT

"I searched his apartment, your house, and Richard didn't have it on him when he died. He was hanging around this cabin watching the two of you. He must have planted it here somewhere." He pulled two cushions off the other couch, looking underneath them while still keeping his weapon trained on Violet. Gray ash formed clouds and he coughed. Violet covered her nose and mouth.

"Look in those drawers," he ordered, waving his gun at her and pointing at an end table.

She slid one open, peered into the empty space, and wiped her hand on her jeans, feeling warm blood soaking one of her legs. "What's it look like?"

"You don't know what a thumb drive looks like?" he sneered.

"Of course I do. But is it any shape in particular? My school one is a cat on a key ring."

"I don't know what it fucking looks like. Keep digging."

"What's on it?" Violet asked. "Why do you need it?"

He took a step closer to her, deliberately looking down the barrel of his gun at her face. "Shut. Up."

Sweat broke out under her arms and her good leg fought to hold her up. The image of Jamie crumpled on the street flashed in her brain. She turned away and opened another drawer.

"Just understand that your life depends on us finding it. Your life and your mother's."

★ ★ ★

Reid heard the vehicle approach the burned-out cabin. Stepping to the window, he barely moved the curtain to look outside. A county sheriff's SUV had stopped in front. He could make out two silhouettes inside.

"Shit."

He turned to check on the girl. *Useless.* Violet had finally collapsed onto one of the couches, crying that her leg hurt too badly for her to move. Rage shot through him. Why had he saddled himself with the girl? They'd searched nearly every square inch of the ashy cabin looking for the thumb drive. He *knew* Richard had stashed it somewhere. *If not here, then where?*

He should search Gianna's home again.

Maybe she'd be home this time.

The slam of a car door turned his attention back outside. Two men stepped out. "Hello!" one hollered at the cabin. Reid glanced back at Violet, silencing her with a stare and drawing his weapon. Her eyes were wide, her hands clasped around her injured leg.

The deputies strolled to the black Escalade and cupped their hands to look in the windows. Their posture was relaxed, no tension or preparedness at all. Clearly they thought they were simply checking on a strange vehicle. They had no inkling of what they were about to encounter. *They're going to wish they'd taken this more seriously.*

The two of them scanned the area and shouted at the cabin again. Inside, he held Violet to silence with a death glare. One of the deputies laughed at something the other said and started up the few steps to the cabin. Reid put his hand on the door handle and took a deep breath.

He flung open the door and shot the deputy in the face.

Violet screamed.

He took two steps, aimed, and fired at the other deputy, who'd frozen, staring at Reid. Blood appeared on his neck and he slapped his hands over the spot. Blood spilled from between his fingers and he spun around to run. Reid took another step in his direction, kicking the legs of the first deputy out of his way. The other deputy lunged, tripped, and fell, his hands still clutching his neck.

Reid slowly moved down the steps, his weapon trained on the deputy flailing in the yard. The man was still by the time he reached him. He kicked the man in the gut. He didn't move.

He turned to see Violet in the doorway, supporting herself with one hand on the doorframe. Her mouth hung open as she stared from the faceless deputy at her feet to Reid.

"Where did you and your mother go when you left this burned-up piece-of-crap cabin that morning?" Reid asked her.

She didn't answer.

"Where did you go?" he screamed. He raised his weapon and aimed at her face.

"C-Chris's cabin."

"Show me."

CHAPTER TWENTY-FOUR

Two county sheriffs' vehicles blocked Chris from entering the winding driveway to Gianna's rental cabin.

"Good," he said. "They got here first. Becker and Hawes must have gotten word to them to check the cabin."

Gianna leaned forward in her seat, eyeing the group of deputies next to the vehicles. "Something's happened." All heads had turned toward them. One of the men stepped forward, holding up his hand to stop Chris and keeping the other hand on his weapon at his waist. One other deputy moved toward Gianna's side of the vehicle until he could see her clearly, but stayed back, his hand also on his weapon. His gaze was dead serious.

"They're on alert," Chris said quietly. He lowered his window. "What's going on?" he asked the deputy.

"You need to turn your vehicle around. This area is closed for now."

Chris gestured toward Gianna. "This is Gianna Trask. Her daughter is Violet Trask, the girl you were alerted about in relation to the black Escalade." The deputy took a hard look at Gianna, his face clearing as he saw the similarity between her and the girl they'd been told to look for.

"Two of our guys were following up on a possible spotting of the Escalade at this location." The deputy clamped his mouth shut, his face paling.

Gianna's heart dropped at the sorrow on his face. "What happened? Where's Violet?"

"She's not here, ma'am."

Her heartbeat returned to normal, but the deputy wasn't done. "Two of our best men were just murdered. We've got every available unit searching for that Escalade and have reached out to OSP and the FBI for support and more boots on the ground."

Chris's knuckles whitened on the steering wheel. "Were they shot?"

The deputy's eyes burned with anger. "Yes. We'd been told they believed they'd found the Escalade back in Portland, so when someone spotted one way up here, I don't think they took the precautions they should have."

"This was the vehicle they're looking for," said Chris.

"No shit."

"I'm so sorry," said Gianna, fighting back tears. *Where is Violet? Please don't hurt her.*

"Thank you, ma'am. We'll find your daughter. The state detectives handling her case should be here soon." His voice returned to a business tone. "You still need to leave the area. If you need a place to go, there's a ranger station not far from here."

"Was there anything else unusual at the cabin?" Chris asked. "You know Gianna and Violet were nearly killed when it burned a few days ago."

Comprehension crossed the deputy's face. "I didn't know this was related to that case. *Someone* has been in the cabin. The warning tape was ripped off and the interior was clearly disturbed, couch cushions on the floor, drawers opened. But that could have happened at any point in the last few days . . . except . . ." He closed his mouth.

"What?" asked Gianna. "Please. It's my daughter. What did you see inside?"

"I didn't see it, but I was told there's fresh blood on some of the couch cushions and floor."

Gianna's lungs stopped. "How much?" she croaked.

"Not a lot," he rushed to assure her.

It was a small thing to cling to.

Chris asked a few more questions, but Gianna's focus was shattered. What had happened inside? Was it Violet's blood? The deputy deflected Chris's questions and suggested again that they go wait at the ranger station. Chris put the SUV in reverse and backed out of the area.

"Are we going to the ranger station?" Gianna asked. "I don't know if I can go sit there and simply wait for Becker and Hawes to show up."

"Let's stop at my place first."

★ ★ ★

"He killed those deputies," Gianna said quietly.

Chris nodded. This wasn't the hiding-in-the-shadows killer he'd first imagined when the two John Does had turned up. Or even the coward who'd shot Frisco from the cover of the woods. This man had shot Jamie and two cops in broad daylight. And clearly didn't care who saw him. Either he'd been pushed beyond caring about his own skin or he had been mentally ill to start with. He thought back to Leo's report. Reid Kruger had had to leave South Africa for his violent ways.

Now he was carving his own violent path through Oregon.

Is Violet still alive?

Beside him Gianna had been silent during the drive to his cabin. He knew her thoughts were on her daughter.

"We'll get her back," he said, reaching out to take her hand. It felt like ice.

"He's a killer," whispered Gianna. "He kills whoever gets in his way. Frisco. My father, Jamie . . . those deputies. Jamie is so lucky."

Please let Violet be that lucky.

"I've tried calling Detective Hawes," she said. "I keep getting her voice mail. I left a message saying where we were and what we'd heard from that deputy."

"Good," said Chris. "I don't want to sit and wait either. After we stop at my place, we can drive around and see if we can spot his vehicle and report it. At least we'll feel like we're doing something."

★ ★ ★

Gianna followed Chris up the steps to his cabin. Had it been only two days since they abandoned the cabin, worried a killer was about to show up on his doorstep? She'd spotted the felled tree that'd ended their escape from the forest in Chris's truck. It'd been pushed to the side of the road and Chris's truck had been towed. It felt like it'd happened a lifetime ago.

"I just want to grab a few things," said Chris as he put a key in the lock. He pushed the door open and stepped back to allow Gianna to enter first. The cabin was dim, and she moved toward the closest window to raise a blind.

A loud crack sounded behind her and she spun around to see Chris crumple to the floor.

She locked eyes with Reid Kruger and froze, her heart in her throat.

Reid dropped the piece of firewood he'd slammed into Chris's head.

"Chris?" she whispered, her vocal cords numb.

"Shut up!" Reid Kruger was big. Bigger than he'd seemed on camera. He pointed at her. "Don't move."

I can't.

Her feet couldn't budge and her knees threatened to collapse. She pulled her gaze away from the giant and looked toward Chris.

"Don't move!"

She lifted her hands and held still but kept her gaze on Chris. *Breathe!* Time started to tick off in her head. She watched his chest, his eyelids, his fingers. No movement. Dimly she was aware that Reid didn't have a gun in his hands. Given that he'd shot three people in one day, she'd expected him to be armed. Had she and Chris surprised him?

Chris's chest moved with a deep breath, and she gasped in relief. She looked up at Reid. "Where's Violet?"

He jerked his head toward the loft. "Upstairs."

Gianna hadn't heard a sound out of the loft since she'd entered. "Violet?" she yelled, holding Reid's eye contact.

Silence.

"She can't talk."

"What did you do to her?" Rage rose from the depths of her gut and fired through her chest. Her fingers curled, aching to rip at his throat, gouge his eyes, and pull his hair out at the roots. Hatred boiled over.

Surprise lit his freakishly blue eyes. "She's fine. I just needed her quiet for a while."

"What did you do to her?" Gianna screamed at him. She took a half step in his direction.

Reid leaned toward her. "I. Needed. Her. Silent," he said in a low voice that made the hair curl on the back of her neck. Seeing her fear, he let his gaze drag over her from head to toe and back up. Sexual desire laced his stare and made Gianna's stomach churn. A new suspicion settled over her and her limbs turned to ice.

Did he rape my daughter?

Touch me like that and you'll never be able to touch another woman.

Teeth. Nails. Knees. Elbows. She mentally prepared her arsenal and spread her feet, rocking up on her toes and bending her knees. She wasn't going down without causing as much damage as possible. She stared back at him, daring him to put a hand on her.

He threw his head back and laughed. "The little tiger has claws!"

She didn't say anything.

Blinding white teeth grinned at her. "She has spice, too. I like that."

"Fuck you."

He found that hilarious. Her anger shot higher.

A glance at Chris showed blood flowing from a gash by his ear. A million questions shot through her brain. *How injured is he? Are the police coming? What will Reid do next?*

Don't know. Don't know. Don't know.

He shoved the door shut and the cabin darkened. He turned on a small lamp. As her eyes adjusted, he reached behind his back and removed a gun from his waistband and a knife from his pocket. He stepped to the blinds and slashed at the cords, then tossed them at Gianna. She instinctively caught them. "Tie him up. And do it good. I'm watching."

She knelt next to Chris. His chest still moved with quiet breaths, and she rested the palm of her hand on his forehead as she would for Violet when checking for a fever. *Hang in there.* She started to tie his hands together.

"Behind his back!"

She awkwardly shifted him to get both hands behind his back. He was incredibly heavy, his limbs difficult to move, but she managed. She tied a loose knot.

"Tighter! Jesus Christ. I'm not blind."

Gianna gritted her teeth and pulled the knot tighter. "You haven't proven to be a very good criminal, have you?" she snapped.

"Watch your mouth."

"How much trouble did you get in when your father found out you didn't have the thumb drive?"

He said nothing.

Aha! He still hasn't told his father. "What about Rafael Jones? What did he do wrong?"

"Shut up."

She lifted her head to look at him, one hand still on Chris's wrists. She brushed her hair out of her eyes. "You weren't supposed to kill your partner, were you? Did you have to do that to cover your initial fuck-up?"

He stepped closer and pointed his gun at her eyes. "You don't know what you're talking about. Now tie his ankles."

She moved to Chris's feet, keeping her focus on the killer. "Then tell me, Reid." She saw his eyes widen the slightest bit at her use of his name. "Tell me how Rafael died. And what did your boss say when he found out my father was dead but you didn't have the thumb drive?"

"Rafael was a fuck-up."

"Why was I drugged?"

The grin that crossed Reid's face would haunt her nightmares forever. "You were both to be drugged. Rafael had planned a little going-away party. But the girl never drank the juice."

"So you started the fire anyway? No thumb drive and one unconscious victim?" She shook her head at him. "No wonder you had to leave your own country. You suck as a crook."

"I didn't have to leave!" His hand tightened on his gun. "I chose to leave."

"That's not what I heard," Gianna said, raising a brow. *Keep him distracted and talking.* "I heard your father had to hustle you out of the country and buy you a new job. Your reputation isn't the greatest."

Irritation and rage crossed his face.

"You're as stubborn as your father was. And you piss me off just as easily." His accent grew thicker as the rage filled his voice. "It felt good to beat the crap out of that old man." The words poured out of his mouth, and she felt their loathing stab her brain. She slapped a hand over one ear as if it could stop the sounds.

"He wouldn't give it up, and I'd never failed before. I know how to interrogate people, but he deflected my questions at every turn." He paused. "He screamed as I kicked him, Gianna." The tone of his voice made her skin crawl. "He screamed like a little girl and begged me not to hurt you and his granddaughter. I took great pleasure in telling him everything I planned to do to you and your daughter. He was crying at the end. He knew his years of hiding were about to come to nothing and that he'd exposed his family to a great risk."

"You're fucking sick," she whispered.

She calmly held his gaze as her stomach threatened to hurl its contents at his feet. The entire time her hearing had been focused on the loft upstairs as she ached to hear any sound that Violet was alive. She wasn't taking Reid's word for it.

"You need the thumb drive to save face with your father," she stated. "You think I'm going to give it to you? You killed my father. I don't owe you a thing. And if you shoot me, then it's gone forever."

"I knew you had it," he said triumphantly. "Where is it?"

"Sorry, Reid. You need to give Violet back to me. Don't you know that a mother would give her own life for her daughter? Keeping her from me gets you nothing." She slowly stood, holding his gaze the whole time.

Indecision fluttered in his eyes. He backed away from her and put a hand on the ladder to the loft. "Don't move. Try to run and Violet will have two holes in her head."

Gianna believed him. "I'm not going anywhere."

He backed up the ladder, using one hand while keeping the gun trained in her direction with the other. She stood immobile and watched him the entire way. As soon as his head disappeared, she bent next to Chris and felt his pulse. Strong. Steady. *Thank you.* She looked up just in time to see Reid appear at the top with Violet clasped in front of him.

Gianna fought back her tears. *She's alive.*

Every muscle in her body wanted to collapse at the sight. Instead she kept her gaze locked on the girl's face, as if she could keep her from vanishing again.

Duct tape covered Violet's mouth, and her arms and legs were tied. She didn't look scared; she looked angry.

Pride in her daughter rushed through Gianna.

How will I get us out of here?

With one arm Reid hefted Violet over his shoulder in a fireman's carry. He turned his back to move down the ladder, and she noticed Chris move his head. He opened one eye and looked directly at her as he tried to pull his arms apart.

She reached to loosen his ties.

"Get the fuck away from him!"

Gianna rose to her feet. Reid lowered Violet from his shoulder and held her in front of him, facing her mother. Gianna studied her daughter, searching for any sign of injury. "Are you all right?"

Violet nodded, her mouth still covered. Reid shoved the barrel of his gun under the corner of Violet's jaw, making her tip her head away from the pain. Her eyes widened, holding Gianna's gaze.

I am capable of killing him.

"Now. Where is the thumb drive?"

CHAPTER TWENTY-FIVE

Nora Hawes was ready to punch through Becker's dashboard. Two good police officers had been murdered at the burned cabin.

What the hell happened?

A false lead had taken her and Becker to the other side of the city and wasted hours of time. No doubt someone had truly seen a black Escalade near Gianna's home, but as soon as Nora had heard there'd been a different sighting in the Cascade Range near the scene of the cabin fire, she'd known they needed to be there. They'd had to cross town in heavy traffic, taking way too much time. Thirty minutes later they'd heard the officers had been killed.

Leo Berg had called her. He'd told her that Gianna and Chris were already headed up to the cabin area. Leo had also provided a name and some background to go with the face she'd seen on the video from outside the furniture store. She'd made some calls and found that Reid Kruger had a short arrest record from the Los Angeles area. Nothing worth shouting about, but enough to show that he had too much time on his hands. And too much money. "This guy has hundreds of thousands of dollars sitting in his checking accounts," muttered Becker. "What the hell? What's it like to have that kind of spendable income?"

Nora had shaken her head. Apparently Kruger's father was worth millions . . . possibly billions. Enough to buy his son a new life in the United States. *This time he's fucked up.* No amount of money would buy his way out of the murders of the two cops in the last hour. And then there were Richard Messina, Rafael Jones, and Francisco Green. The attempted murder of Gianna, Jamie, and Violet. And now kidnapping.

Her gut told her Reid Kruger had pulled the trigger every time.

She wanted to see Kruger's father try to make that go away.

"From what Saul said, this guy is brutal and dangerous. If he's hurt Violet Trask . . ."

Becker didn't answer. They'd both already imagined the worst. Several times.

"How far away are we?"

"Twenty minutes. Depending on the traffic."

"I've tried calling Gianna and Chris. They must be in a cell phone dead spot."

★ ★ ★

From his position on the floor, Chris stared at Reid Kruger's boots. After Reid carried Violet down the ladder, he'd been too close for Chris to crane his neck to see his face. His ankles and wrists were tied tightly; someone had been efficient. His head hurt like a bitch and double vision came and went in waves that nauseated him.

Gianna stood between him and Kruger, arguing about a thumb drive.

Chris was no help. He knew nothing about it, but it sounded like Richard Messina had stolen some private information that could destroy Kruger's father's business. *Does it really exist?* Gianna's father hadn't been right in the head. Perhaps he'd made up this storage device to threaten the man who'd ruined his life?

Chris closed his eyes against an avalanche of nausea. *What if all these people died because a crazy old man made up a story?* What if three more were about to die?

Reid Kruger had left multiple bodies in his wake. Three more would be nothing.

His lids flew open as the ground shook while Kruger took two steps and shoved Violet onto the couch. She flopped on the cushions and fought to keep her balance, her terrified gaze meeting Chris's. Her hands and feet were still bound, but Reid had ripped the tape from her mouth. Chris twisted his neck and rolled to his side to look up as Kruger stepped closer to Gianna, his weapon inches from her eyes. He took a quick glance down and made eye contact with Chris.

"You! Scarred man! You want to see your woman's brains turn into a pink mist?" Fury sparked from Kruger's pale eyes. "Where is it?"

Kruger took a step and kicked Chris in the stomach.

Bright lights exploded in his vision and his lungs refused to let him take a breath.

He wheezed.

Kruger laughed. "I think you've been beat on before, scarred man. I know those round marks. I've given plenty of them."

A too-white face from the past rose up in Chris's mind.

He's dead. The Ghostman is dead.

Kruger's accent resonated in his brain. He sounded nothing like the Ghostman. *That's not him.* Chris looked over at Violet on the couch, her brown eyes wide in horror. In the depths of her eyes, he saw every child who'd vanished with him but had never returned. The pain in his chest echoed with the memories of torture. *Burns, chains, knives.* The other children's voices filled his mind, their names, their faces. He'd sworn never to forget any of them.

Were he, Gianna, and Violet about to join their ranks?

Who would keep alive the memories of the children who'd died?

Had he deceived fate for too long? He should have never survived. Now nature was catching up.

He gagged and his lungs sucked in oxygen. Kruger laughed at his desperate gulps of air. His leg swung back for another kick and Gianna stepped in the way. Her legs tangled with Kruger's, and he hit her across the face with his weapon. She collapsed to the floor, falling across Chris.

Kruger fired.

Chris felt Gianna's body heave and jerk at the impact of the shot, and her shriek burned his ears.

"Fuck you all," Kruger shouted. "I'll find it!" He strode toward Chris's tiny kitchen.

Chris twisted his body under Gianna as she shook with silent sobs. He stared as blood soaked through her shirt near her abdomen. The warmth of the liquid touched his arm.

She's crying; she can't be dead.

"Gianna! Can you move?" he begged. She pulled into a ball, shaking her head.

Smoke registered in Chris's senses. Flames rose from his kitchen stove, and he watched Kruger rip the curtains from the kitchen window and add them to the blaze. The flames grew higher. Kruger pulled the top off an old-fashioned oil lamp and threw the oil across the weathered boards of the kitchen wall. He grabbed two more and did the same. The flames followed the new path and eagerly licked the dry wood. Smoke gathered at the peak of the roof and quickly filled the loft.

He turned toward Chris, a silhouette in front of the red-and-yellow fire, but his gaze burned with a cool intensity.

He's fucking nuts.

Kruger paused and grabbed the last of Chris's emergency hurricane lamps. He dumped the oil over Gianna and Chris, smiling as the oil soaked into their clothes. Chris flailed as if he could shake the flammable liquid off his body.

This isn't happening.

Kruger strode to the door and glanced back at the three of them. "Burn in hell." He opened the door, stepped out into the night, and slammed it shut.

"Gianna!" Chris shouted, shaking her with his body. "Get up!"

She shook her head and burrowed it into his torso, her legs pulled up to her injured abdomen. More of her blood warmed his side. She hadn't flinched when Kruger flung the oil over them, but Chris was more than aware of it for the both of them. He looked over at Violet, the sound of the growing flames starting to fill the cabin. "Get out! Just get yourself out! Roll if you have to."

The girl slid awkwardly off the couch and scooted on her butt toward him and Gianna. "Is she going to be okay?" Tears streamed down Violet's face.

"Yes," Chris lied, "but you need to get out. I'll get your mom out."

Violet's gaze said she knew he lied. "Let me try to untie you." She scooted around him and tried to line up her hands behind her back with his. Her fingers fumbled uselessly with his bindings. The heat of the fire toasted the skin of his face as he willed Violet to untie the knots.

"I can't get them!"

"Then get yourself out!"

"No!" she shrieked, turning. "Not without my mother! Mom! *Get up!*"

Gianna lifted her head, and Chris saw her gaze lock with her daughter's. With a shaking hand she reached out and plucked at the knots she'd tied at his wrists. They didn't budge.

"Can you get to the kitchen?" Chris asked Gianna. "Get a knife."

Gianna pushed to her knees and the bloodstain on the side of her shirt expanded. Her arms quivered and she closed her eyes in concentration. Chris fumbled up to a sitting position, knowing he'd have to try. "See if you can turn the doorknob," he ordered Violet. He moved to the kitchen, scooting in the same way Violet had. A small voice in his head worried that Violet would add more oxygen to the fire by opening the door, but the flames were still expanding, showing they had an ample oxygen supply in the cabin. She wouldn't create a backdraft explosion unless the oxygen inside had been nearly depleted.

He pressed his back into the wall of the kitchen island and scooted his way up to standing, feeling the heat on the back of his head. Violet mimicked his movements at the front door, concentration on her face. With his hands behind him, he yanked open a drawer and fumbled for a knife. A slice along his finger told him he'd found a good one. He felt carefully for the handle, trying to ignore the growing heat.

His fingers wrapped around a handle.

He hopped back to Gianna and fell to his knees beside her, dropping the knife. "Cut the ropes."

She picked up the knife, her lips pressed together in a white line, and sawed at his bindings. His arms jerked apart and he grabbed the knife out of her hand. He slashed the binding at his feet and swept her up into his arms, acutely aware of the warm wetness that immediately soaked the front of his shirt. Violet shuffled out of his way and he opened the door and stepped out into the cool night air and sucked in a deep icy breath.

The rumble of a V8 engine sped away in the distance.

CHAPTER TWENTY-SIX

Twenty-four hours later

Gianna smelled smoke and jerked open her eyes. In a chair beside her hospital bed, Chris leaned forward, concern crossing his face. "Do you need the nurse?"

"Where's Violet?" she rasped. Her throat was unbearably dry.

"She's fine. She's with my parents. She's not hurt."

Relief flowed through her and her lids fell shut.

My baby is safe.

"You've asked me the same thing five times," Chris said softly.

She realized he was the source of the smell of smoke. He hadn't showered and he wore the same clothes that—

"How long have I been here?" She lifted a hand and gently touched her side. It burned under the thick bandaging. "I remember you carrying me out." Her mind was fuzzy, and she recognized the floaty sensation of narcotics pulsing through her system.

"Since last night. You're going to be fine."

She struggled to focus on his bandaged hovering face. "He hit you in the head."

"It's not much."

"He shot me," she whispered, remembering the sound of the gun.

"Yes. But the bullet went through cleanly. A couple of inches another way and you would have bled out immediately."

Her brain created an image of her cold body on a stainless autopsy table. Dr. Rutledge probing the opening in her corpse.

We're fine. Violet is fine. Everyone is okay.

Chris's warm hand took hers as he leaned his elbows on her mattress. "I wasn't sure you were going to make it. Your daughter had pressure on your wounds before I could even think straight. She's a level-headed girl."

"What happened?"

"The detectives showed up minutes after we got out. They'd spotted the smoke from the other cabin and when they saw your injuries, they radioed to call back the paramedics who'd responded to the shooting. We're lucky they weren't far away. I would have had to drive you out to get cell service."

"Kruger?" She hoped he was dead in a ditch.

"Gone. Don't know where. We'll find him." A fierceness entered his voice. One she'd never heard from him before.

"*We* will?"

"I mean the police."

She studied his face. He was up to something. Between him and Michael, no doubt they were exercising every resource they had to find the rock Reid Kruger had hidden under. Then she remembered the thought she'd had at the cabin.

"I know where the thumb drive is," she said.

His jaw dropped. "You do? Becker and Hawes have been all over me about that. I was convinced it didn't exist. I think Kruger might be, too."

"I *think* I know."

"Where?"

"Are my clothes here? The stuff I had on?"

Chris stood, looking around the room. He walked over to a small closet and found a plastic bag. He opened it and pulled out the shirt she'd been wearing. He wrinkled his nose. "Do I smell this smoky?"

"Yes," said Gianna. "Now look in the pocket of my jeans."

I think I'm right.

He set down her shirt and removed her jeans. He slid the folded drawing of Violet out of her pocket along with the Darth Vader PEZ dispenser. He froze for a second and then looked at her with wide eyes as he flipped back the plastic head.

"Is it there?" she asked.

"How did you know?" Chris shook the Star Wars figure and a slim silver USB drive slipped into his hand.

"I didn't. I grabbed it because it was the only thing in that whole apartment that represented the man I remembered. He'd collected all sorts of Star Wars memorabilia. At some point during the night, I realized that it was the right size and wondered if he could have hidden it in there."

Chris closed his fist around the small drive and handed the dispenser to Gianna. "There's probably another one in the other dispenser. I'll tell Hawes to check."

Gianna stared at the small plastic figure. "Hiding in plain sight. That sounds like something my father would have done."

He died for this device.

She smiled and looked at Chris, who was eyeing her with a bit of awe.

Her heart filled as she spotted a smudge of ash at his jawline. He'd washed his face and hands, but hadn't taken the time to do much else. She imagined the nurses had urged him to go home and change while she was unconscious, but she knew he hadn't listened. *She knew.*

His expression changed to bewilderment. "What is it?"

"Thank you," she whispered. "That's twice you've saved Violet and me."

He held her gaze. "I guess someone's trying to tell me something. I've tried my hardest to stay away from people for the past two decades. It took both my sister and Michael to yank me into their lives, and I've never regretted it. Now someone has forcibly placed you and Violet where I have to practically trip over you to get me to open my eyes again. I think it's a sign."

Her lips curved up. "A sign? Do you remember asking me if I believed in fate on that first night in your cabin?"

"I do." His expression was deadly serious. He reached out and gripped her closest hand.

"You said you thought you were sent to help Violet and me."

"I've changed my thoughts on that," he said.

"Oh?"

"I wasn't sent to help you two. You were sent to save me."

Gianna couldn't breathe.

"The last two years of my life have been a series of small steps. Learning how to live in the real world. Being human again. I think someone felt I was ready to take a huge leap. I've never felt more alive than in the last few days. I feel like . . . something has settled into its rightful place inside of me. I *knew* something was wrong, but I couldn't put a name or description to it. There was an empty spot and I couldn't figure out how to fill it."

"It's better now?" Gianna asked. Her mind spun as he spoke, knowing the exact sensation he was talking about. Violet's father had left a hole when he'd died. It'd healed over, but she'd never felt the same. A constant nagging empty sensation had followed her for years. She'd tried to fill it with work and her daughter, but it had been like placing a paper patch on a fabric hole. It protected the spot, but never felt right.

"It's like it was never there." He paused. "It's you, Gianna. I've been waiting for you for a long time, but I don't think I was ready until recently."

Tears streaked down her cheeks. "I feel the same way," she whispered. "I don't want it to go away."

"Hell. I'm not going anywhere." The familiar stubbornness settled on his face. "We've got all the time in the world. And I know what I want to do first."

"What's that?"

"Introduce you to my son."

She couldn't wait.

★ ★ ★

One month later

Chris sat on the rocky wall and stared out at the Caribbean at five in the morning. Even in the early hours, the Kool-Aid shade of blue was stunning. White sand under his toes. Palm trees overhead. The beach on the Yucatán Peninsula was straight out of heaven. He'd never visited this part of the world before. It was an odd mix of Mayan ruins, sleepy towns, tourist traps, and poverty.

The sweat under his bulletproof vest ran down his back.

"The local girl said it's the second tent," Michael said softly. He crouched on top of the wall, his gun balanced lightly on his knee. Weeks of searching, digging, and payoffs were about to come to fruition. They'd tracked Reid Kruger south into Mexico and east to Cancún and then south again. Twice they'd been hours behind the man, finding dirty dishes and angry women who said he'd promised them money.

Reid Kruger was out of money.

The USB drives in the Darth Vader PEZ dispensers contained information that'd brought Kruger's father's company to its knees. War crimes, hate crimes, international crimes. His father had been a part of all of it, and he no longer had money to send to his son on the run. Evidence of Reid Kruger's brutality in his home country of South Africa was also on the thumb drives, but it paled in comparison to the crimes of his father. Hawes and Becker had been stunned by the amount of information and passed it to the right international authorities.

Chris didn't care. He simply wanted Reid Kruger to pay for shooting Jamie and Gianna. The women had spent the last month looking over their shoulders, wondering if the blond giant would reappear. Michael and Chris were determined to give their women peace of mind. Their latest lead had brought them to a camp on a quiet beach where young international travelers gathered. College dropouts who wanted to see the world on a budget. Young people in their twenties who wanted to live by the water this week and climb a mountain in Tibet next week. A transient group, constantly changing and evolving. Their most recent addition included a *very* tall and large blond man.

"Let's go."

Chris followed Michael between the palms, staying low and stepping quietly. His brother moved like a panther. He crouched next to the second tent and looked in the open flap. "Tent" was a misnomer. It was several tarps strung together between two trees. Large openings allowed the coastal breezes to flow through. Michael looked back at him and nodded, his eyes serious. He held up one finger.

It's Kruger and he's alone.

Michael started to enter the tent, but Chris grabbed his shoulder. He shook his head and pointed at himself. His brother held his gaze for a long moment and then stepped back. Chris had spent decades looking over his shoulder, expecting to see the face of his torturer, wondering when the Ghostman would find him again. Chris might have been locked up for two years, but he had spent even more years in a mental and emotional prison because he never felt safe. Ever. Chris could eliminate that life of uncertainty for the women.

Chris took a deep breath, studied the inside of the tent, and stepped inside. The smell of unwashed male slapped him in the face. Even the salty breeze couldn't clear the sweaty odors from the blankets. He crept closer, his weapon trained on the head resting on the small pillow, and he recognized the profile. The man was leaner now, his beard growing out and his hair in need of a trim. The smell of alcohol mixed with the other odors of the tent. Judging by the empty glass bottles off to one side, Kruger drank a lot. And often.

Here was the source of Gianna's, Violet's, and Jamie's nightmares.

He thunked his weapon on the man's skull and stepped back. Kruger lunged up from the ground and froze as he saw the men and the weapons trained on his face. He stared at Chris and muttered something in a language Chris didn't recognize. Alcohol fumes and bad breath drifted from his mouth.

"Yes, he did survive," answered Michael.

In the dim light, Chris realized the man had lost more weight than he'd originally guessed. Life on the run was a thorough diet. He hoped Kruger had been scared shitless the whole time.

"I knew someone was following me," muttered Kruger. "Are you the police?" he asked, looking at Michael.

Michael's lips twisted. "I'm not."

Kruger looked from Michael to Chris and then scooted back a few inches. "What do you want? I can get you money."

"No, you can't. Daddy's deep pockets have dried up, and I'm sure you're very aware of that fact," said Chris. "What we want can't be bought. We want the women in our lives to be able to sleep at night and not worry that someone is going to burn their house down around them or shoot them in the stomach."

Kruger's white teeth flashed. "I read she survived. She is a hot one, your woman."

Chris's arm shot out and whipped his weapon across the man's face. Blood dripped from his nose. Kruger wiped it with the back of his hand and eyed the blood smear.

"You Americans think you're all John Wayne," sneered Kruger. "You don't know what real power feels like."

"I have your fucking puny life in the palm of my hand," said Chris, lining up his weapon with Kruger's right eye. "No one will care if I kill you right now. The United States wants you for murders of police officers. Do you know what we do to cop killers back home? South Africa wants you for some of the sickest crimes I've ever heard of. You should be happy that I'm going to save you from that hell."

Kruger's bravado faded at Chris's words. "I still have friends with money. I can pay you well."

"They can't be very good friends if they let you sleep in this filth," answered Chris. "I've got no reason to let you walk out of this tent. No reason at all."

Kruger lunged for the tent flap, and Chris leaped on the stinking man's back, clubbing him in the head with the butt of his gun and forcing him to the ground. Kruger fought to throw off his weight as Michael flung himself onto the backs of Kruger's legs. Michael grabbed one of the man's arms and wrenched it behind his back. Chris heard the click of handcuffs and transferred his weight to the man's shoulders. Kruger swore with foreign words as Michael wrestled with the cuffs.

A second click.

Chris rolled off his back while Michael kept his weight on the man's legs. Chris crawled to the tent flap, pushed it aside, and looked out at the four waiting men. "He's all yours." The men were dressed in cheap tourist shirts, but Chris knew they wore body armor underneath. They were impatient to take their prisoner back to South Africa.

Two of the men ducked inside and Kruger shouted in anger at the sight of the newcomers.

Michael crawled out of the tent. "It fucking stinks in there."

The two remaining men shook hands with Michael and Chris. "Thank you," said one.

"No, *thank you*," answered Chris.

"Let's go home," said Michael.

"Home," echoed Chris with an eager smile.

CHAPTER TWENTY-SEVEN

It's over.

Gianna stood in the waiting area of the tiny regional airport, shifting from foot to foot, watching out the window. Heavy rain had fallen for the last few hours, delaying several flights. Behind her Brian patiently explained the nuances of his video game to Violet as they sat with their heads together, peering at his small screen. Violet's interest was genuine, and Gianna's heart warmed at how the kids had taken to each other.

The first meeting between the three of them had been stiff and awkward, with Chris uncertain how to introduce Gianna and Violet to his son. Brian had looked from one woman to the other, a puzzled look on his face as he listened to his father fumble through an explanation of a cabin fire and snowstorm.

Gianna couldn't take her eyes off the boy, stunned at his strong resemblance to both Michael and Chris. She'd pulled her gaze away for a second and raised a brow at Chris in amusement. He halted his jumbled story and held up his hands in exasperation. "I like her," he finally blurted. "A lot."

Brian frowned as he processed his father's statement, and then his face lit up. "She's your girlfriend?" he said with a grin, looking eagerly from Gianna to his father.

Gianna could have sworn Chris blushed. "Yes."

"Awesome." Brian's smile filled his face. "It was about time, Dad," he said seriously. "I was getting worried."

"Ah, jeez," muttered Chris, running a hand over his face.

Gianna wished she'd recorded the moment. After that, Brian acted like he'd always known her and Violet. He'd had a bit of a crush on Violet for the first two weeks, but lost it after she beat him in almost every video game he owned. Now the two of them argued and teased like siblings.

"You need to pause a second when the werewolf appears," Brian instructed. "If you shoot too soon, you'll miss."

"Like this?" asked Violet.

An explosion sounded from the game. "You got 'em!" exclaimed Brian. "Nice!"

Gianna sighed.

"Their plane landed ten minutes ago," muttered Jamie, stopping next to Gianna. "In this rinky-dink airport, it shouldn't take more than two minutes for them to walk in. The plane had only four people on it, so why don't they *hurry up!*"

Gianna understood.

In the two weeks Chris had been gone, phone calls and video chat hadn't filled the void. She'd worried constantly that Chris and Michael wouldn't find Reid Kruger. And she'd worried they would—and not survive the encounter.

It's over.

The words repeated over and over in her head.

Now come back.

"Dad!"

Gianna turned around to see Chris wrap his arms around his son and lift him off his feet, his face buried in his son's neck. Next to them Michael tipped Jamie backward in a flashy move and kissed her soundly as Jamie's hands gripped the front of his coat.

Chris looked over his son's shoulder, and his hazel gaze locked with Gianna's. Her heart did a flip and she smiled, her legs unable to move. He was tan and his hair had lightened in the constant sun of Mexico. He set Brian down, tousled his hair, and slapped the high-five palm Violet held out to him.

Then he moved toward Gianna, a grin on his face.

He looks relaxed.

He gathered her into his arms, and she melted into him, laying her head against his chest, listening to the rapid beat of his heart. They stood motionless, simply drawing what they needed from each other.

"I missed you," she whispered into his coat. His arms tightened around her.

"You have no idea how much I thought about you while I was gone," he said gruffly.

"Thank you," whispered Gianna. "Thank you for stopping that man and helping Violet sleep at night. She's been a different girl since we heard he was on his way back to South Africa."

"I couldn't let the two of you always wonder," said Chris. "I didn't want to see you with a black cloud hovering over your head every day."

"See me every day?" Gianna asked, lifting her head.

His gaze held hers and his mouth lifted into a smile. "Yes, every day. Is that all right?"

She turned her head and saw Violet and Brian watching the two of them, big smiles on their faces.

"Absolutely."

ACKNOWLEDGMENTS

Ever since *Buried* was published, readers have begged me for Chris's story. I knew when I sat down to write this that I needed to do justice to my readers and Chris. Since I already knew Chris and Michael, I believed this book would be a breeze. It wasn't. To my surprise, I'd never had such a difficult time writing a book. I have to thank my husband, who practically held my hand for the last six weeks of the writing process. Many days the only reason words made it to the page was that he sat beside me, tapping on his own computer keyboard and keeping me focused.

A big thank you to Charlotte Herscher, who helped me make sense out of the jumbled mess of words. More thanks to Melinda Leigh, who puts up with my procrastinating and is always ready at a moment's notice to help me plot through a problem. My always-stellar Montlake crew: Jessica, JoVon, Thom, Hai-Yen, Marlene, and Anh. No matter whom I work with there, everyone is consistently fabulous and supportive. New thanks go to Meg Ruley, agent extraordinaire; I'm glad to have you on my team.

My three girls. My heart. So proud of their mom. I do it for you.

ABOUT THE AUTHOR

Born and raised in the Pacific Northwest, Kendra Elliot has always been a voracious reader, cutting her teeth on classic female heroines like Nancy Drew, Trixie Belden, and Laura Ingalls. Kendra won the 2015 and 2014 Daphne du Maurier awards for best Romantic Suspense. She was an International Thriller Writers finalist for Best Paperback Original and a *Romantic Times* finalist for best Romantic Suspense. She still lives in the rainy Pacific Northwest with her husband and three daughters but looks forward to the day she can live in flip-flops.

Made in the USA
Monee, IL
15 April 2020

25981214R00201